THE BLACK STATE

THE BLACK STATE

A Novel

JOHN DELACOURT

CANADA

Library and Archives Canada Cataloguing in Publication

Title: The black slate : a novel / John Delacourt.

Names: Delacourt, John, 1964- author.

Identifiers: Canadiana (print) 20230577571 | Canadiana (ebook) 2023057758X |
ISBN 9781989689608 (softcover) | ISBN 9781989689646 (EPUB)

Subjects: LCGFT: Thrillers (Fiction) | LCGFT: Political fiction. |
LCGFT: Novels.

Classification: LCC PS8607.E4825385 B54 2024 | DDC C813/.6—dc23

Printed and bound in Canada on 100% recycled paper.

Now Or Never Publishing
901, 163 Street
Surrey, British Columbia
Canada V4A 9T8

nonpublishing.com
Fighting Words.

We gratefully acknowledge the support of the Canada Council for the Arts
and the British Columbia Arts Council for our publishing program.

I.

The wind from the sea washes everything clean. One storm could take away all you want to forget.

This is what Hacene said to Henry this morning, in his musical French. So musical that Henry presumed there was a song about the Mediterranean, and these were the lyrics. Maybe it was about drowning a lover. A murder ballad. Songs of love and death—here, they would never go out of style.

Hacene was the kind of old man who would know every word. He would keep such songs in his head from when he had first fallen in love. On the wall behind the counter of his cafe was a calendar page hanging from March of 2009 with a photo of a desert flower. Royal blue petals seamed with purple. Perhaps Hacene's wife died then; he still wore a thick gold band. His thin, tapered fingers were like a pianist's. He carried sadness and lightness in equal measure in the way he moved, qualities in balance like the sweetness and bitterness of the espressos he served each morning with cardamom.

"Take water for your drive, Monsieur Henri. And you should not go by yourself in case you get lost."

"Thank you, Hacene. I understand."

But understanding is not the same as taking heed. Henry had to drive from Rabat to Temara alone; he wouldn't risk anyone else's safety. He'd waited until mid-morning because the downtown traffic wouldn't be quite so bad as it was at 9 am, with the din of horns blaring, the rippling air heavy with smog.

"It is like you're going hunting, monsieur."

Henry smiled and nodded as he slung his camera gear over his shoulder and swallowed the last of his espresso. It was true, he was hunting an image down and he would not return until it was there, alive, trapped in his camera.

It did not take long, once Henry took the beachfront drive to Temara, for him to find the route to the forested outskirts. The shacks diminished to hovels of breeze blocks and plastic sheets, with corrugated steel roofs. Then along the road there was a small squib of concrete and rebar, faded white, which, judging from the litter and the newspaper on a bench, was a bus stop. There were ghost sounds bleating from a moped radio that looked more discarded than parked.

Farther along, where Henry could glimpse the edge of a forest, there was a Shell sign leaning over two gas pumps. The garage behind it was scraped clean of paint by years of disuse. There was the wreck of a school bus parked by a phone booth, which Henry slowed for so he could read the Arabic logo on the steel box. Such things still existed; it was at least a decade since Henry had seen a phone booth on a city street back home.

On a barren stretch of hardscrabble, two soccer nets marked a field just past a grazing land for a congress of goats. The goats were kept off the road by a fence of stacked rock and rusted wire. A few scrambled away from their grazing spot as Henry sped past. The strangeness of their eyes, slowly blinking, acknowledging his intrusion. They looked to be the last sign of life before the wheat-coloured patches of grass thickened into a lusher green with a grove of cork trees, a blue sky streaked with cirrus clouds. The colours, much like the terms of existence, went primary.

Out here there was no country any more, nothing governing but the ancient wild. This old forest swallowed up everything, including time. What better place for a secret prison: the landscape of forgetting.

Henry remembers a film by Antonioni he watched at seventeen. Jack Nicholson portrayed a man slowly coming apart in a desert. Why not a forest like this one? That would be more to Henry's liking. There was so much silence in the film. Such slowness. He had wondered why all films couldn't let the silence bleed into you like that.

It was not soon after he had watched that film that Henry got rid of his video camera for his first old Leica. The moving image, he decided, created an expectation of conventional storytelling.

That was exactly what he didn't want to do—and he had no interest in subverting the medium.

Now as he sped along, feeling the chassis thrum beneath him, he rolled down the window. The road smelled faintly of diesel and charcoal. He reached for his phone on the passenger seat, poked the icon for his camera app and turned the phone on its side. Any shot he took from this vantage point would have a panoramic aspect ratio. Through the screen he took in the tops of the trees. A line of dark craggy clouds suddenly loomed above. He sped up, moved his camera hand until the image blurred. Aside from his work on this day, such shots were all he wanted to take. All remnants of place and time, he had written in the morning, he wanted to "push into abstraction." This was on the page after the rejected/crossed-out words ~~do violence to, erasing the facts of the story~~. He was not quite sure where this violent impulse was coming from, but to move fast through this wilderness promised all the exhilaration of forgetting.

He was now far enough along the unpaved road to run the application he'd grown to trust: the phantom GPS. Designed by new friends of his, Marci and Kathy. It told him, as Kathy had said, "where the ghost world is."

The ghost world ladies were representative of this new tribe of followers he never imagined were out there. Mostly Americans, mostly damaged but brilliant introverts who had stumbled into deep state secrets through no fault of their own. They represented a subset of people who bought Henry's art. And they existed outside of the growing list of ageing plutocrats that his English dealer, Garry Fry, lured from their gated seclusion to drop thousands a show. Henry would have given ghost world people his work for reduced prices if he could, and this was probably why Garry just quietly demurred from following up with any serious inquiries from such people.

Marci and Kathy had come to Henry's first Chelsea show and weirded him out initially.

Close talkers, dressed like truckers. They said they didn't know anything about art but knew what they liked. And then Marci sang the next line over Kathy's shoulder—"surfing in a swamp on a Saturday night"—and Henry had laughed in recognition. He could spot old guy punks like those he once called friends by their dad jeans and their black basketball shoes—and here they were, the female equivalents.

Marci and Kathy said they had met while working for "Christians In Action," doing classified work but nothing glamorous—that work was "too far up the chain" for them. No, they focused on encryption, "nuts and bolts, code-monkey work." They fell in love, "got declassified or cashiered, I still don't knoe, rully," Kathy said. Once out of the CIA, they went to work on their own projects. They bought themselves an alpaca farm just outside Roanoke and called their first stud Salvador after Allende. They dropped a fortune for Michael's Romanian airport triptych and invited him out to see where it would hang.

At their dinner table, eating vegan pizza and drinking bourbon, Henry had felt like he could ease into a tribe like this in America, now that he was settled into his part time teaching gig in Pullman. They were like-minded rejects from the last years of that grand old military industrial complex. He wondered if there was something fundamentally American about him too, given that his grandmother was born on the south side of the border. She was Lizzie Raeburn of the Seattle Raeburns, the family's failed painter, resounding success as a suicide. She could be the ministering spirit watching over him. Saving him from his Canadian father's bag man pretensions, his German mother's repressed guilt and self-loathing. It wasn't soon after his Virginia trip that he legally changed his surname to Raeburn.

This was all just a couple of years ago but why did it seem so much longer now? Was it the money, the success, whatever that might mean… that had created a density to his new identity? It was hard to imagine how he could ever go back to being Henry MacPhail from deepest, leafiest Vancouver. He had lost those co-ordinates, there was no phantom GPS for their recovery.

A murky green square started to take shape on the screen of Henry's phone. First it appeared like a treasure chest at the bottom of the sea. This was what happened when he was closing in on where he would photograph. He started to visualize the interior of the site: the terraced floors of cells, the guards in unmarked uniforms, the German Shepherds straining at the ends of their leashes as they patrolled beside each barred door. From kennel to prison, all the dogs had learned to smell was fear. Henry could imagine the sounds in there: the barking, the clanking of bars, the muttered prayers, the faint sounds of screams behind steel doors. It was the chamber music that played in Henry's version of hell.

The green square faded into shadowy grey and Henry felt his pulse quicken. To be so close caused him to imagine his own incarceration—a brief moment of animal fear in a cell, bars and cot captured in lurid shadowless light—and then he squeezed his eyes shut to banish the image.

He knew that there were hidden cameras in the branches of the argania trees, motion detectors buried in the last few hundred metres before the electric fence lines. Yet there was nothing he could do but pull the rented Renault over to the soft shoulder and begin his trek.

He had, in his backpack, a tube of toothpaste, toothbrush and sunblock, three bottles of lemon water from Hacene's café, two oranges, houmous toast and a plastic container of yogurt in a thermal pouch, his digital camera and his chamois satchel of lenses, his tripod and his long black leather case with the Orion refractor telescope. Check, check, check: nothing forgotten and everything of value that he would care to bring with him if this was his last shoot.

But before he zipped it back up again, there was also the small photo in the black woolen frame, bejeweled with plastic rubies and emeralds. It could be a passport shot except the woman was smiling. Coal-black eyes, just a few wispy dark curls poked out from the scarf framing the crown of her head. Henry could have taken many photos of her; they should have all been on his phone. But he erased them because this is how the woman, Yasmin, had framed herself in a photo booth, the day she had seen him off at the Frankfurt airport . It was how she wanted to be seen by him. And so he had bought this little frame for the photo in an Algeciras market. It was originally a pendant for a saint's image. Taxi drivers hang such keepsakes from their rear view mirrors. But it would have been too much to hang this photo around his neck, too soon to say whether this could be love. He touched the photo as if it contained a little juju that would rub off onto his trigger finger.

Yasmin was all he wanted to think about apart from his work. He would stop himself from imagining any kind of future for them together. From what he had learned of love and relationships, he knew they were in the phase where it must not be overthought. He focussed on the present tense every time he wrote her and yes, so far, it was working. He had considered dedicating this series of photos to her, maybe with a quote from her beloved Darwish. *In her absence I created this image: out of the earthly the hidden heavenly commences.* Except there was nothing heavenly that could exist in what he was about to photograph, save for hope of eventual freedom, eventual justice for those inside.

About a quarter of a mile away was the hill he had chosen as his ideal vantage point.

It was a stubborn fist of earth, punched up from the dust and the sun-baked dirt. There were no trees along its highest point, not much vegetation to speak of from here to there. This heightened the risk, given his visibility from a distance. But he was going with Hacene's reassurance to him: "If the army wanted you they would have taken you days ago, Monsieur Henri." Hacene had been in prison for eight years before he had opened his little café, he knew of these things. And yet it was just too quiet: all Henry could hear was the sound of the dry earth crunch under his engineer boots.

A black bird soared above him. At first glance he thought it was a crow but then, as it lowered and circled, it looked too ragged, misshapen. Henry remembered a black and white photo of a street vendor in Lodz. It was from a show in Spitalfields he happened on to as he was walking through the neighbourhood, hungry for new images to fill him up. Call it wartime scavenging: he and this ragged bird were allies.

The sun on the back of his neck felt as intense as midday when he had finally found his spot. The rock was flat and square; you could have lain a prayer rug down and it would have aligned well with the dimensions. He imagined a hermit finding this spot, centuries before. Years in the wild… was a faith like that even possible anymore? Henry took out his tripod, then the refractor telescope. From this distance, this was what he needed.

From his first look through the viewfinder he knew the image would be grainy and distorted. The drinn grass would become abstracted into patches of floating greenish cloudlets. But this was exactly what he wanted: irresolution, behind the barbed wire chain link fence was a grey box of a building, like a warehouse for forgotten goods. The more the photos looked like shots of Mars from satellite footage, the more the black site would seem alien.

Verfremdung—making strange. His father had aped his mother's German with fake irony. How that must have driven her crazy, the years they were together. Still, the word carried the weight of the strange better than the English phrase.

You could never translate it into estrangement. Not to describe how he and his mother were now. There was no way to fix the state of their relations, and yet he couldn't imagine it being forever. He just had faith that time would wear away at the impasse—as it had with his father. An eventual unraveling of the knot of unknowing. She would see the man he'd become in public and want to love him again.

But this might be wrong. Estrangement itself could dissolve all desire to reconnect.

The one thing he had come to realize with this particular photography project was how powerful the weaponizing of solitude was.

That was the point of this photo series, really. The deeper he could reflect on these structures, the better the shots. All at a distance, the viewer reflecting on the design of these machines for constant surveillance that slowly crushed the soul through isolation. *New versions of Piranesi's Carceri*, he had written in his notebook that morning, they eluded the relentless photomapping of the earth.

But to capture these sites accurately you needed patience. Henry dug with his thumb into the skin of an orange, conscious he was salivating, anticipating the sweetness of the first section in his mouth. Anticipation was all.

Photography is a bringing to light. Where had he read that? Sounded like the monkish Hungarian who had the show in Toronto. Lajos something... Henry had been too young and foolish to take note. Back in his bartending days when you could have just walked off the street along Queen and found the real thing. It took about nine hundred shifts to scrounge enough for his first Hasselblad and finally ditch the Leica. He missed living in that state of hunger.

And a decade of working had taught him to endure the waiting better. *Bide your time.* Wait for the light to transform as the minutes become hours.

He waited.

And clicked.

And then waited some more. He watched his shadow recede and fade on the surface of the rock. At some point in the middle of the afternoon the wind had picked up. He could smell the ocean in the air and remembered how close he was to those wind battered stretches of rocky coastline he had glimpsed from the road on his way here. Crusades, pirates, desperate French refugees fleeing Petain's France... this little grove of no man's land swallowed up time, leaving no trace of those incursions, no texture of history. Down there, through the trees... angle, frame, click... what better plot of land could you find to house the forgotten and condemned? The characterless functionality of the buildings, like warehouses in an industrial park, the fenced off, barren perimeter... it could have all been built last week or decades ago. No way of knowing. He hoped the images he captured might distill this sense of historical depletion, just hint at what horrors might have been happening within.

It was almost five when Henry decided it had been a good day of shooting. He had about two hundred photos to pore over that night, back at the pension. As he packed everything back up in his bag he felt the tiredness of being all day out in the sun. And it pleased him, made him feel that he had completed a good day of work.

He remembered the summer days fishing on Canim Lake when he was a boy. In a way this was so similar. The silence, the waiting, the moment of great promise seized. Some shots were prize catches, others deserved to be thrown back. Not the same river though; not the same man.

He began to walk back down to the road. He was surprised by the length of his shadow as the sun's rays darted through the canopy of branches above the path.

Out in the west Texas town of El Paso, I fell in love with a Mexican girl, Henry sang in his deepest voice. Grandpa Dougie MacPhail would trill that to himself, out in the canoe. Grandpa had a couple of Marty Robbins albums back in the rec room of the big house in Kerrisdale. His second wife Ruth Ellen liked her country and western. A birthday pool party, a piñata, Japanese lanterns strung across the concrete deck. He was not sure why this was all coming back so vividly now as he was walking. Put it down to how time had slowed during the course of the afternoon. After hours of silence it was as though there was a blank canvas for memory.

Henry did not hear the car approach while he was walking. The path along the stretch of road was hardscrabble, and it was loud under the heels of his boots as he walked. It was only once he had gotten into the Renault and pulled out from the soft shoulder that he saw the white SUV in his rear view mirror. It was a figment quivering, as if he was looking at it through smoke.

The SUV was going so much faster than Henry was, and soon it was only a few metres from his bumper. A bare arm emerged from the passenger side window and pointed in the direction of the soft shoulder with a quick sharp stab. From the force of the gesture Henry knew it could only be one thing: he was being arrested by the special police.

Blacker than night were the eyes of Felina, wicked and evil while casting a spell. Henry decelerated and glanced at the SUV moving with him, gliding off the black road. The pounding of his heart surprised him; he thought he'd be less afraid. It was worse because of the tinted windows, the mystery of who these police-men were. The concealed are truly free.

"You are Henry Raeburn, yes?"

"Yes."

"You are under arrest, Monsieur Raeburn."

The officer was surprisingly young, with bare, sinewy arms, the golden brown eyes like the Berber girl who had trailed Henry when he first hit land in Ceuta. She had been holding an orange and when he refused her—*la choukran*—she finally hissed and cursed him. Was this the result ? There was a crudely done tat-too—an anchor ?—in the crook between the officer's thumb and forefinger. Those hands were rifling through Henry's wallet, fin-gers flicking the American bills with disgust.

"Why am I under arrest?"

The officer looked surprised by Henry's French, almost impressed. He then returned his gaze to the wallet. "You know why, my friend."

"I know nothing."

The officer tilted his head. What Henry had just said—that he knew nothing—was worth considering. "Come." He ges-tured for Henry to get out of his car.

Once he did he heard the other door of the SUV open, the driver's side. As he turned to look the police officer grabbed him by the shoulders and spun his body until he was flat, facing the door. He felt the metal of the handcuff against his wrist, heard the click of one, then the other locked shut.

The last thing he saw in daylight was the other policeman, the driver of the SUV, reaching into the back seat of his Renault to take his bag. He wore clear plastic gloves, his fingers chapped and whitened through them, as if they belonged to a refrigerated corpse.

The evening wind, sharp as the chergui in the desert, had already begun to pick up. He heard it faintly in the back of the SUV, felt its force on the chassis. It would erase all trace of him here today. Without the shots he took, in the camera in the trunk of the SUV, all might be forgotten.

It is just like Hacene had said this morning, about the wind. That seems so long ago now.

But if Henry could intuit anything, it was that time was about to become more of an abstraction. Days might contract or expand, depending on the intensity of his loneliness. And perhaps his despair.

2.

The walls of the Canadian embassy featured some well-chosen works from the national art bank, just installed to mark the sesquicentennial year back home. Ambassador Ashwin Khadilkar liked to take his guests for a tour, usually before dinner, and show them some of his personal favourites.

"Here is the Canada where I live, no matter where I am." He opened the doors from his office and the light filled the hallway. Motion sensors glowed over the potted halogens above the Riopelle. Security surveillance marrying aesthetics: this made Ashwin smile. He led, Pisco Sour in hand, and behind him his three guests from the Astana delegation followed.

Ashwin had a terrible habit of forgetting names. Or mispronouncing ones he'd read in briefing notes. This should have been career limiting. But he had learned to remember one name from every group he hosted. Here it was Adilbek, who could have passed for a bouncer save for the English shoes that betrayed the fortune he'd made in oil back in his country. Ashwin turned to him, gesturing with his drink hand, "This one, Adilbek, this one is my favourite."

Adilbek nodded, turned to the young woman walking two steps behind him. Her English was better and he'd need her for this part of the evening. She was serious, wide eyed, and she had been focussed on Adilbek since they had arrived at the embassy. She was making notes in the red book she clasped with both hands, shielding her breasts. A gazelle out in the wild among the hyenas.

"And this is Canadian also?" Adilbek asked.

"This gentleman would have preferred the distinction that he was Quebecois and Canadian. Politics, my friend." Ashwin cast a rueful look Adilbek's way and sipped from the tumbler in his hand. "It can't be escaped, even in abstraction."

Adilbek laughed and his two colleagues from the delegation laughed also. But it dissolved quickly. Not even Adilbek seemed sure this was the correct response. Yet Ashwin had said politics then paused before his next sentence—what else could it have been but a punchline?

Only the young woman remained unmoved. Only the young woman had understood what Ashwin had said.

Still, Ashwin was pleased with how they were all getting on. And he was used to finding his own amusement in his casual observations. Some of his best thoughts emerged like this. Off the cuff. The lingering feeling of l'esprit d'escalier marked his days. He could use an amanuensis to get his best thoughts down for posterity. Amanuensis, just the beauty of the word itself justified the position. Imagine it filled by someone from old money, 'old stock"—like Torquil Forsey, his Head of the Political Section. But younger than Torquil, younger and far more charming.

Maybe that's what this woman was for Adilbek—a Kazakh Boswell. She could have been writing down all his gems in that book of hers. The little red book of Adilbek. But there was nothing about the man that suggested he was anything more than a very corrupt, former petroleum engineer who had made friends with the right oligarchs among Putin's gangsters. Well, the right friends for now. There was a remote possibility she was Adilbek's mistress but she was not dressed for it—no heels, no bling—and Adilbek, with his pasha's belly, looked like a man who would gravitate to such trappings.

"What I love about this work are his brush strokes. You know, a photograph can't capture what standing in front of a good painting reveals. If a photograph of a painting does reveal all you need to see—the painting's not that good, in my view."

Serious nods from all. It was unclear to whom Ashwin was speaking as he gazed into the painting. Possibly himself. He had let the moment overtake him. When Adilbek had asked, back in Ashwin's office, "What is your faith sir?" Ashwin should have responded *art is the only faith I have.*

Yes, that would have been Ashwin once again speaking for the sound of his own voice.

But what was the harm in being your best audience? Especially here in this country. *You are welcome, sir, to Cyprus. Goats and monkeys!* Cyprus would be better than Rabat.

★

Henry had about two minutes left before they took him from the interrogation room and put him back in his cell. It was quaint—the chunky black phone with the touch-tone dial pad. Old French design, the last touches of the imperial project. He had no internet access so he couldn't send a message to his father to tell him he was calling. Unsurprisingly, when he finally did get through his father did not pick up.

So he tried Yasmin—the call he preferred to make anyway. She could have been at the law office or at Amitas where she was volunteering. But surely when she saw the area code she would know it's him.

And yet, for that very reason she might decide to let the phone ring. That's where it was with her. She was a keepsake photo but there was no deeper relationship. No real obligations. At one point, not so long ago, Henry had imagined that would be exactly what he wanted. No longer.

"He-llo. Henry? Is this Henry?"

The melody in her voice, the sense of calm and peace. He had to find a way they could be together.

"It is me, Yasmin. I'm here and I'm in trouble."

"I heard, Henry. Did they arrest you for your photos? How did it happen?"

"I was in the desert at a black site. They say I might be tried for espionage. I'm looking at ten years at least. I don't know how much time I have on this phone. And I know they're listening."

"I can get there. I can come to you. We can make sure you'll be okay."

"Yasmin, I'm going to give you my father's number. Can you call him? Introduce yourself?"

"Of course I can."

"Yasmin…" He looked up at the punctiform pattern in the soundproofing tiles that covered the walls. The window view was of a cloudless sky, a high chain link fence, a circular track of paved concrete. My life as a Moroccan dog in a pen, a photo essay by Henry Raeburn. "Yasmin, I have to say this because I don't know when we'll talk again."

"Henry, what?"

"Yasmin, I think I love you."

"Henry, I'm scared for you now. Let's get you free."

She didn't say I love you back. And he couldn't push the point of course. Despite all of the trouble he was in, this was his first real moment of anguish. His love might be unrequited.

★

Torquil Forsey received the email about Henry Raeburn while dining alone in his apartment. His last lover's recipe for turmeric eggs and kale. He resolved to make it for his mother when he returned to Ottawa at Christmas. He thought about her most nights when he was home alone these days, deliberated on emailing her. She had been a widow for over a year now. The old man's last stroke in Sarasota was supposed to be a liberation after three years of his constant care. But she didn't quite take to it that way; she was less liberated than shell-shocked. She'd settled in her new condo in Ottawa and she still couldn't quite figure out her laptop. And yet when the email came in, his first thought was that it was her.

"NOTE: Henry Raeburn is the son of Senator Gordon MacPhail." So this was serious, he had better get back to the office. Ashwin was cc-ed but of course he hadn't seen it. He was entertaining someone; it was the only part of his job he was capable of doing.

Torquil emptied half the plate of scrambled eggs into his space-age garbage compactor—one of the few attractive features of his apartment when it worked—and quickly brushed his teeth over the kitchen sink. His teeth felt old and crumbling; he ground them at night. "In my line of work," he had said to his last dentist in Ottawa, "if that's the least of my problems I'm happy." Happy was relative, of course.

He was almost out the door when he realized his wrist was bare. He wasn't wearing his father's gold watch and he couldn't walk in that embassy and play his role without it. He had turned taxis around and been late for meetings when he forgot it. Not this time though; he caught himself. He hated the old man for thirty years but ever since he died his old watch was the only thing that completed Torquil, made him feel that be could play his role.

In the taxi, he scanned the technicolour chaos of the streets but took nothing in; he was ruminating on his own neurosis. How did this happen? When he was thirteen and sent off to Lakefield School he had felt liberated. The last thing he would have cared about was anything handed down from his father. That felt like just a few years—not decades—ago. Possessions and attachments had been for other boys and he was in a hurry to be a man.

This was why it was so hard to quit smoking, the doctor had said, because he started then. Determined to be dangerous and elegant.

Torquil and his brief, late-adolescent turn as an artist. He had loved the idea of writing for the stage but he realized his writing was bad. He'd been concocting a new identity, some eighties version of Noel Coward who emerged, fully formed from the snowy wastes. He was the only character he was really interested in creating. What followed were two years in Manhattan after high school being nothing more than a nanny, chattering and typing through his shame.

Daddy to the rescue, Daddy and his friends in the Privy Council. God, that was decades ago now. *I grow old, I wear my trousers rolled*. Prufrock, the only poem he could ever memorize when he was young. Odd that he couldn't see the significance of that at the time.

"Just here to the left," he instructed the driver. "That's my office."

No matter how you approached it, the best way to describe the new embassy was that it had all the character of a small city's airport. Lots of natural light, sure, but there was a blankness to the bleached white walls, a puritan disdain for anything but straight lines and pure function, flat shadowless light. Safe in his office Torquil felt sealed off from all the unpredictable energy in the streets, this new restiveness in Rabat that seemed to cough out moments of street violence like the first signs of a new virus—call it an Arab spring flu.

Still, Torquil always felt better when it came into view from the back of a taxi. It was where he did work that his colleagues depended on, and he was well liked. He quickly tapped out his next steps for this Henry Raeburn in an email. He felt proud about the fact that, what, five years ago now, he had realized he was very good at what he did, As Ward Jellicoe, the Director General back home had so charitably said, "few can read a room like Forsey." He should have been the ambassador rather than Khadilkar.

"Merci, monsieur." Torquil gave the taxi driver a generous tip, as he always did.

And why not? Whatever expense he racked up, it wouldn't come close to Ashwin's entertainment report each month— never mind the salary of Ashwin's driver. Torquil presumed that was a calculation Ottawa made each month as well.

He buttoned his blazer as he emerged from the taxi. The paunch, like the receding hairline, he owed to this posting. In the smoked glass of the front doors he barely recognized himself. All at once his body was middle-aged. Two glasses of Bordeaux a night have become three but there's nothing he could do about that, there were no good therapists who spoke English in this diplomat's burg, imagine.

He got through security and decided to take the stairs. He could hear the muffled white noise of vacuum cleaners on one, on two. Many evenings in the past, that sound would prompt him to pack up. This was before Ashwin; only he could make Torquil nostalgic for his workaholic days.

He saw Ashwin and his guests halfway down the hall. They were crowded around the Mary Pratt—lemons and oranges in a red bowl. The Kazakhs looked as if they were straining to smile.

They must have been thinking these Canadians have such long winters that just a few lemons were worthy of veneration. Oligarchs dragooned into the tour ritual; Ashwin was at least predictable in his vanities.

Torquil would handle this diplomatic emergency passive-aggressively with Ashwin. Consider it a tribute to his mother and how she had managed to get anything done. Nothing to see here, just an old mandarin working late.

"Torquil, forget something?"

"Oh hello. Not at all, just responding to a couple of messages."

What was irritating Ashwin the most about Torquil's sudden entrance was that he had to introduce Torquil to every member of the Astana delegation and of course he couldn't remember their names. He gestured to the first man beside him and Torquil saved Ashwin by shaking hands with each, saying his own name and asking for theirs. Ashwin just stood there, sipping another one of those bloody Pisco Sours and glowering. *I am not doing this for you, I'm doing it for the embassy.*

That would normally be it; just another potentially awkward or embarrassing situation Torquil had managed. Yet once his door was shut and he'd logged into his computer, he was not two lines into his email to Ottawa when he heard Ashwin's sharp knock on the door. Of course he entered before Torquil could rise from his desk.

"Did someone die? I can't imagine what else would have you here one minute after six."

Torquil's eyes remained on the screen. It was less than respectful, sure, but we were working after hours here, an inch or two of the mask of decorum could drop. "Not a death, no. Just an arrest. You haven't seen the email."

"No I haven't seen the email. I'm working. As one does most nights. What's the urgency with the arrest?"

"The son of one of our senators."

"What? Why didn't you call me immediately? Jesus Christ, Forsey. Which senator?

One of the goddamn independents your Liberal friends have appointed?"

There was a time when if one were to have spoken of partisan politics this way, it would have been cause for a stern reprimand. The time before seemed so much longer than a decade ago now. Progress was provisional. Things could return to a more combative state at any time.

"His name is Henry Raeburn. He is the son of Senator Gordon MacPhail, appointed in 2014. So, someone you might know, ambassador."

"I can't believe you didn't call."

"I did call. And then I came down because we should conference in Ottawa." Torquil's voice was without drama. It was almost conciliatory. Note the 'we.' *I will survive you.* This was the mantra that blared in neon behind his smile for Ashwin every day.

"Why can't this wait until tomorrow? If I don't know MacPhail—and believe me, I don't, really—I doubt anyone in the PMO will view this as urgent, given he's Conservative."

Torquil's eyes remained on his screen. To return Ashwin's gaze would validate his preening self-importance. "That was my thought initially but then I Googled Henry Raeburn. This is complicated."

"Google Adilbek Zholy while you're there. Estimated two hundred million net worth with an interest in Saskatchewan potash and he's out in the hall, wondering where the hell I am."

"Henry Raeburn won the Windauer two years ago. He photographs black sites all over the world. He was caught taking shots of a detainment centre which is not supposed to exist here."

Ashwin gently placed his cocktail on the ledge of Torquil's desk. He put his hands on his hips like a sprinter walking off his last heat. "Oh fuck."

"Yes, precisely."

Torquil hated the sound of his own fingertips on his keyboard. Like the claws of a small rodent scurrying across the counter.

"Like we can do anything here. Like we're in any kind of position to piss Washington off with the Trump people running the White House. I better go and see this Henry Raeburn."

"Yes, your excellency."

There was not a trace of anything but pliant obeisance in Torquil's voice as he addressed the ambassador formally. He wouldn't even give Ashwin his contempt.

"So you're setting up the conference call?"

"I'm setting up the call."

"You know, we weren't the ones who started the whole issue with the detainees. It was your friends working with the Americans. We just inherited this goat fuck."

"I'm not sure whom you mean by my friends."

"Oh please. Fine… I'm going to need another fucking drink. Just set up the call."

Torquil pressed send on his email. There was the hushed sound of something launched, suddenly aloft, like a drone.

3

Gordon learned of his son's arrest on the Sunday morning of the Canada Day weekend. He was a couple of hours outside of Ottawa, staying in a condo he'd rented in Mont-Tremblant park. Off on his own, he really didn't want to be found.

He missed the three urgent calls and the text messages to his phone because he was out running. Yet even out there along the trail that snaked along the ski hills, he'd had a bad feeling. He'd startled two young white-tailed deer, grazing for wild berries. The sudden clamor, white patches on the flanks that flashed through the trees and then… gone. He'd been thrown off his rhythm, head a-swim with the kind of memories that came so vividly to him these days.

When Gordon was a boy, his father had bought a broken-down little cabin on Canim Lake. This was in the old man's salad days before his time in the BC Legislature; he'd been a junior partner at McLeod-Crawley. The shack couldn't have cost him more than a grand. Gordon's mother had taken her own life and this was Dougie pulling his boy close. The wilderness wasn't a place of loneliness and despair: it was where son and father came together. Gordon learned to hunt and fish there; the project was to transform him, a boy prone to daydreaming, into a young man with skills on the land, his heart slowly hardened and his nerves sharpened by concentration and the focus required to stalk and kill, and to cast a line well into the silence of the lake.

One year, in the first weekend of November, Dougie took him along the old South Road that cut through the forest to bag the first deer of the season. Young Gordon had spent the summer months without a gun in his hand, feeling loose and free. But now he felt the weight of seriousness and obligation dissolve his summer into winter over the course of one shivering morning.

The old Remington his father had given him was oiled, heavy, blunt, and unpredictable. The force of the shot jolted and wildly sprayed the possibility of death. Their breath had become smoke. One "lucky" shot and there, just fifty metres off a clearing was the fallen buck, its black, liquid eye widened, startled out of its innocence, the joy of its running days juddering out in the last few spasms before its long lashes closed forever.

He'd never tell Dougie how much he hated the moment of the kill. In the worst period of his adolescence, he even took up range shooting with a pistol to prove how he'd refined some measure of ruthlessness within him. But it was a pose, the Walther PPK a deadly little prop in his hands. And this was despite his talent for the target. He quietly abandoned the pistol, put it back in its box and left it on a shelf in the cellar just before he left for Montreal and Lower Canada College for his final two years of high school. His father never asked him about what he'd done with the birthday gift; he must have sensed how Gordon was changing and knew the futility of tamping down his only son. Gordon was becoming his own man.

Now Gordon is four years younger than his father was when he died of a heart attack. The smokes and the half-bottle of Chivas a day hurried along Dougie's exit, just a year after he'd quit his last role in cabinet. Gordon would like to run from that fate, thank you very much. Up most mornings, in lycra and cartoon colours, "a moving fashion violation," as fellow senator Mona Kaufman had teased him, with that wink of hers in the committee room. Maybe she imagined it was his vanity that got him out the door like that, the need to still appear as a man in his prime. It was a common enough affliction among his colleagues; Ottawa was a good town for blue pills and hair products that turned that touch of grey to dull magenta. But he was happy to walk off that dance floor of flirtations and long-rehearsed steps before the last song. Loping along in the mornings was simply a way to ground himself now. It was precisely because he could feel the age in his body, the twinges in his calf muscles, the tightness in his shoulders, that he felt stripped of artifice, simplified by the force of time and still faintly surprised by his own resilience.

But he knew immediately, as he panted and tramped up the stairs inside the condo, that the chime of his phone was a call too early, too insistent… that whatever news this brought, it would test this resilience.

The voice of this Yasmin woman sounded like it was coming to him through a long tunnel. He wondered if that was because of additional security on the line or something, if she was truly Henry's "good friend." He sat on the stairs, felt his temples prickle as his heart pounded. This was different perspiration, caused by a surge of adrenalin. Yes, it was bad… regarding Henry… bail would need to be negotiated, and soon. Even before he was off the phone, Gordon was checking flights for Vancouver. Had to get to Henry's mother, Marithe. Had to figure this out with her, and fast.

But first Gordon did the best/right thing, what a man who understands loyalty does naturally: he called Ginny McEwan, the real chief of staff for the Leader of the Opposition and his office, the OLO—though she was still one of the busiest lobbyists in town with her own shop just a block away from Parliament Hill on Metcalfe. Yes, it was inconvenient. Surely she would rather be with her partner this evening. But in less than a half hour there she was, primly positioned on the sectional couch in the living room of his condo. He'd poured her a glass of white wine, a Canadian Sauvignon Blanc he'd had for two months in the fridge and couldn't bring himself to try. She had already drunk half of her glass before she completed the text message she was writing… presumably to the Leader, who was back in his Alberta riding for the Canada Day weekend. She sighed for punctuation. All this while he tried to explain the situation to her. Here he was, being helpful and he already felt like he'd done something wrong.

"Can we say he was vacationing there?"

"I don't think so. He's built a career on these kinds of photos."

"These kinds." Ginny tilted her head and pursed her lips. She was demonstrating her puzzlement like a primary school teacher to a child. "Exactly what kinds?"

"Photos of black sites. Henry's a visual artist."

"I knew he was an artist. But black sites?"

"It's what he does."

She sighed again and put her vintage blackberry on the end table, where it promptly buzzed. Her fingernails were painted the same ivory as her golf skirt. "Gord, that's important information. You never thought of sharing that with any of us?"

"I didn't think it was relevant."

"Not relevant? We never would have had you at committee in May. We would have subbed you out."

"What does my son have to do with committee?"

Ginny smiled, affected a puzzled look. "Come on, Gord. We met on this. All of you in caucus got the briefing. You saw the draft of Cornwell's motion."

"The motion was about the extraordinary rendition of detainees."

"You didn't see a conflict? I mean when we asked... there were four of you there... who is prepared to filibuster this..."

"No, I did not see a conflict."

"Gord."

"First. That was about classified information. It was national security."

"Where the hell do you think these detainees went?"

"We did not initiate this practice. Christ, Cornwell probably heard all about it when they were in power."

"You know that's not the point. We're wearing it. And now..." She shook her head, ran her fingers through the tinted blonde strands of her new bob cut. She looked younger. They all looked so young, the Leader's new people. Like a fertility cult.

"I do not see a contradiction in me blocking a motion on the treatment of detainees and defending my son's right to a fair trial. On trespassing charges, for Christ sake." His hands were jittery as his voice went up an octave. He gripped his glass of wine tighter and the skin whitened around his knuckles.

"That's great that you see it this way, Gord. No one else will. Least of all the press gallery."

"I don't care about the press gallery. They already screwed me on the filibuster story."

"They screwed you because you didn't talk to us first. Let's not make that mistake again."

"What are you saying?"

"I'm saying if you get any requests to comment on this, you come to us. You say nothing. We'll handle it."

"I've got nothing to hide."

Ginny re-crossed her legs and folded her arms in her lap. "Respectfully, senator… it's not what you have to hide that they care about."

"I'm aware of that."

"Are you? Gord, please just leave this to me and the Leader's D-Comm, okay? Your office gets a call from Pfeiffer or Leroux, moaning about their deadlines, you direct them to the OLO."

"I have to go get my son out of jail. I will inevitably have to comment."

Ginny got up from the sectional couch. She rotated her right shoulder like she was working out a muscle cramp. Her expression changed to suggest sullen concentration. In her thoughts she was already back on the back nine with her beau, that retired colonel with his cop haircut and his dad jeans. "Will you, Gord? Really?"

"You think I'm going to just forget about him over there?"

"No. Not at all, Gord." She was at the door. She turned to face him, unsure whether she should hug him or shake his hand. She revealed an awkwardness that almost suggested vulnerability. Almost. "And we're not going to forget him, either. Just let us handle this our way, 'kay?"

It was all he could do to nod as he shook her hand and mumbled his goodnight to her.

4.

The cell where Henry was being held had twenty-one men in it. One smaller, older man had his lawyer visit, a young, scholarly looking fellow in a new tan suit. They were both escorted out behind the grey metal door, a few hours passed but then the little man returned, his eyes still glassy from tears. Although Henry briefly drifted off to sleep, slumped down in the corner, a few kicks to his legs from a scuffle that broke out roused him, and he decided sleep had its dangers. A kid that looked to be no more than fifteen eyed Henry's cheap digital watch, and Henry dutifully took it off, just handed it to him. Tribute for the journey ahead in here. This was at hour 32; that could have been a half hour or two hours ago now. The tedium of the old play-ground fear made time elastic.

It was surprising to him how effective the constant blinking wash of shadow-less fluorescent light had been to increase his suffering. He could understand the rationale: the surveillance cameras required it for the safety of everyone held in here. But after a full day of standing he was barely awake. Dream-like snippets of nonsense dialogue slipped through the gate of his consciousness. For a few moments he was not in the cell but in a bus station, he believed, near Bucharest. It was a figment of memory from a previous shoot. The smell of body odour, urine and an industrial strength cleaning agent pulled him back from his reverie. He realized that, if only in the effect rather than the intention, his sense of dignity, that he was someone whose human rights mattered, and that they had already been diminished.

Not anything close to the diminishment those in the black site in Temara were going through. Levels of despair: Dante knew what he was doing with his circles of hell. Still, as Henry looked up and took in those he was among, the variations on private suffering—the hollow eyed gazing at one's shoes, the compulsive scratching at a rash on one's neck, the crouched rocking on one's heels—this was quite a circle, all things considered.

And he couldn't shake the feeling his otherness should cause him shame. Even the faded tattoos on his forearms, the circled "A" for anarchy, the sword etched with Caravaggio's creed "nec spe, nec metu" (no hope, no fear), struck him as just reminders of his callow tourism among the desperate and lost as a teenager, when he spent some dark months cast out from the family home, living on the streets of East Vancouver. Even in the throes of his crack addiction then, when he had smoked his inheritance money over a year, he knew there was a home to return to. Henry just seemed to inherit the ability to plunge deeper into depression and isolation, the low pain threshold that his grandmother, the painter and "sensitive soul" Lizzie Raeburn passed on to him. It was just all so much physiology, really.

And it his physiology he was determined to overcome. You could put it down to the vanity of "self-dramatization," as his dealer Garry Fry called it, that he would not listen to sense and admit he did not actually have to be here. He could, with just a couple of signatures, get his bail guaranteed in forty-eight hours. Garry, God love him, had flown from London the minute he had heard Henry was arrested. He was his first and only scheduled visitor so far. Pale, hairless arms exposed in his tennis shirt, unslept and looking, as he put it, "worse than his passport photo," Garry was his angel of rescue. And he gave him little quarter in the fifteen minutes they had to speak.

"You should be out right now. It's an outrage."

"They've set the bail at half a million, Garry. That's extortion. I'm not paying it. I'm fine."

"Half a million American? That's three works from the Salt Pit series. I could auction them off within a week." Garry nodded, as if to reassure himself of the veracity of his claim.

"Yeah but then I go to trial. I guarantee you the legal fees will be crippling."

"Henry, you will earn it out, mate. You don't think I have some experience with this? Bella Steadman was in for possession.

They were going to give her five years. She did one show and covered her bail."

"I'll be fine. You worried I can't focus on my defense from here?"

Garry shook his head, ran his hand through his lank, chestnut coloured hair. It was cut like an ageing schoolboy's. Only over the last year or so had it started to thin and go grey at the temples. "I'm worried you'll be your own worst enemy in the courtroom. You should let me get you a lawyer."

Henry gave him the briefest of smiles. "My father's handling that."

"The senator back there in Canada."

"That's right."

"Henry, I'm not leaving until this is settled. And you get your work back."

"One thing at a time. Got to get through the hearing."

"It's infuriating. You want to make a larger point here? Fine. We can make sure this government is embarrassed over this. It's a trespassing charge they have you in for. You shouldn't have spent a minute behind bars. I can get an open letter written. We will have a long bloody list of signatories. I can get Emin, Doig and Ofili… bet you Damien will sign."

"Not sure about that, Garry. That could make it harder. Let's just get to trial. If I pay a fine, so be it. A fine that I will earn out for you."

Garry huffed in disgust, shot the guards in the room a quick glance and then reached into his back pocket for his wallet. He pulled out an ivory white business card, placed it on the table between them. "That name mean anything to you?"

"Peter Bishop? No."

"Best lawyer in London for this kind of case."

"I don't need your Peter Bishop. Ninety percent of the guys in that cell with me, the ones who probably don't even know why they've been arrested, they're the ones who need the celebrity lawyer."

"And your case throws light on theirs. And this government."

"This is my point. You've been representing me for six years, Garry. Four of those I've been doing this series. Bangkok, Kabul, Bucharest."

"You've done a lot of great work, Henry."

"Meaning I made some money, yes? Had nice, smart people write nice, smart things about the art."

"You telling me nobody cares, Henry? You know when you took the Auden quote about poetry making nothing happen and painted it on the doormat for the group show at Graves? I thought that was too bloody cute. I never told you that, I suppose."

Henry grinned, looked over at one of the guards as if he might share in the humour of the moment. The guard was not amused. "Well… this is a good time for confessions, I guess. I'll have to work on mine."

"All right then. If this is how you want to play it, let me actually make it effective. Let's make something happen, Henry."

Henry picked up Peter Bishop's card from the table, examined it carefully. "Nice font."

"I can get an open letter in the Times for Sunday."

Henry exhaled, stared up at the bank of caged fluorescent tubes on the ceiling. "All right. I will take your wise counsel. I don't need Peter Bishop. Just your particular talent for publicity."

Garry leaned back and nodded sternly, taking back the business card. "This is you bucking up and I like it. At least we can get somewhere. I'll be back in two days. You keep it together, all right?"

They embraced. Garry smelled faintly of the cologne Henry remembered from the office above his gallery. The thought of London in March, the last time he was there, filled with him a sense of longing for freedom that was so overwhelming he could feel himself tear up. He looked away and promptly moved towards the door that would lead back to his cell.

Maybe it was just his contrary nature, his ability to stoically inflict pain on himself that Henry had resisted giving Garry what was his most powerful point of leverage for his trial. The police had taken everything upon his arrest. But in a moment of grace as they processed him in Temara, he quickly snatched the SD card with his photos from his camera. From his drug years he was not squeamish about concealment. Yet an uncomfortable insertion wasn't even necessary; a young guard had watched Henry furtively pluck the card out of the camera, nodded, with the briefest of looks that suggested quiet complicity, and then made a show of handling all of Henry's equipment himself in front of two of his superiors. Henry thought of Hacene's not-so-cryptic answer of "spring is coming" when he had asked him about graffiti outside the pension. Now here was the card, in the breast pocket of his black t-shirt. Back in his little corner of the cage, as he patted by his heart, it gave him some sense of consolation that it was still there. He wouldn't trade it for anything now but one thing: his little bejeweled photo of Yasmin. And this little treasure, the card the size of a postage stamp, was not for his "money man" but for her.

What was it about her that had made him so smitten? Of course he loved her mind—the library in her head—but it was also her kindness to her friends and her family at the opening of the exhibition in Ottawa. And, these feelings aside, he kept thinking about the two times they had slept together.

The first was in Ottawa a few days after that opening, in her small apartment after her instructor and 'mentor' (her words) Mehdi Mekhounam had left following dinner and drinks. He wanted to like this man but there was no ease to the conversation. Mehdi was at his most didactic about how the government was a willing partner in the crimes of what he called 'the new imperium,' how the attacks in Paris and Belgium had brought the old conflicts back in the foreground, made the rendition and detainment of Daesh suspects a fait accompli. Yes, he was probably right but even Yasmin seemed disappointed by how humourless he was. She had said he was too young for his new beard. Once Mehdi had left, it was as if she wanted to prove to Henry there was nothing intimate about her relationship with her old professor, that she had chosen him. She took Henry's hand, led him into her bedroom, whispered "this is what I want to remember tonight for."

The second time was in Montreal, after his show had opened there. So many old friends in the room at his friend Christian's new restaurant in Mile End but the only person he really wanted to talk to was her. And she had come back with him to his hotel, whispering in the cab that he had gotten her drunk on that Spanish wine that was so good, that she was only so impulsive with him.

In both instances it seemed as if she was giving in, not to him but to the part of herself she kept hidden from the world. She had given it a location—"our secret hiding place." The only person she wanted there was him. Given all the pleasures there, why would he ever want to be anywhere else?

She was working on getting a flight to Rabat, she'd said on their one call. She was trying to figure out how long she could stay. She probably had no idea what she had done—given him the kind of hope that made him still feel human.

★

Back in his cell he felt a kick at his feet. There was a sudden commotion, a parting of bodies in the crowd like doors opened up in a crowded train and he looked up from his crouched position to see the young man he gave his watch to. He reminded him of some street urchin from a Caravaggio painting. The full lips and round cheeks of a child only made the sense of menace from him more disturbing—evil, not innocence as a natural state. He was smiling, hectoring in Tamashek, pointing to the breast pocket of Henry's shirt.

"Money. Money there."

Henry shook his head. "No. Je n'ai rien." He pulled out the SD card to show him. And then he felt the boy's spit as it sprayed across his cheek and left eye. The boy pushed him back and he slammed into the wall of the cell as the bodies parted around them. He could hear shouts and jeers, the sound of men suddenly hungry for violence.

Henry looked wildly around him and he could see the fear on the face of the little man who was weeping earlier. One soul who was worried for him, no one else.

And then, from the corner of his eye, he glimpsed a flash of metal. The boy pulled out an exacto knife from the pocket of his filthy green soccer warmup. The blade was small but it would do the job, no question. The shouts around him sounded like a cheer.

The boy lunged, slashed. Henry shielded his face and felt the knife break the skin on his forearm. His heart was pounding wildly as the pain was searing, and he felt the muscle memory of his street fights in Vancouver take over.

He kicked at the spot behind the boy's knee, where he knew the blow could break a leg. And indeed it hobbled the boy. Another wave of shouts from the men around them, the pleasure of sudden reversal of fortune. He grabbed the boy's wrist and hammered it against the bars of the cell. The knife dropped to the floor. With one more sweeping kick it was in the corridor for the guards to find.

Henry could sense how unfair his self-defence looked now. It was a thought that flickered up as the boy spun and he rabbit punched him, sending him sprawling. Henry saw them both as if he was levitated out of his body. The boy was unconscious.

He realized he just might have killed him.

5.

It was more than two years since Gordon had made the trip to Marithe's house but much looked the same. No pines felled for new development, as Marithe had feared. The road wound through the close corridor of shade and you could suddenly be miles from the city. Each home was set far back in the woods but you could still spot some ranch houses, a couple of boxy cabin frames blown up to twice a cabin's size. Signs of life flickered like pilot lights in the few windows where the curtains weren't drawn. This was now a neighbourhood for the old, not the young.

A ropey-armed, bearded old man, dressed all in black, emerged from a garage with a racing bike. He climbed on, hunched over the handlebars and began to accelerate, his gaze squarely set on Gordon's oncoming car. An old neighbour scowling like a doomsday prophet.

You're not welcome here anymore.

Gordon remembered Henry first riding his bike without training wheels on this road.

Running behind him with one hand on the back seat to steady him. Breathless, as Henry found his balance on the pedals. Gordon had put his hand on the seat, then the back fender, then his little boy was speeding ahead, laughing. Henry always had joy in his life growing up. How did he end up so serious, so angry?

Time, maturity and success had softened the hard edges, thankfully. They had also brought father and son to a state a good deal better than the simmering détente reached during Henry's years at art school. Marithe, however, seemed content to maintain her own state of detachment and exile from both of them.

And yet surely she had to care, she would be moved enough to act with him now for the sake of their child. This is what got him in the car this morning. He would do the work; he would make more of the effort. She could remain contemptuous of him and all he has become but this was not about him. Position this as two worried parents doing what's right, how about that?

Marithe answered the door and smiled for him. It was the same one of broken consolation she had perfected once their divorce was settled. She said his name—Gordon, never Gord— and took him in her arms. It was an embrace one would expect from an audience with the queen: firm, quick, with a perfunctory pat on the back. And then he was freed and standing, unsure what to do with his hands.

"You look great. The hair, I mean."

"The grey? Ha." The laugh sounded like it had been punched out of her.

"No, I mean you've let it grow long."

"Oh it's been this way for k-vite some time, Gordon. I suppose it's been a while, yeah? Come in, come in."

He entered and walked directly into the kitchen. This was the home he had walked out of on a rainy Sunday night in July of 1995, the first act of the marriage's end. The walls have been painted a muted grey. Everything's neutral in tone, including her cardigan and linen dress. How many women have lived here with her? Two, Henry had reported, his source a sculptor friend who knew one of them. No one any more though. Now it's the house as she always wished it was—the tastefully appointed shelter on her island of solitude.

"Can I get you a glass of wine? I'm having one."

"That's probably a good idea."

She walked to the fridge and pulled out a bottle of German Riesling. Alsace—he remembered the pension where they stayed together in Strasbourg. One month after he had finished his MA in History at the London School of Economics—she still had a semester to go there. They were newly in love and he was discovering her country, her language. For a while it seemed as if their love would remake him as a man far more European than any MacPhail could have ever imagined being—there in the land of his grandfather's enemy. So much possibility. He's loved German wine ever since.

"To your health, Gordon."

"Thank you, Marithe." He turned and took in the living room. On the wall was a painting of a warehouse along a river bank. He'd say it had a Scandinavian quality of light—words he'd keep to himself discussing paintings with Henry. It has to remind her of Hamburg. But she would never admit to being sentimental about her childhood home. "How are you liking the university?"

"Ah, the teaching." She ran a hand through her hair at the crown of her head, stared into the zinc counter as she sat in the stool opposite him. "We shall see if I can survive it. I am a visiting lecturer. I have an out. Though I'm sure that is exactly how they want it too."

"I don't believe that. I'm sure they love you. Students, especially."

"Well thank you, Senator MacPhail. You remain so very complimentary."

"I am being my best self, as the kids say."

"Do they?"

"The kids on the hill anyway. The ones running our government."

"It must be so strange to be in that world." She shook her head. She has done everything she can to convey her contempt by the way she said the word 'strange' despite the ambiguity of the statement. Teaching public policy to students after twenty-five years as a bureaucrat, she must frighten the hell out of them. "But you were always heading in that direction, weren't you?"

"Oh if you had a sense of that, I certainly didn't. I mean I saw what it took out of Dad."

It's been years since either of them has mentioned his father. But there was a time back in the eighties when even Marithe called him Dad. It was a word she'd never call Herr Heinemann, still very much alive, still very much in charge of the corporation back in Hamburg, no doubt: the terrifying Papa. You could say that at least they had this in common: they were still getting over their old men.

"But you said yes to them, Gordon. You could have turned them down."

"I suppose that's true. I suppose I wanted it."

The place on his knuckle where the wedding band used to be is still visible. As he spoke he covered it with his other hand. It bothered him that she had left her mark. Not always but certainly right now.

"What do you want to do with it?"

"With it?"

"Your new title. Your new life."

He took a sip of wine and swallowed. It tasted like a summer of possibility long ago. He was going to write history books, live in foreign cities, speak three languages. Marithe had nothing to forgive him for then.

"I think I'm there for the right reasons, Marithe. I know you may not believe it but it's true."

"Doesn't everyone believe that of himself in your line of work?"

"I think we have to get our son free."

She looked past his shoulder and focused on a distant point out the window. It was like she was sensing something approaching. "One of your lawyer friends will be working to get him free. Let's be clear, Gordon. You're here for money."

"Is that wrong?"

"If I had no money, would you be here?"

"He's your son too, Marithe."

"My relationship with Henry is none of your business."

"None of my business?"

"None of your business beyond the obligations we both agreed to. If you'll recall, I spent years reminding you of those obligations. Nagging you to do the bare minimum as his father. Set some boundaries."

"This is about how he spent his inheritance, isn't it? And you still haven't forgiven him. Unbelievable."

"We were talking about obligations. It's predictable, you changing the subject."

"You'll never believe it was just his addiction. That he was ill. For you it remains some deliberate act of rebellion."

"I don't want to go over this again."

"And yet you raised it when you mentioned boundaries."

She smiled. A quick tight wince before it evaporated in veiled acrimony.

He remembered picking Henry up from a night in jail. Henry had turned to him in the car, crying, telling him he was trapped in a nightmare. He smelled like an ashtray. He said he could not even remember many of his lies. Yes, Marithe was right when she had called him a thief, a compulsive liar, and yes there was indeed a conviction for credit card fraud. But in that moment of breakdown Henry was still his boy.

When Marithe had found out that all of Henry's inheritance was spent, she had made her mind up and closed the door on him; she had said he'd never be welcome in her home again. It revealed a harshness, a streak of cruelty that evoked the worst of what she'd told Gordon of strict Herr Heinemann, Marithe's father. If she had been conscious of that, she would not admit it. The whole episode was a hollowing-out of whatever remained of the family for the three of them.

"It was twelve years ago, Marithe. I guess I'm still surprised nothing has healed between the two of you. I'll never regret standing by him."

"And I'm sorry. You can say nothing has healed. I would just say he and I are clear about our boundaries. We speak. We're cordial."

"How unconditionally loving of you."

"Do you really want to talk about unconditional love, Gordon? I'll never feel guilty for the decision I made at the time. You can try now once again but there is a more pressing concern, yes?"

He nodded, folds his hands together as if ready to pray. "Okay. Yes, I'd be happy to. I'd just like to preface it by saying that everything I'm about to tell you here, it's what I was advised from the government."

"I would have liked to be in that meeting."

"It was a call. A guy I knew who could help."

"Like a plumber."

"Sure. Listen, what he told me is this: Henry can't handle all of the expenses alone."

"He's done well for himself. His art."

"I talked to the guy who manages his portfolio. And then I talked to his dealer."

"That English man I met at Henry's show here in Vancouver, yes?" Marithe took a sip of the Riesling and frowned, as if she suddenly found the wine to be bitter.

"Fry. Garry Fry, yes."

"Man looked like a banker."

"Bankers buy Henry's work. Bankers and the Russians who bank with them, anyway."

"Photographs of prisons. That is all I need to know of contemporary art and the world he's in now."

"Marithe, he's not as wealthy as you think. All in, with his assets, a couple million. Because he's a foreigner in one of their facilities… as they say… they're charging him for everything. And if he gets off with a fine—best case scenario—they'll bankrupt him."

Marithe turned from him, shaking her head. She was staring out the window at some indeterminate point past the boxwood hedge. She was doing everything she could not to show her grief. "We have to get him out of there."

"I spoke with him yesterday on the phone. He asked me to find a lawyer for him. So I've contacted an old friend, Hisham Mahmoud."

"An old political friend?"

"It is through politics we met, yes. But he'll be right for this because he speaks Arabic and French. He knows the region, he's been to Rabat."

Actually he was not sure about that last statement. But if it helped to make a convincing case, he would use it.

"You're not doing him a favour or anything?" She folded her arms. This was a tone she had perfected in the last years of their marriage. A mix of the cynical and the maternal. As if Gordon was a teenager that had to be managed. He and Henry were the two boys she'd needed to distance herself from in order to live, as she put it, 'aut'entically.'

"Quite the contrary. He said he'd waive his travel expenses."

"Does this Mr. Mahmoud think he can get Henry off?"

"He thinks he can make a strong case in appeal to, at the very least, get the sentence reduced. Henry could serve six months and then be freed. But if that's going to happen other people have to get paid. It's the way it works in Morocco."

"Wonderful."

"Hisham is at least direct about all this. More direct than the people in Foreign Affairs."

"I'm sure he is. He's talking about a transaction. He's a lawyer."

"Marithe, Henry was doing nothing more than taking photographs."

"That we know of. You, me and your friend Hisham. There could be more information in the trial."

He drained his glass of wine and took a deep breath. Controlling his twinge of rage. That she could still do this to him was an indication of some residual love, wasn't it? He needed to believe there was some part of him who was still the person who married her.

"Marithe, I guess it's a question of trust. Is Henry's work my cup of tea? Your cup of tea? Maybe not. Did he trespass on government land? Violate their security laws? Yeah, sure. He's not a spy. He's not a criminal. He's still our son."

"I am being lectured by you on the question of trust. Permit me if I reflect on the irony." She rose from her chair and walked toward the hallway closet. There her purse was hanging on a hook. No matter how big her purses were over the years, he remembered each one of them as overstuffed, pockets of chaos and disarray that she would never permit in any other part of her life. She removed a chequebook and a pen and returned to the table. "I have cashed in some of my savings."

"I did too."

"Gordon, you would think, for all your years in the back rooms with your friends, you wouldn't have to do that."

She wrote quickly, with a slant and a crabbed cursive that seemed from another era. Love letters from an ocean liner long since sunk below the waves. One, two, three, four, five zeros. This felt like their very last ritual of parenthood together.

"I'll set up the account. You'll have full access. It's nothing but his legal fund."

"This is all I can do."

"I understand, Marithe. The trial, though… will you come?"

"I suppose I haven't decided yet." She ran her hand through her hair. A big turquoise ring… that was new. She'd never choose something like that for herself. Perhaps a lover's gift. "I will let you know in a couple of days once I get a sense of my teaching schedule. How's that?"

He nodded, slipping the cheque into the chest pocket of his jacket. If he had learned anything over the years since their divorce, it was when to make his exit.

But as he passed her he felt her hand brush his arm and he turned to her once more.

"Gordon, I love my son. You tell him that, please."

And as he saw the tears well up in her eyes he had to stop himself from embracing her. "I will, Marithe. I'll bring him home."

He turned away, his gaze fixed on his car in the driveway. If he doesn't leave now, he won't know when or how to leave later. Far too much could be said.

6.

They were going to have lunch on a patio, Hannah Eisenberg and Yasmin. It was Yasmin's request, and Hannah was pleased her articling student, her favourite, was opening up to her this way. And why shouldn't they get outside? The good weather was so fleeting, you had to take advantage of it, Hannah cautioned to Yasmin. This was something about this logging town Hannah had never gotten used to after more than two decades. A scrap of swampland amid a boreal forest, that was Ottawa—even the term boreal sounded harsh and primeval. The stunted growth of her tomato plants in her small garden over the last five years was testament to the fact the summers were only getting worse too. But the buildings along Sparks Street did not block out the sun, and the restaurant food was actually much improved these days, so it was worth the short walk from the office. They could talk on the way about other things than work, really get to know each other.

And then it began to rain. Not a light sprinkling—angry torrential blasts that felt like icy nettles on her bare arms. Hannah and Yasmin had to sprint to a food court underground. As they took the escalator down, Yasmin turned to Hannah, wide eyed, thrilled by the power of the storm and what they had escaped. Hannah's long white linen shirt was soaked through and she was more irritated than thrilled, yet she laughed with Yasmin, as if this was a little sisterly mischief they could share.

But the truth was that Hannah felt less like a sister than a woman fighting off her displaced maternal feelings for Yasmin. The young woman was like an orphan far from home; over drinks at the beginning of the summer Yasmin had told Hannah she was an only child who had grown up in Philadelphia, after immigrating from Lahore. An over-achieving immigrant's child

(Hannah knew that drama), Yasmin had played piano well enough to enter state competitions until she was sixteen. This was information Hannah had felt she could have guessed, because she had played cello well enough to tour with a quartet at eighteen, and she sensed Yasmin's same awkwardness around other young women who had less disciplined study through their childhoods. To counter her own awkwardness as a teenager, Hannah had tried to affect a casual, hippie-from-the-kibbutz persona after she had come back from Israel and enrolled (early) at UBC, and she detected a similar attempt at granola bohemianism on Fridays, when Yasmin would wear her Birkenstocks and boyish jeans to the office. At those "5PM Socials," both Hannah and Yasmin worked harder to sound cheerful and witty with their colleagues, and it didn't always come off as authentic. The two of them were like women from another era who expertly concealed their introverted selves, and pretended they were oblivious about their attractiveness and the petty resentments and jealousies their looks could cause. You could say Hannah overthought how connected they were but truly, Hannah was incapable of not overthinking—and this too she saw in Yasmin.

"I should eat something healthier but they've got a Broadway Bobby's down here," Yasmin said.

"Broadway Bobby's?"

"Burgers and fries. And Tex-Mex poutine."

"I thought you were vegetarian."

"Because I didn't take anything from that charcuterie plate last Friday?"

"Ah yes. Okay. Pork sausage."

"Which looked delicious, I might add."

"It wasn't, if that's any consolation."

As they stood in the long line at Broadway Bobby's, and the silence between them deepened, Hannah was already feeling too serious, wishing she could have taken her last words back.

"It's a good idea, those Friday socials," Yasmin said, her voice an octave higher than usual.

"I know!" I always say I'll stay for just a glass of wine and end up taking a cab home at seven. I'm glad you're enjoying them."

"I feel the office is just big enough so you can really get to know everyone. I don't know what I would have done if I had gone to Blake's. Me and a hundred other articling students."

"Oh you'd be doing fine anywhere."

"No, really! If I hadn't met you through the Amitas meetings, Hannah, it would have been totally different. And not better. I'm so grateful."

"Oh… you're welcome! You don't have to say that."

Hannah didn't know what to do with all this stiltedness, the sudden obsequiousness. Thankfully, the line at Broadway Bobby's had moved quickly enough that they could order, joke about the menu as if it was a shared, guilty pleasure, and take their odd little numbered sticks on quoits to their table along a tiled walkway. Hannah could sense, in how "grateful" Yasmin was, something coming in the conversation. No, it was not a bonding moment Yasmin was looking for when she asked her to lunch. That was not how this young woman worked. It was best to get out ahead of it.

"Yasmin, I'm glad you invited me to lunch because I was meaning to check in with you, to see how you were liking it. I know not all the client work is particularly riveting."

"Oh listen… I know I have a lot to learn. It's all experience."

"That's true." An extravagantly tattooed young woman in a black t-shirt and Broadway Bobby's apron was squinting in their direction. She was carrying two trays with cheeseburgers wrapped in paper. Hannah raised her hand like she was waving down a taxi. "I feel like there's a however coming. A however with fries."

Yasmin did not laugh. She only looked down at the table, as if she was putting her words in order in her head. "Hannah, I wanted to tell you about a case of possible imprisonment. In Morocco."

"Possible imprisonment?"

"He's a photographer. Henry Raeburn. I went to his show in Ottawa some months ago. We had heard about it through Amitas. Henry takes photos of black sites."

Hannah picked up a french fry and examined it before chewing a small section from it, as if it were a crudité. "Ah. Okay. Yes, I remember. I couldn't go."

"It's complicated. For a couple of reasons." Yasmin was etching out a circle with her index finger on the table between them. She had not touched her hamburger. It was still wrapped up, as if she'd briefly enthused about it and then forgotten it existed. Which was odd, unless you considered that Hannah had mentioned her weakness for hamburgers and poutine over drinks at work two weeks ago, and Yasmin probably filed that away. Well what did that say about her, other than she was ambitious? "First, his dad's a senator."

"Raeburn?" Hannah's gaze went above Yasmin's head, as she was trying to recall if anyone by that surname had recently been appointed.

"No. MacPhail."

"Gordon MacPhail?"

"You know him?"

Hannah was remembering a young Gordon, in the backyard of his parents' home in Kerrisdale. He was standing on a diving board on a cloudy summer afternoon. Lean and tanned, like he was carved from blonde wood. He was sixteen, she had just turned seventeen before him. He was smiling for her before he jackknifed into the water. He was her first love after she had lost her virginity in Kibbutz Shamir to Yuval, the boy who had broken her heart. Gordon was a 180 turn, the WASP ideal all of her girlfriends never thought she would date. He was sweet natured, curious about the world but had none of the passion, the earnestness of Yuval. Why would he have? Gordon was a boy for whom the world was bound to welcome and ensure he got all the presents; he would never have to work as hard as she did for anything—and everything would come his way as long as he didn't let the old side down.

And so there was an unfortunate sense of destiny fulfilled when last she had seen him. There he had been, in that largest of committee rooms over in Centre Block, the point man among his fellow senators as he filibustered the motion for the government to look into whom the ground troops might have handed over to allied forces in Kandahar, only to have those detainees sent to black sites in Bangkok, in Bucharest… maybe even somewhere in Morocco. No one was ever going to know, really, the government would make sure of it.

She had caught Gordon's eye in that committee room and for a brief moment she could see a crack emerge in his composure, a pleading look in his eyes. All she could do was give him a serious nod. It was all her fury permitted. Then she remembered turning to Yasmin and Mehdi Mehkounam, the U of O professor who had been so assiduously filing access to information requests in the hopes of nailing these useful idiots who were doing the devil's work for their government for at least a decade or more. She had pretended she was checking to see if Yasmin was taking notes (but of course she was). She could not give Gordon MacPhail any more of herself that day.

"Yasmin, he was one of those senators in committee the last time we were on the Hill for Amitas."

"Seriously? God, that's right, I'm remembering the Hansard I transcribed now."

"His son's in jail in Morocco?"

"Uh huh. Well it's this, Hannah. I… um… I have become involved with Henry." Her eyes wouldn't meet Hannah's. There was a sudden formality, a stiffening of her movements as she sat straight up in her seat, gave her hijab a light tug as if she could conceal her mouth.

"I see. My God, you must be so worried."

"I am, yes. And Hannah, I want to thank you for everything but I'm afraid I'm going to take a leave of absence. Indefinitely. I have to be with him now."

Hannah gently pushed her tray aside. She was no longer interested in lunch. She was trying to figure out why she felt so angry. Would she feel this way if it were another articling student? A boy, some doughy, hockey playing kid she could have never imagined being her child? This was definitely some motherly protectiveness coming through. Twenty years ago she would have torn such a reductive, physiological argument about her irrationality to pieces. Not anymore. But that didn't mean she had to give in to her anger either.

"Yasmin, before you do this... and I'm just assuming you haven't bought a ticket and made arrangements yet."

Yasmin shook her head. She crossed her arms and legs, a closed book.

"I just want to suggest that you might be able to be more effective in Ottawa. Either through Amitas or our office... I mean, Mehdi knows people in Rabat. You don't have to put your life on hold."

Yasmin looked her in the eyes now, once again. And yet she held her gaze too long, as if she was willing herself to look sincere. "I thought of this, Hannah. But thank you. I want to tell you I know how competitive these articling positions are. I know what I could be sacrificing."

"So don't. Seriously. Let me help you with this. We have resources. I've got Mehdi's card. I'm going to call him when we get back to the office."

Yasmin shook her head and then gently touched Hannah's hand across the table. Such a tender gesture, full of real fondness. "No, Hannah please. I thank you. I thank you for everything. Maybe you have felt this once? This feeling that you cannot be apart from someone?"

Hannah looked at the backs of her hands, remembering the brown blotches on her husband Isaac's, the way his wrists became so thin and child-like when he was in palliative over those last three weeks. They hadn't lived together for the good part of a decade when he got the news about the cancer coming back but, as she said to her mother, she couldn't not be there for him. She took all four weeks of her vacation; she never saw the sun that August. Just the bluish white light of his hospital room, her afternoons reading him Bellow and Caro's Johnson books as he faded in and out of sleep. Isaac her mentor, her lover, going out like a lamb not a lion.

"I suppose I do, yes."

It made her feel a little better about herself to say this. It almost sounded true.

7.

In his nine full days of detainment, only one image made Henry feel that all might not be lost—one, apart from the gradual stirring back to consciousness of the boy who attacked him of course—and it was Yasmin's shy smile, sitting across from him.

They didn't say much to each other that was memorable when she visited. He asked her about her articling with Hannah Eisenberg, the lawyer she had idolized for her work on the stateless around the world, but all Yasmin would say was that it was fine, it had gone well but she didn't know when she would return to the office. She was more concerned about him, of course, how he was managing.

The problem was they gave him no books here. The library only had one in English: Dale Carnegie's "How to Win Friends and Influence People." There had to be a story about how it got in this hell hole that would be worth listening to but no one here could possibly remember. Who would befriend an American who read that?

Yasmin promised she'd bring a few paperbacks for him upon her return. He only wanted history, and no contemporary writers: how about Herodotus, Gibbon, Carlyle. Why not Mohammed al-Qadiri or even Muhammad Iqbal? Too close to home, he told her, not quite seriously.

He said he'd trust her to decide, and that he was just appreciative of any time he had with her at all. Which didn't necessarily follow but what could he do? He couldn't think that straight when she was in the room with him; he was just overwhelmed by all the things he wanted to say, now that she was in this country.

And then, as he reached for her hand, she glimpsed a corner of the SD card from his camera, under his fingers. She touched his and like a card sharp snatched it and looked up at the clock on the opposite wall with a sigh. What a performance, she was a natural.

She would return soon—in a couple of days, she had promised. She was trying to figure out how long she could stay, she'd said. She probably had no idea what she'd done—given hope and imagination back to his waking hours.

He would save such thoughts for his walks in the yard. They were twice a day, in the mornings and evenings after the prayers of his fellow prisoners. The chanting voice of some ancient Imam blared from the speakers of a nearby mosque. Were those clerics ever young? All over the old city, they sounded like they might have been alive at the time of Mohammed himself. In the evenings, the angle of the sun and the spare contrast of the guard towers and the minarets out in the suburbs made him feel like he was sleepwalking through a Dali painting. With his thoughts turning to painting as he circled the fence line, his loneliness briefly transformed into a bearable solitude.

Of course he reflected on when and if he would work again. He wondered if he'd unconsciously willed the arrest. It brought to a close the series he'd grown tired of; he had long been suppressing his own objections to each finished work. He thought of Courbet, imprisoned at the end of Commune, painting still lifes of scarred apples. Maybe that was the way to revive what creativity was still in him. Back to painting—wouldn't that surprise everyone?

But a change in approach could be perceived as surrender. He could best expose his intentions by painting like a Soviet social realist. Pastoral Canadian scenes with just the subtlest visual cues to the dirty work abroad. But if he could work this all out in his head, what was there left to discover on the canvas? Irony wearied him, made him feel dumb.

His politics didn't make him feel better.

Once he had finished his degree in Montreal and had his first studio show, he said to himself he'd complete a painting a day. Didn't matter if they were any good, he'd just grind them out. He'd moved to Toronto, got a basement apartment in Little

Portugal where, lucky him, the garage was empty. He could use it as studio for free. So he cleaned it up, cleared enough space for a couple of easels. He collected photographs from magazines and plates from old books, pinned them up on the walls. These were images that sparked him in some way. He'd take them in, close his eyes, and begin to paint.

He was concentrating so hard on his technique that he decided he needed to paint in absolute silence. Yet the problem was the walls of the garage were too thin. The noise back there—the kids dealing dime bags and smoking dope, the dog walkers ("Caesar, no! Caesar!" became the name of one painting), the cars rumbling along the rutted pavement—it began to enrage him. He'd bellow his curses in frustration, especially at the cars.

One hot summer morning, he hit what he reported in his journal as "a breaking point." He'd heaved open the garage door, blaring his loudest music through old stereo speakers. He wasn't just surrendering to noise; he was embracing it. He radically altered his technique and his palette, quickly slashing away at the images. He'd become a guitar player who had reduced everything he knew to three chords, played loud and fast. This had all felt so liberating until he realized one or two finished works interested him and the rest just seemed derivative. Still, this was what the imperative of engagement had become for him—filling his ears with noise, throwing the old garage door open to the light and the chaos of the alley. He had to start again from the premise—and the promise—that his art wouldn't deny those sounds anymore.

Last night he had written to Yasmin, without irony, that it wasn't with dreams that responsibilities began (the phrase his mother put in a letter to him): it was with politics. Dreams can will an escape. Not so the effort to understand the other, the noise and the desire and the desperation of people. That clamour was one window thrown open on a working day. But here was a secret: he was now tired of responsibilities. Could you blame him if this is where they led?

Only Yasmin could ~~solve~~ him no he meant save him.

He heard a guard's footsteps. There were four prisoners in individual cells down this corridor—all older with the same proud bearing, their own clothes. They must be wealthy or politically connected to the government or both—the guard might be coming for one of these "neighbours." But now there was something about the cadence of the guard's steps that affirmed it was he the guard had come to summon from his cot in this new cell. The official march for the foreigner.

"Come, Canadian." The guard's voice was low but melodious. He probably had as much talent for music as he did for menace. "Your ambassador's here."

Henry lifted himself up from the bed on his elbows. "My ambassador?" He pantomimed great surprise. He was slowly becoming a silent screen actor in here.

"Yes. Come! Come!"

Once the barred door was open and he began to move, he felt lightheaded. If one were sentimental, you could say it was the possibility of diplomatic intervention rather than his crap diet in here that brought on the dizziness. Who else could have caused Ashwin himself to come but Henry's father? The old man—always there for him, no matter how down-to-business and disappointed he'd sounded on the phone the last Sunday. The necessary distance between them never felt harder to bear than in moments like this, when gratitude about being loved and cared for couldn't be denied—or expressed well.

He and the guard entered the long bank of carrels that made up the visiting room, and there was Ambassador Ashwin Khadilkar, the only person on the other side of the Plexiglas screens along a row of chairs. He looked dressed for a funeral in his pressed black suit, white shirt and black tie. Guy must go from air conditioned room to room all day.

Ashwin stood up once he saw Henry entering. From his expression this gesture seemed less out of respect than curiosity about what kind of person this fellow Canadian might be. He looked Henry up and down, apparently concerned by the cheap rubber sandals the prison had issued him. Henry felt self-conscious, as if the sandals were somehow his choice.

As they took their seats across from each other, Ashwin was the first to hunch over and speak into his microphone. He introduced himself then remarked that Henry looked thinner than his photographs. Was he eating enough?

"It's bearable. After the fight they moved me. I seem to be in a wing with business class prisoners. There are no cockroaches in the food."

He surprised himself by how casual he sounded about the violence within him, his ability to still do damage to another human being. He felt no shame about it. This was new, a coarsening he wasn't even aware of until the words left his mouth.

"That's good to hear. I'll tell your father. We spoke this morning for about a half hour. He says you and he have been speaking quite a bit since you've been imprisoned."

"We have, yes. And he always asks if I'm eating too. It's the first thing he puts to me on most calls."

"Is that a surprise?"

"I suppose not."

"We all want you to stay healthy. Keep up your strength."

"Thank you for your concern. I guess I say your excellency?"

Ashwin allowed himself the start of a smile and then looked down at the wooden desk in front of him. Names and places carved with penknives, it looked like. How were the visitors allowed them in here? "Oh I am too young for such an old man's world... sorry, I meant word. Call me Ashwin."

"Ashwin, I appreciate you coming here. I imagine this is not something that happens for every Canadian who finds himself in trouble."

"That's true. Your arrest merits greater attention for all concerned. I mean, I understand this is... well, your practice, isn't this right? Taking these photographs?"

"It's a part of my practice, currently. That's correct."

"It's my understanding that not all of this work you do requires that you trespass."

Ah, the media: Ashwin had read some stories on him. Of course Garry would have put out a press release about his arrest. He's working on the open letter, no doubt. Here was a cynical thought he couldn't deny: this had to be good for the market value of his work. Garry—not Henry—stood to make quite a bit more money.

"It sounds like I've made the news."

"A little bit, yes. Few details right now. I'm sure there will be more interest in the days ahead. Not just in Canada."

"Not just in Canada but probably not here."

"No. You can't be arrested for photographing a site that doesn't officially exist."

"That's our government's position too, isn't it?"

Ashwin clasped his jaw, ran his hand across his mouth as if he were tracing a goatee he had shaved off. "Let's just say it has to be."

"Why?"

"You asked why this was not a story in the media here. That's what I can tell you. That a tourist was arrested for trespassing on government land is not anyone's idea of a front page."

Henry gently pushed himself back with his hands flat on the desk before him. He frowned, peering through the Plexiglas at Ashwin's steady gaze, and slowly nodded to suggest he understood. "You think I am in serious trouble, your excellency?"

"I think this is serious, yes."

"I think they have destroyed my property. My camera. Taking photographs is how I make my art. It's how I make a living."

"I understand that, Mr. Raeburn. I'm not here to advise you. I imagine your family's hiring a good lawyer to do that. Your father—"

"I haven't committed to anyone."

"Nevertheless, I can tell you that the government here might be prepared to lighten your sentence if there was some indication you were going to keep those photos to yourself."

"Ah. You heard. So you think I should make a deal."

"We can negotiate a fine. You were trespassing on a protected cultural site, a nature reserve of one of their princes. The beggars in the city, they go out there and dig for trilobite fossils, petrified shark's teeth. They'll jack your fine up, say they want to make it clear to foreigners that their culture will not be exploited."

"I spoke with my dealer. Some friends of his in London. They do finance."

Ashwin cocked an eyebrow, allowed himself a look of sullen approval. There was something about the phrase 'do finance' he liked.

"I mean it's simple. This is extortion by a corrupt state. My only leverage is exposing this, really."

"Before you came to Morocco did you know much about this country at all, Mr. Raeburn?"

Ashwin was choosing his words for maximum effect. That effect being an understanding he would not be fucked with. He had come to this hellhole where Henry was languishing because it was his job. And because Henry's father was who he was.

"I know enough about how it was colonized, what the French did while they were here. It's no surprise to me this current government is what it is. No surprise I'm here. Is it a surprise to you?"

Ashwin leaned back in his chair, primly crossed his legs, folded his hands together on his knee. Taking the measure of Henry. "Surprise would be too strong a word. I'm not surprised by anything. I'm just amused. I mean I'm obliged to offer you my best counsel."

"Thank you for your service."

"I'm telling you you should play ball and just start talking about paying the fine. I'm telling you your government can't work for you with one hand tied behind its back. You want to embarrass the prime minister's office here, expose what you view as his complicity with the Americans, still fixated, almost two decades on, with their 9-11 phantoms—"

"Oh I think we're just as complicit."

"I would argue we're not complicit at all but pragmatic. It's a winning quality, in my book. My point is you're putting this government in a defensive position. Please listen to me on this: your trial will not go well. They do not care. Your art, who your father is… you know what I'm saying?"

"Oh I think I do, yes."

"Aside from a more pragmatic perspective, if I were you, I'd also be thinking about my father and the position this puts him in."

"What position?"

"You're affirming activities our government does not want to address in a foreign court of law."

"Okay, here we are. I understand your pragmatism now, your excellency. Rendition. Detainment without trial. Enhanced interrogation techniques."

Ashwin uncrossed his legs, leaned in to speak. His gaze was fixed on the small microphone. "Help me help you." From his tone, if you did not understand English, it sounded like Ashwin had just threatened him.

"I thank you for the offer. I realize now I should go ahead with this trial and not try to negotiate this fine you speak of."

"You know, after that little skirmish of yours in here, who do you imagine got you the private cell?"

"I'm sure it was a pragmatic decision of this government. They don't want to see me dead before they can make money on me."

"Like an art dealer, no?"

Henry could not help but smile. He liked Ashwin's sense of humour despite himself.

Ashwin had found his moment to exit. His chair coughed and scraped as he turned to the door. But then he paused, turned, pulled out his card from his breast pocket and slid it under the Plexiglas. "My direct line is there. If you change your mind on your approach, please give me a call."

"I will, sir."

Henry watched him turn and head for the door. Ashwin had a quick, wide stride, as if he were measuring out yards by counting his paces. Couldn't leave soon enough. He nodded to a guard on the other side of a set of iron bars and then there was the faint buzzing sound. The door clicked and he was gone.

And yet, as Henry got up and headed for the corridor back to his cell, he could see Ashwin talking with someone, at the door to an office. It was another suit nodding, looking down.

Henry took the business card in his hand and ran his finger across the raised lettering of the ambassador's name. Seemed a bit regal and unusual for such a position. His father didn't have government business cards like this. *My old man.* Here he'll be soon, back in a courtroom, once again believing in Henry.

He closed his eyes, saw a soccer field in White Rock, British Columbia. The game was over and his team had lost. The evening sun dipped below the grey-blue mountains and he was full of anger at his eight-year-old self. Not playing good enough, not winning. There behind him, a hand at the small of his back, "It's all right, Henry, it's all right." His dad right there. What he put him through to compete and become fearless.

He felt tears well up. The first time since he was arrested. He rose from his chair and hurried to the door. No one, not even the young guard, was going to see him cry.

8.

Since his arrival in Rabat, Gordon had developed a new appreciation for terrible seventies architecture. Marithe, over dinner with him two days ago, had called, not quite accurately, the newer government buildings "brutalist." She said it reminded her of London when they were students. That was the London nobody wanted to remember. She said Thatcher's people were right to want to flatten all the brutalist projects back then. But Gordon was taking comfort in anything remotely familiar right now: the concrete and steel boxiness of a six-storey block, the empty plaza with the sculpted abstraction stranded in a shallow fountain and now, the fluorescent, migraine-inducing half-light of the courtroom in mid-afternoon. You could be in Ottawa or Croydon or Hamburg, save for the molten caffeine tar from the canteen. Consider it the international style of cultural amnesia.

This was where he and Hisham had met for the last two mornings. Marithe came for the first meeting but grew impatient the longer the two men talked. She hadn't returned since. There was nothing Gordon could do about it. It was Hisham's methodical, discursive approach to make everything that was said in Arabic absolutely clear and yes, he had spoken mainly to Gordon, not giving her much eye contact at all. And so the rapport the two men had once as law students returned; perhaps it was too coded and laconic for anyone but them to understand anyway.

Bags under Hisham's eyes. Back in Vancouver, he came on as an ageing dandy with silk scarves and bangles on his wrists, but not here. His mottled, crabbed hands looked shrunken. The trial has stripped all his vanity away; he's even cut his hair to a monkish stubble.

"I'm not sure why we're back here," he said, eyeing the espresso grinds in his cup, the small plastic bowl of couscous he'd ordered and then decided he wasn't hungry enough to eat.

"There are no tea leaves to read, my friend," Gordon said.

"We could have wrapped this up yesterday, gone to the sentencing."

"I keep waiting for Khadilkar. I am hoping he's being effective behind the scenes."

"What's he afraid of? The perception of complicity or something? If that's the case, then don't have your Head of the Political Section show up and sit here like an errand boy without an errand."

"This government's prepared to fight a publicity war. This is my worry. There was no other reason for that guy from the culture ministry to be on the stand yesterday. Positioning."

"My translation was correct, I hope. I was hearing heritage site."

"That was right. Fossils in the El Harhoura cave or something. 'Dents de requin'... Christ, who knows."

"He was making the case for a culturally protected area."

Hisham nodded. "A lesson to all North American tourists. This is why I think we're looking at the fine."

"You think. How can you be sure?"

"I can't, Gord. You don't fuck with these guys." Hisham shook his head, his gaze fixed on some distant point past the elevators. "I'm worried about the provocation."

"That's not going to involve us. Henry's working with his art dealer, that guy Garry who was at the table last night. A PR flack playing at art dealing."

Gordon was no longer trying to be the soul of diplomacy. Marithe had warmed to Garry Fry, and to this Yasmin Raza, whom Henry seemed to be dating. During the dinner at the French restaurant, the three of them had fallen in like conspirators, leaving Gordon and Hisham to talk BC politics over a Morgon that tasted like bitter cherries. To be left to themselves was fine because really, there was something about Garry Fry that he had found frivolous. He took the opportunity to put himself in the foreground of the conversation, descanting on the menu and what he learned about French cooking when he was a waiter at Julian Cataldo's first restaurant of renown in Spitalfields. And who the hell was Julian Cataldo? Then he just had to pick up the tab because the restaurant was his choice. Dressed like a vacationing banker in his pink linen shirt, Fry said Corbyn was the best thing that had happened to Labour. Fervent nods from Marithe and Yasmin followed. It left Gordon thinking that there were people Garry Fry wanted to charm at the dinner table and people he wanted to piss off—Gordon being the latter.

"I'm just not sure we're helping ourselves with this approach."

"It's the threat of the money on the line. You know what Fry told me last night? Henry was sick a week ago. Really bad nausea and diarrhea. At first they thought it was dysentery."

"Why didn't he tell us that?"

"Fry said Henry told him not to tell me. Said I'd worry."

Hisham shook his head. "Of course you should worry! This is what I'm talking about, Gordon. There's a split focus here."

"I find out it was probably something in his orange juice. A guard could have tampered with it. A day later he was okay. Except the hospital trip and the night in the infirmary came to five thousand dollars."

"See, this is important information. The government's playing us. That's a message. They're saying you don't want to fuck with them by making too much of this black site. If Henry's sentenced, worse might happen."

"I don't disagree."

"That's a politician's thing to say, Gord."

"I mean I agree but I don't know what to do to stop it. It's Henry's choice to play it this way."

"Gord, he's your son. I've tried to talk to him but…" Hisham raised his right hand, stretched out his fingers by the side of his ear as if he was willing a cartoon light bulb to flick on. "He has to realize these people are serious."

"You know as soon as I heard he was arrested, I should have just said that's it, I'm paying the bail, gave him no choice in the matter. It's martyrdom he's playing at."

"I too do not disagree." Hisham sipped from his empty cup, ran his fingers through the stubbles on the crown of his head. "But here we are. We should get up there and meet him. They'll be bringing him in."

As they headed for the elevator, a small fat boy came out of the mens' washroom. He could have been a putto with his long eyelashes, soft dark curls, the flush of pink in his olive complexion. He dashed for the closing elevator doors and, huffing noisily, slipped in like a seal under a wave. He was in a pressed navy suit jacket and matching shorts, thick woolen knee socks. Must be a French school here. The boy didn't smile; he looked straight ahead, focused on the point where the doors met. Then he blinked when the bell for the door opening pinged. Whose little tragedy was he? The old empire, it was still everywhere, still making broken boys.

As Hisham and Gordon walked into the courtroom, they negotiated their way through a small group of journalists, two with video camera equipment slung over their shoulders. This was new and puzzling in the worst way. Why media all of a sudden? No one from the embassy staff was here; for the last three days Torquil Forsey had been sitting one row behind, furtively sending messages via his phone. He had said little, but his presence was at least something; as Hisham noted, he had the manner of a man of the cloth who doesn't believe anymore. Now the familiar faces were only Marithe and, one row behind, Garry Fry and Yasmin Raza. Those two as chummy as old friends now. So many necessary episodes over the last few days felt edited out of Gordon's own film. Like Marithe's time with Henry. Maybe there was a true reconciliation. The fluorescent lights flickered overhead.

The judge entered through the back of the courtroom. He swam within the long black robe with its turquoise sash. With his rimless bifocals and dictator's moustache, he looked embittered by his own formality as he squinted to take in the people in the room. As if he'd prefer to be peering over the windshield of a jeep on the battlefield. Such martial pride radiating from every functionary and bureaucrat in this country. That old dictator aesthetic permeated through to the core of the government.

The police brought in Henry through a side entrance. His jumpsuit was Christmas red, the stubble on his sunken cheeks had darkened into a patchy beard. He smiled for Gordon and Marithe but it was like a brief wince of pain.

Marithe turned and looked to Gordon. Two decades of sadness in the tears that welled up in her eyes. And yet she was trying to smile, summoning her last reserve of hope. Gordon closed his eyes and looked away to stop his own tears from flowing.

Henry took his seat beside Hisham at the desk and they nodded to each other like two commuters on a bus. Hisham murmured something into Henry's ear while Henry looked to Yasmin and Garry Fry. It was unclear to whom Henry was nodding in affirmation; it could have been all of them. Yet there was nothing positive that could be affirmed in the moment.

The resolve is all. Gordon had heard the voice of his grandfather, that growl of a brogue. You couldn't get farther from Dunfermline than here.

Gordon unraveled the plastic wire of his earphones, jacked into the small metal box on the wooden pew in front of him. His French had improved over the last year. Like riding a bike, all his boyhood diligence at Lower Canada College forty years ago, finally paying off. Yet the translator's intonation was so different from any French out of Ottawa or Montreal. Gordon caught phrases, just a general sense, but what he heard more than anything was the calm, remorseless tone of power that would exercise its authority.

The judge had asked for any final submissions from Hisham. He understood there was some question of the accused's private property being returned to him. A satchel with two cameras and sundry items, was that not correct?

Hisham looked to Henry who turned, murmured something to the nape of his neck. Both of them nodded and Hisham turned to face the judge once more, bent lower to speak into the small microphone on his desk. "I understand my client's personal articles will be returned upon the conclusion of this trial, your Honour."

The judge said there was never any question of Henry's property not being returned. But with the camera and any film, there was "a question of cultural property that still must be decided." He scowled at the journalists seated at the back of the room. The volume and the force of the judge's intonation rose; he couldn't help but be provoked as he spoke of the state's duty to protect culture from pernicious influences.

Henry's gaze was locked on him but he was calm, impassive.

The judge droned on about the responsibility of the state towards its homeland. To preserve the past was their duty to the future. He mentioned a railroad built by the French, the antiquities stolen by the foreigners' government.

The bailiff, an older woman in a boxy checked suit, yawned into a fold of her hijab. It suddenly felt like there was a greater depth to the silence in the room.

"Those from outside our borders, like Mr. Raeburn, must understand this is a question of justice for all of our people—those who have come before us, and those who have yet to be born—in the face of desecration, of violation, of our shared property, our shared understanding of our history."

Gordon heard one spectator huff and shift in his seat. He turned to see it was Garry Fry, dressed for a funeral. His formality only made sense if he was poised to be photographed and videotaped. And true to his new role in Henry's life, he was ready for his close-up, already avoiding any eye contact, gaze fixed on the judge. He could have been a player-coach for a soccer team back in his England, keeping his eye on the ball.

The judge proceeded to his decision. He paused, took a deep breath, peered through his bifocals with a tighter squint. The wrinkles at the corners of his eyes were like the folds of skin on a large reptile. He mumbled his sentence in Arabic and Gordon could not make out the French in his earphones. But it mattered little; Gordon heard Marithe and Yasmin gasp behind him, as people rose from their seats. Finally the translator's words came through: "Mr. Henry Raeburn, you are sentenced to five years in prison for trespassing on government property. Your terms of parole will be reviewed after six months from this day, the twentieth of July, two thousand and seventeen. That is all."

Henry nodded at the judge's words, looking down at the steeple he had made of his hands. He glanced back from the desk, first at Gordon and then, just for a moment, at Marithe and Yasmin. His lips moved and his words were easy to read. "It's okay, it's okay." His eyes were glassy with tears.

Garry Fry shot up from his pew. His right hand clasped the top button of his suit jacket and slipped it through the eyelet. He poked his horn rimmed glasses back up against his eyebrows as he moved past his fellow spectators, left hand raised to hail down Gordon.

Gordon turned to gaze at Hisham at his desk. His old friend had suddenly aged as he slumped in his seat. Was it Cezanne who said you could read a whole man's life when you viewed him in repose from behind? Henry had told Gordon this when they walked through the streets of Venice late at night after a thunder-shower, but Gordon was always forgetting which artist said what.

Gordon felt a tug on his sleeve and he turned, smelled a musky cologne. It was Garry Fry.

"Mr. MacPhail, when I leave this courtroom, those reporters are ready to ask me some questions about a release I had translated and sent out this morning."

"A press release?"

"That's correct."

"You didn't tell anyone about a press release."

"That's correct. It was Henry's wish to keep this quiet."

"Jesus Christ…" Gordon shook his head, put his hands on his hips to steady them from trembling. "Why didn't you tell us?"

Garry brought a hand up to stroke the stubble around his lips and chin. "It was Henry's decision. If you ask me to speculate on his reason, I'd say because he knew you would oppose him."

"You're damn right we'd oppose him. We want to get him out of here alive."

The two police officers that ushered Henry in approached him, nodding and gesturing for him to stand. Henry complied, his hands needlessly outstretched. A martyr pose for the media. He affected a serenity that was strange, un-Henry-like. He was performing for somebody and it was neither Gordon nor Marithe.

Marithe would be oblivious anyway. She was just staring down at the floor a few feet in front of her, shaking her head. Nothing else mattered but Gordon going to her now. He moved with a sense of purpose that parted those in his path.

He clasped her hands in his but she did not look up. She was still shaking her head, but slower. "Oh what now... God what now."

"It's going to be all right. We'll appeal. None of this is final. This, this is just theatre."

She looked at him, smiling. The smile was not one of endearment though. Perhaps she thought he was even more of a fool now than the man she divorced.

"Let me say something, Gordon, something I've been thinking about. You know, when Henry was younger, when he told us he wanted to paint... I was struck with something like wonder. This was our son and he was completely mysterious to me."

He squeezed her hand, took in her thick, stubby fingers. At one time he loved how they betrayed her pretentions to elegance. Now her elegance was authentic.

"I'm sitting here, in this foreign place, listening to its lies. The first time Henry was on trial I chose distance. I would not give him his claim to truth. Now..."

"I know."

She looked at Gordon, her brow furrowed as she fought back her own desire to snap at him. And then she breathed in, wiping at her tears before she continued. "Now I know it's the world that lies. Not our son. I understand his work is his attempt at truth. I feel so sorry for how I've been. And it's too late."

"It's not too late. Goddamn it, if I know one thing."

"Gordon, I always hated your family's love of politics. First your father and now you. It was too much when I saw it take you. But now... now I know we need it."

"We need what?"

"Your awful work." She smiled as she said this. It looked as though she could begin to laugh through her tears.

Gordon shook his head. "You know I'm beyond excuses for myself, Marithe. But this won't stand. This is the beginning." He took the hand he hadn't let go of and squeezed it. Talking this way was like dancing in a suit three sizes too big. He was fully aware of his ridiculous pose but he couldn't leave the floor. "Come. Let's see what this Garry Fry has orchestrated to keep his money coming in."

When they get to the main foyer area there was a squat, moustachioed reporter standing in front of a videographer the size of a night club bouncer. The shot he was framed in captured the long corridor with the columns meant to evoke Rome. The outer limits of empire this was, as the Pillars of Hercules in Ceuta confirmed, the home of mad proconsuls and the exiled cast-offs of Augustus. The marble in this building was the colour of vanilla ice cream. The reporter was speaking loudly in Arabic and it was impossible for Gordon to make out anything he was saying. Behind him was Garry Fry, already miked, he looked like he'd never been more confident.

He read from a piece of white paper in his quivering hand. "This trial has proceeded under false premises. There has been a denial of the very reason Henry Raeburn was in the desert on the afternoon of July the first. This government's collaboration with the Yew Ess and its partners, perpetrating the war crimes of rendition, unauthorized detainment and enhanced interrogation techniques— the latter plainly known as torture—is the open secret at the heart of this court's decision. The Bataclan bombing and the threat of ISIS is the true explanation for what we're seeing play out today."

As they watched Garry babble on, Yasmin approached them both. She carried copies of the press release in a black file folder. Her fingernails were painted the deep red of revenge. "Senator MacPhail, Henry wanted to say he's sorry he didn't tell you and Hisham about this."

She handed them both copies of the release. "He just discussed it with Garry and me."

"Yasmin, you're seeing him or something, right?"

She blinked and smiled bashfully. "We've become good friends, that's all. I introduced him to Mehdi. Mehdi

Mekhounam, my instructor at U of O. You know him, don't you?"

Gordon looked to Marithe. He was wary of her judgment. She still had that highly tuned antenna for his prevarications.

"Yes, he appeared at my committee. He and I have spoken off line a little."

Yasmin let out an upbeat little "oh!" She was either charmed by his quaint, fogeyish way of sounding contemporary or she knew more about how he and the other Conservative senators tried to deal with Mehdi than she let on. A tricky one, this young woman.

"Mehdi might be of help here. He knows a lot about this black site and those who are in detainment."

"You're absolutely right. That's a great call. Thank you, Yasmin."

He realized he was saying this for Marithe. Once again he needed her approval. It mattered to him that she saw him as responsive to this young woman.

As Garry Fry spoke in a higher, louder register they turned to watch him. The three of them nodded in the right places with his speech. It all felt like a stunt. Gordon was cynical enough to believe it was all designed to inflate the market value of Henry's work, to get him that prized commission for the Biennale.

Hisham shuffled away from this scene. There he was, at the front doors of the courthouse, on the other side of the glass. He hunched, cupping the small flame of his lighter in his hand as he lit his cigarette. He was shaking his head, muttering to himself, maybe in Arabic. The places your life takes you to, the frustrating persistence of banality. Even here… especially here… just another old functionary, just like Gordon, vain enough to believe he could control forces this large, this immovable.

A force as large as real justice.

9.

The streets bellowed and thumped with club music rumbling out of ancient Mercedes Benzes. The smell of *kif* in the alleys was the residue of the young men without means, getting high, their rage at life's limitations blunted for another hour, another day. In the traffic the sun pounded down on tasseled windshields, and the dark fog of smoked glass reduced every driver to a shaved head. Through a rolled down window, a Gulag silhouette. The streets wailed with the klaxons of ambulances. Mid-morning heart attacks, knife fight casualties in the workers' cafés.

This is no place for the boulevardier or the flaneur. What could you peruse? Auto and scooter parts? Cigarettes and soccer magazines? You would have to be a determined romantic to sit on a terrace with a capuccino and the Herald Tribune and pretend that the century hadn't exploded and destroyed every remnant of your precious culture. You would have to be Torquil Forsey.

He waited for Gordon at the Roma Café. It was at the end of a boulevard as wide as an Olympic pool. This was the part of Rabat blanched of old, cosmopolitan aspirations. Nobody passed here on the sidewalks but large women in chadors, carrying plastic bags full of groceries. There was a laundromat across the two speeding lanes of traffic where migrant workers in shell suits and flip-flops sat outside in plastic chairs, folding themselves into the tedium of the afternoon. Torquil, in Panama hat and khaki suit, ordered another espresso from a stout, silver haired man with a jaunty red bowtie. This was someone's idea of Rome, but it was decades out of date. Torquil checked his father's watch and realized the white flowers in the boxes that lined the wrought iron railings were fake.

It was his sudden look of disdain that Gordon saw as he approached in a cab, instructing the driver to pull over. He gave Gordon a heavy-lidded nod as he glanced in his rear view mirror. For eight blocks this man was mumbling into a headset that glowed like a large blue beetle behind his ear. He chewed and spat the shells of sunflower seeds out his window. Gordon fidgeted in the back seat, wrestling with his disgust and losing. Ever since Henry's sentencing, his reserves of detachment were diminished. It would be liberating to play the ugly American. He passed the driver a crisp 100 Dirham bill he had snatched from his waiter at breakfast, and he didn't wait for his change.

"Hal-lo!" Forsey raised his freckled hand. As if Gordon would miss him; the only other patrons were two old men solemnly in conference at the far end of the terrace. One would need to form an allied front to grow old in this country. Gordon waved back and looked for the café entrance.

As he neared the table, Forsey tipped his hat upwards to reveal more of his face. "Senator MacPhail, thank you for meeting here. I know it's out of the way but I wanted to make sure no one from the embassy staff was around."

"I understand. This is a private conversation."

"As off the record as it could possibly be."

They sat and Gordon took in the fake flowers. "That's charming. I suppose real ones would die in this sun."

Forsey made a quip about anything of value perishing sooner or later in Rabat and called the waiter over. But his heart wasn't in it, he mumbled the last words of his remark. Then he shifted tone, spoke in Arabic to the waiter, ordering Gordon's espresso for him. He was so full of deadpan confidence. In his old life as a lawyer and backroom suit, Gordon would have found anyone performing their language skills pretentious, but now he welcomed the effort to impress him.

And any place that brought to mind his last trip to Italy, just father and son, couldn't be all bad. He remembered Henry insisting on taking him to get the best espresso in Venice. This was what, two summers ago now? They ended up in one of the smaller piazzas near the fish market with so many pigeons…

another St. Somebody's Square. Henry was a guest at what he had described as the "alternative biennale." He was taking his father as his travel companion. The wonders. That restaurant where they had served black pasta they called Medusa's hair. Everyone in masks, the smell of tobacco in cologne. The world was changing so quickly for Henry, and Gordon was trying to be excited for him.

Yet Gordon's Europe had never been like that, when he was traveling with Marithe that first summer they were a couple. So many German university towns then. Marburg, Freiburg and then at last East Berlin. The sadness, the drab clothes, the bookstore with nothing but cloth-bound copies of Gorky, Dostoyevsky and Tolstoy. That side of the wall had held no surprises, no mysteries—a culture pulped and readied for recycling.

In Venice though, with Henry, the surprises and mysteries were in every vaulted room. Gordon wanted to be focusing on the art but the women got in the way. This he could not reveal on the trip. The loucheness of being that kind of father.

Besides, it was too late for seduction, despite the beauty of the middle-aged Italian wives in the coffee bars, dressed down as if for the English countryside. With their dachshunds and their terriers, the lapdogs' jolting leaps for biscotti. These women were Renaissance ladies of the court in profile. The force of sudden fantasy struck him unaware.

Back in an earth-toned Ottawa two days later, what a relief to lock into his celibate frame of mind again. It was like he rediscovered his membership in a Masonic order, back in his office in the East block with his view toward the Prime Minister's office, where all his caucus colleagues plotted to claim as their domain once again. The dignity of that old sandstone. Yes, anything structural, anything that spoke of true durability, that was in Gordon's wheelhouse, thank you very much. Durability apart from marriage, that is.

"So Mr. Forsey, what is your take on Henry's sentencing? I saw you sending so many messages when you were in the courthouse. I imagine you've come to some conclusions."

"I have, yes. May I express my condolences once again. It didn't have to come to this."

"Thank you for saying that. I felt the same way. I just don't think Hisham could have done much more."

"Your son's lawyer."

"That's right. They're making an example of Henry. We'll of course appeal."

"Of course. And you can count on the embassy, in the coming months, to assist you."

"The embassy but not the ambassador?"

Forsey planted his elbows on the table and folded his arms. He was looking off into the distance, just over Gordon's left shoulder. One last review of the words he must have rehearsed.

"His excellency Mr. Ashwin Khadilkar. It is probably no secret to you that we see things differently."

"What things?"

"Most things."

"Like Henry's innocence?"

"I believe the ambassador has a certain perspective about your son's politics."

"You're saying he could have tried harder."

"I'm saying it has been a frustrating experience to get clarity on our strategy. As in how we would approach this government. For this I am sorry, Senator MacPhail."

The waiter in the red bowtie brought over the two capuccinos and Gordon glumly took his, paused to sip and stared into the street. There was not much to savour really, the coffee was just vaguely reminiscent of how it tasted in Venice.

"You're risking quite a bit, aren't you, Mr. Forsey? You're presuming I'm going to disregard my own suspicions about you."

Forsey took off his Panama and reached for the handkerchief stuffed in the chest pocket of his jacket. He wiped his forehead and his eyes brightened. He looked as if he was enjoying the candour.

"I would understand such suspicions. I can only give you my commitment to do all we can here in the months to come."

"Let's hope they are only weeks."

Forsey paused, pursed his lips. "Yes, let's hope. But in the meantime, I could not let you return to Canada without as much context as I could provide."

Gordon placed his elbows on the table, his pose a subtle mimicry of this man sitting across from him. "Forsey. Would you be any relation to the former Clerk of the Privy Council?"

"My father. I'm impressed, Senator. That was more than thirty years ago."

"My dad was Dougie MacPhail. He was in the BC Cabinet when your dad was in charge in Ottawa. My dad was Minister of Natural Resources."

Forsey arched his eyebrows in surprise. "Ah, okay then. I'm sorry, I didn't pay much attention to my father's work when I was growing up."

"I recall that your father got a bit of a rough ride. My dad, he used to rail about Ottawa. He used to say even the 'crats are Liberals. 'Crats like your dad."

So much more could be said. But to summarize the years of arguments across the dinner table between Dougie and the earnest teenaged pedant he'd been would bridge the divide between him and Torquil Forsey. And if Gordon had learned anything in Ottawa, it was that unknowability was useful.

Forsey leaned away from the table. He was going to be a touch more cautious here. "My father told me when I entered the public service that he loathed partisan politics. He said it was the enemy of good policy."

"You think he was right?"

"I think Ashwin Khadilkar is a case in point. He keeps his head down with the new government, concealing his old affiliations for the right people. But it's all a bit of theatre."

"The same PMO that made his appointment possible made mine before they lost government, you realize."

"Of course I realize. It's for that very reason I'm speaking to you. He's made some dangerous friends. I would think you'd care about this."

Gordon shrugged, almost convincingly. "This is a dangerous country. You'd prefer him making enemies?"

"There are always advantages to transactional relationships. But he's openly courting some of the regime's worst trading partners and I don't see how this helps us, in the short or long term."

"He strikes me as ambitious. There are worse traits for an ambassador."

"Russian Petro-money? These fucking oligarchs sucking up to Putin?" Forsey, as soon as he cursed, managed to glower at Gordon for a moment before his rage dissolved in a casual glance out in the street. "Ambitious for what?" He exhaled with an athsmatic wheeze, recovered his composure with a prim tug at his collar and tie.

"Potential trading partners? That's the liberal project, isn't it? Sorry, I mean small l. I don't want to quibble on partisan lines with you. But surely you know how it all works, right? We bring 'em into the market and they come to love our democratic ways."

"You sound even more cynical than I am, senator."

"I'm just trying to be realistic. And I guess I'm jerking your chain a little. This is not a trifling accusation, if I'm hearing you correctly. Wouldn't it be better for you if I didn't take it seriously?"

Forsey retracted and ran his pale pink tongue along his bottom lip. He looked at his fingernails, as if he suddenly approved of the manicure. "I wouldn't have invited you here for this conversation if I didn't want you to take me seriously, senator. I believe the ambassador's advancing the interests of a few of his friends. One or two might have Canadian passports, perhaps. But he's colouring way outside the lines. And in your son's case, he has taken his direction from this government rather than our own. I'm not quibbling on partisan lines either. Your party could benefit from these revelations and no one would care about Ashwin's own political affiliations from ten years ago."

Gordon drained his cup and folded his hands in front of him. This was his performance of inscrutability. "So you're suggesting I exert some influence. You're saying I should talk to the OLO, tell them how one of the ambassadors we appointed when we were in government is working both sides of the street. Though I have no evidence beyond hearsay to support this claim. I'd ask you who wins from a conversation like this. How are we going to lay a glove on this Liberal government with such a claim? Sorry. Don't see it. I'm thinking the only person who'll benefit might be you, sir."

"That might be so, senator. Though I do have evidence I could share. It's you that I'm thinking of, you and your son. I'll never be a father so I don't want to be presumptuous. But I would not want to have any regrets when this is over."

"It's a long way from over."

"I'm saying I would want to know I did all I could, given what I knew."

Gordon looked Torquil Forsey in the eye. And the curious thing was that Forsey was ready for it. He coldly returned his gaze. Forsey must have known this strategem of his could boomerang on him, take him out. Yet it seemed he'd be okay with that. It would give him a legitimate cause to martyr himself, most likely. One better than his own ambition.

"Trust me, Mr. Forsey, I'm ready to fight this with everything I have. I'm choosing my battles here. If the ambassador disengages, then I'll get back to you on this. But thank you for your consideration and your diligence. You're a good man, sir."

Walking out of the café, Gordon did not dwell on Forsey's puzzled look. There was simply nothing more he had wanted to say, the temptation to be candid was too great. And Hisham would be at the airport by now, ready to check in. If only out of gratitude, he needed to call him.

As he settled into the back seat of another taxi, he checked his emails. Too many ended in parl.gc.ca for him to feel compelled to open them. He had become a daily item for the issues management squad in the OLO. The Little Rascals gang was now on his file. Fat kids in their suits from the some old mob extra on Bank Street, with salt stains on their unpolished shoes. There were four meeting requests for conference calls he'd have to click on at some point. Accept, maybe, decline, decline and propose new time. None of the above for now.

Torquil Forsey might actually be a good man. Sure, you could say his motive was one of self-interest. If Ashwin Khadilkar was suddenly out of favour with the Prime Minister and that court of Versailles the young dauphin had put in place over in the Langevin Block, then Forsey's star might rise. But there was more to it than that; Forsey was too prepared to be challenged. And it was clear, given how pale and underslept he looked in this hot country, his work was everything to him.

Gordon suspected there was a standard that haunted Forsey, handed down from his father, the clerk. He knew this only too well; it was how Dougie MacPhail haunted him every day. And at least Forsey was self-aware about this legacy and tried to honour its first principles: service before self-interest, providing the best counsel possible, honouring the office. Were they walking anachronisms, him and his new diplomat friend? It felt like that—rubes on a casino floor, oblivious to the gangsters around them.

There were decades when Gordon was in denial of following in his father's footsteps.

Over something stronger than espresso, this was what he would have eventually revealed to Forsey. He would have told him how he spent almost half his life hating politics—his father's conservative politics especially. He would have added that after thirty years of reflection, he still felt defeated by fate, that his own success was nothing more than an admission that the ideals he once aspired to were weightless, callow. His efforts at self-definition were dyed in nothing more than adolescent rebellion and were sure to fade once he had begun to wear his beliefs as a man.

The beginnings of his resistance to his father's choices were still so vivid. He could conjure them staring out at foreign streets in this speeding taxi, scanning unknowable faces, feeling the alien awareness of another self still pulsing within him. From those first few months when he was packed off to Lower Canada College, thousands of miles away from home, no one would let him forget the shadow Dougie MacPhail cast over him. The old man looking like a young Gregory Peck in the photos on the walls of the McBroom Building. The hockey team, the tennis team, the "Ciceronians" of the old debating club. There was nothing Dougie couldn't excel at; surely Gordon his boy would cut the same figure soon enough.

But nobody there among the sons of the great knew of the event that destabilized such a pat reading of Henry's destiny. He kept the photo of his mother, the one they used for the obit in the Vancouver Sun, in an old pewter frame, tucked in the top drawer of the dresser in his room. Elizabeth Raeburn of the Seattle Raeburns. Painter, board director of the Kitsilano Arts Circle, alcoholic and suicide. Gordon was furious with Henry when he changed his surname to Raeburn. But he understood only too well why he did it. Henry wanted to trace a direct line from her to him. It was like a cord Gordon had never cut either.

Now it would have to serve as a lifeline to Henry.

10

"Hisham, you're still here. I was worried I'd be calling too late to catch you."

"Oh hello, Gord. Yup. My flight's delayed for three more hours. Nowhere to go. No point in going back to the hotel."

"So this is lucky. I was just going to leave you a message. I thought we'd only meet back in Vancouver for a debrief."

"Three hours in this airport is not my definition of lucky but sure. Here we are."

"I'll be right there."

Gordon redirected his taxi driver in his halting French. The man sighed as he yanked his steering wheel and accelerated down another street. *Ghaouri…* idiot foreigners, yes. Gordon would agree it would be better if he was back in his own country.

It was all he kept thinking about after his time with Torquil Forsey. He closed his eyes, rolled up the window, and as he attempted to drift off into a quick nap there was the image of his mother, slender and elegant in a sleeveless white summer dress, approaching him on a sunny afternoon, holding out a tumbler of her homemade iced tea. Ready for her role as an avenging angel, it seemed.

Elizabeth Raeburn was everything Ruth Ellen Coleman, from 'an old Baptist family' in goddamn Delta, BC, could never hope to be. Ruth Ellen the vulgarian, who went from legal secretary at his father's law office to lady who lunched as soon as the funeral for Gordon's mother was done and paid for. Ruth Ellen who got her hooks in to the "most handsomest" junior partner once she found out he was the son of the Murdock MacPhail who ran Northwestern Forestry Products. Only Dougie could enable her transformation into this hillbilly Lady Macbeth, avenging her own father's pratfall into ignominy when he lost his mayor's seat over a land flipping scandal. Yes, she'd ensure Dougie's courage was stuck to the sticking post.

"Bottle blonde and double D since before I could drive my daddy's Caddy"—Ruth Ellen drew herself in one line at a pool party in the backyard, openly flirting with the other partners of the firm and not really giving a damn if Dougie's little boy overheard.

Once married to her, the future minister's fate was decided. She ensured he continually won his seat by keeping it local, keeping it retail. Bake sales, car washes, ribbon cuttings—'that Dougie McPhail would show up at the opening of an envelope.' Every move he made was done with Ruth Ellen coaching him from her father's playbook. And Dougie submitted, determined to remake his life. The young man Elizabeth Raeburn fell for on the tennis court became unrecognizable, fifty pounds heavier from pancake breakfasts and the compulsory nights of drinking—the latter necessary to forget the better man he could have become.

But maybe it was reductive and wrong to blame his descent and the fundraising scandal Dougie barely survived politically on Ruth Ellen. This belief in naivete was a convenient family fiction that relieved the old man of any agency. Dougie, sliding into less-than-functional alcoholism, was not even sleeping in the same bed as Ruth Ellen at that point. Which suited her fine; she was dressing in muu-muus to conceal her girth. The weight she put on must have heralded her retirement from serial infidelity.

Still she probably had her own private tragedies, no doubt some long buried guilt about the love for some yokel she sacrificed for revenge on all the fancy people. Always battling the mob that dragged her daddy's name in the mud.

Gordon rolled down the window, took in the first few floors of a jumble of office towers the taxi passed. The sun bleached out their contours into the faint lines of a grid of windows. It was reflective glass, each square was like a painting of azure and cloud tinged with rust. Maybe the family dramas and the struggles for power were really the same here. They have probably seen Henry's kind before, all the burning, monkish young men dressed in djellabas, have the same quiet intensity. That might all matter but Gordon suspected not. Despite the espresso coursing in his veins, his eyelids finally began to flicker, that deep hunger in the bones for sleep pulled him under. He was no longer awake by the time the taxi took the exit onto the highway.

He dreamed he was running down a long backyard that was somewhere in the Vancouver of his childhood. The grass was faded-vivid like in an old Polaroid, and the lawn ended in a thick, dark grove of Spruce Pines. He still felt the anxiety he was living through in the moment of the dream—a feeling that he was searching for something back there, deeper in the wood. Whatever was lost had him waking with a heavy sadness, and he felt barely out of the dream when he walked through the sliding doors of the airport terminal.

Hisham was exactly where he texted he would be: under three potted palm trees, camped on a couch, his stockinged feet propped up on one of his suitcases. His glasses had slid down his nose but that was all the better for him to scan the screen of his laptop. He looked diminished, humbled by the whole ordeal in the way his shoulders sloped. As he looked up and saw Gordon coming he just nodded, not even pulling back from his screen.

"You want to do this call with legal at Foreign Affairs on Friday?" Hisham sounded like he'd just woken up as well, drawling out the question.

"There's a call?"

"Just got the request ten minutes ago."

Gordon took a seat beside him on the couch. They both stared out on an empty runway. The sky was clear and deep blue as a cowboy's desert. He and Hisham always talked more comfortably without direct eye contact. Two introverts pushed into the extrovert's world.

"No down side, I suppose."

"I suspect they'll talk us through the appeal process. Stuff I already know."

"But it's the gesture."

"That's it. We're a team working together now."

"How deeply reassuring."

"I'm already in a better place."

"You're not serious."

Hisham turned his gaze toward Gordon, wearing a goofy grin. "Nope."

"I just sat down with Torquil Forsey."

"The charge-D?"

"The same. What do you think of the guy?"

"If you're going to be a wolf, stop making sheep noises. That's what I think."

"That's what I think too but he was on about Khadilkar."

"Of course he was."

"Thing is, he's probably not wrong. It is plausible that Khadilkar backed away from Henry's case, done less than he should have. Forsey says he has evidence of this. Emails… I'm sure he's written his own reports."

"We've got to choose our battles, Gord."

"This is what I told him."

"That guy you said who came to your committee, the one who had filed all the access to information requests on the detainees…"

"Mehkounam. Mehdi Mehkounam. He's at U of O."

"I feel like we've got to talk to him. Whatever's going on in that detention centre or prison or whatever you want to call it…"

"The black site. That's the term Henry's partial to."

"It's really all this government cares about. All ours as well. Everybody just wants a quiet way out of this story."

"Everybody except Garry Fry. And maybe this Yasmin." Gordon shook his head, watching a plane approach the runway in descent. He knew that the problem with all the bad influences around Henry was that Henry was one of them. It was a quip he wanted to try out on Hisham, but not now, Hisham was looking too serious.

"We're going to have to deal with that grandstanding. Why is Henry running with this crowd of activist types and… shall I say well-heeled fellow travelers like that Garry Fry?"

Gordon shrugged, watched a bird that looked like a pheasant peck along a crack in the pavement of the runway. Game birds reduced to scavenging. "He makes him money. Henry, he lived on the streets for a while there, in East Van. Nothing I could do for him then. I don't know all that happened… we weren't talking… but I think it gave him the fear of God of ever being poor again."

"If we're going to do this, Gord, if we're going to get him back soon, there can be no side shows."

"Agreed."

"Can you talk to Henry? He doesn't quite trust me yet."

"Of course."

Hisham leaned forward in his seat and stretched, then slipped his feet into his loafers. Blue suede shoes. He used to play the oud, listen to Miles Davis. Elvis was probably nothing but noise to him.

"I better catch my flight. When do you get back to Ottawa?"

"Fly out tomorrow. Marithe, she's already left, you know. Didn't even call me before she got on her flight."

"Maybe she's working on this as well. Another side show."

Hisham slipped his laptop into his shoulder bag as the two of them stood and squinted at the big screen with the flights listed. Gordon felt stiff and creaky in his joints yet it had been days since he'd run. Trotting out of his hotel in his superhero colours, bare arms and legs, he had suddenly felt too much like a western caricature and quickly returned after a couple of kilometres along the smog-choked expressway. Must get back to familiar ground again.

"Let's sit down when I'm in Vancouver next. It should be on Friday."

"Gord, this whole thing with Forsey…"

"I know."

"I just think we have to be cautious. Guy's probably right but I'm more worried about the distractions we're creating ourselves."

"I hear you."

They reached the line-up for the security screening. There was a wall of frosted glass, and behind it, the faint outlines of the anonymous amassed around grey tables. Two figures doing the slow disrobing dance. No seven veils, no metal objects. Hisham and Gordon shook hands like they'd just met. Gordon wondered when it had become normal for him to behave as nothing more than an acquaintance with everyone. Was that the price of politics?

"Don't worry, Gord. We'll fix this and get him free."

Gordon could only nod, try to smile and walk away. He couldn't look back until he was out of the airport.

Henry,
Should I start with the obvious? I miss you. I'm writing this from the café outside my pension, the one where you stayed too. I think of you walking these streets, maybe sitting here in this café just three weeks ago, and I will not accept you won't be with me again, and soon.

I'm not going to leave you here until we get you free. I spoke to Hannah, my old boss, and told her the situation here. I said to her that I regretted taking this leave of absence right now, that every case is important, but the very reason Amitas exists is defined by your situation, Henry. I could hear some disappointment in her voice but I think she can tell what this is about for me. She told me to take all the time I need.

I don't want to bring up our disagreement again but truly, you do not have to worry about me doing this. I have my savings, and Safae, one of the journalists Garry and I met, has become a friend and is helping me find translation work. Opportunities come when you're working from your heart. I will be fine.

I think you'd like Safae too. In the time I've gotten to know her, she has told me so much of what's really going on in this country. It is clear that the old regime is crumbling, and their ties to the Russians and their friends willing to be their proxies is an open secret. She's been making notes, interviewing people who will talk. These are all the stories she cannot write for the newspaper she's working for because she would get arrested and the newspaper would probably fire her editor in what would officially be called a management restructuring. It's happened before. Yet she's still getting it all down, risking her life. So brave.

And the stories. Long before the incidents in Paris and Belgium and these trumped up threats of ISIS, the government was torturing and working with the usual suspects to ensure the detainees sent here had no legal representation, no rights to speak of. And it's not just the Russians or the Chinese who have interests here and are making a few people in the government very rich. There's so much she could tell. Safae could get a book published with everything she has on her laptop but of course she'd have to leave the country, and that's no guarantee she would be safe. I left our last dinner together feeling that the more I encourage her about finally releasing all this information, the more I could be jeopardizing her life.

Anyway, the important thing is that she's not alone, that's clear. She's introduced me to a few of her friends from her university days. Everybody I met knows about what happened to you and who you are, it doesn't matter that no paper ran that press release on your lawsuit. And from everyone who was at this party she took me to, I think Safae was the only journalist. There's a network here, it's not like I needed Mehdi to introduce me to any of his old friends—the ones who've given up and discourage the generation under them from actually resisting.

I can imagine that each day where you wake up in there must pass like it's an eternity. I feel guilty that each day on this side feels like it's too short for me. Aside from the translation work, I have found a legal clinic where I can volunteer. All of this is going to help your case, I just know it. I just don't want you to despair. Every day, I get a little more hopeful about how we can get you out.

It's that hope I want to send to you in this letter. With my love.

Yasmin

Despite everything else in this letter, the last word, aside from her name, that Yasmin put to paper was *love*. Henry would like to be a lot cooler and reserved about this, but hope was as powerful as any drug he could be given in here, and certainly better than any he could buy.

Sitting in the visitor's area just one last time with Garry, before his friend was scheduled to fly back to London, Henry's opportunities for brief, mental escape was of interest to him.

"I heard you can get heroin to smoke. From Afghanistan or Kashmir."

Henry slowly blinked, in a performance of boredom. "Apparently, yes."

"I mean I would get that. It's a bloody survival tactic."

Garry winked. He needed to assert his credibility on this topic. It was the louche side of him Henry's always found tiresome but he felt too politely Canadian to address it.

"Not interested. Seriously. Maybe I went through all that at too young an age. It bores me. It's like television."

"Suit yourself, mate."

"Yasmin wrote me."

"Yeah, she told me that."

"You two are staying in touch?"

Garry nodded, as if he'd barely given this much thought. "She said she'd help out the campaign back in London any way she can. I invited her over. She can stay in the loft in Spitalfields."

"That's very kind, Garry. Thank you for that."

"You fancy her, don't you?"

"I might, yeah."

"Hard to tell." Garry smiled, mostly from the delight of finally seeing Henry lighten up.

"You know she's meeting a lot of people here. People who can help."

Garry looked down at his hands, nervously spun the gold signet ring on his baby finger. "Yeah. We met a few in a café together. If I were her, I'd be careful of that lot."

"What do you mean?"

"I know the type. I'm sure you do too. Bit rough around the edges. By choice not necessity."

"That's your definition of choice."

"Or yours of necessity. Look, I don't mean to be a prick."

"You're paid to be a prick."

"Well said. But seriously. There is this one bloke who calls himself Gato. Has a Unabomber complex. He fancied wearing his sunglasses a bit much while we were sitting there."

"Maybe he had a reason. CCTV cameras everywhere in this fucking country."

"His mates didn't seem to care as much. Nor the girl they had with them."

"Point is, they might be able to help."

"You know, out in the countryside in China, during the cultural revolution, if your tractor broke down, you know what the government would give you to fix it? A copy of Mao's Little Red Book."

"I don't follow you, Garry."

"I'm just saying it's always good to question those who want to help, I suppose."

"I've never questioned your motives, Garry."

"Well let's hope I never give you cause, yes?" Garry gently pushed himself back from the table, his gaze going to the door behind them. "I'll call you, after the auction for the Sand Pit series."

"You like her?"

"Who, Henry?"

"Yasmin. I mean do you trust her?"

"I do, yes. I think she has your interests at heart. I think she'll help. I just want you to be careful."

"Thank you, Garry."

"Of course."

"I mean for everything."

"You just stay healthy. Don't drink any more of that bloody orange juice in here."

"I promise."

"Good. Let's get you out of here soon."

And with that, Garry was gone. Henry didn't know what to make of the fact that Garry never looked back as he walked down the corridor. He wasn't going to think too much about it, though. No, he was going to imagine nothing but the best about those who said they could help.

12.

The Spitalfields Gordon remembered was one stained by misadventure. But that was almost forty years ago; he'd prefer to think his misadventures were behind him now. He looked out this third floor window, here in this room of taupe walls, bone white doors and ivory coloured chairs, the clean lines of anonymous new money as if painted by Magritte. He'd forgotten how much he loved the London skies—the islands of tarnished clouds floating across the silvery blue emptiness that darkened so softly in the evening. Responsibilities have made of him such a different man and yet this city's spires and towers returned him to the years when he was learning so much, actually becoming interesting, at least to himself. He can drift into nostalgia despite the odd unsettling episode he still can't help but puzzle out… he's sure it had happened just a few doors down from this place.

There was a party he and Marithe had gone to… this would have been… what, '79? They were invited by Marithe's friend Rosalind DeCourcy—or Roz, as she liked to be called. Roz from Sydney, doing international law at the LSE. She had big hair, leopard print tights, and was determined to be loud and vulgar with the fervor of someone who had been brought up to be neither. Her father had made his fortune mining silver and she needed to outrage him from a safe distance. The Spitalfields party was at the squat of an old boyfriend of hers. He was an art student, in a band with three other desperate characters, and they all lived on one floor of an old bottling plant. There were empty cans of lager piled up on the kitchen counter with plates of congealed beans, crusts of toast. And kelly-green wallpaper, torn down to the plaster, creating little islands of ancient ugliness. It had looked like the place had barely survived the Blitz and nothing much had been done to it since. Throughout the night ska selections and three chord squalls of grey noise had played, fingered from a stack of 45 records by a white plastic phonograph. He and Marithe had attempted dancing on a beer-soaked Afghan rug. Those on this makeshift dance floor roughly collided into each other and, just after midnight, Roz vanished into a bedroom with a painfully thin American boy no one recognized— and that was the cue for Gordon and Marithe to leave.

Once outside there was an altercation on the street as they were waiting for a taxi. Two desperate boy-men in leather, who had seemed high and excitable, approached them. They wanted money but because they were making such a commotion on the corner an old prostitute took exception. She hurried over, scowling and muttering, her pug-like face coated with a thick layer of foundation and pink sparkly eye shadow. She didn't need no trouble, nobody bringing 'round the filth. She pulled out a switchblade to scare the boys off but one of them figured, unwisely, that he would just grab the knife from her. The violence was all over in maybe ten seconds, with the boy stabbed in the palm of his hand. Marithe's scream—he can still hear it, so high pitched and girlish. The boy held the wound up to the white glow of the streetlight and it bled like a parody of the stigmata. His teeth were stunted and yellow, little tombstones of decay. He and his friend fled a moment later, shouting their curses, sprinting through the puddled streets that shimmered under the streetlights.

Marithe had broken down and cried once the they were safe in a taxi. She swore she would never be so reckless and foolish again out in London. He had realized she was still so young, so unworldly, just like him, and he had felt that much closer to her in that moment.

Fifteen years later, little could make her weep. She hadn't cried when she announced to him she wanted to separate; she knew by then there was nothing worth reflecting upon, nothing to be learned from the needless drama of his infidelity.

She would approve of Garry Fry's gallery space and office here. The dinginess of this old dive had been transformed, it could pass for a well-appointed apartment in Hamburg, just like her father's place near the harbour.

Yet Marithe will never know of this address nor of this meeting. She had remained what she described as "agnostic" about Fry's influence over Henry's trial. As Garry and Yasmin Raza nattered on to each other in the kitchenette, preparing tea, Gordon could not help but admire how cleanly Marithe got away back to Vancouver. He is the only one who will have to contend with all the contradictions of Henry's life, his ability to navigate this moneyed set of Garry Fry's Knightsbridge friends while appealing to "Henry's other network"—a collection of old radicals and clever young students working with Amitas and all the international NGOs the OLO and his colleagues in caucus had nothing but contempt for.

"Senator MacPhail, I've got some Scotch, I realize. Can I at least interest you in some of that?" Garry said this as he re-entered the main salon area, cradling his cup and saucer close to his broad chest. Garry moved a touch too daintily for his big, lanky frame, an Englishman doing his version of suave Gallic charm.

"It's a little over eight AM back in Ottawa. I should probably hold off."

"Ah, yes. Give yourself a day to catch up."

Yasmin followed Garry into the salon. She gave Gordon nothing but a nod and a shy smile as she chose the chair near the window, balancing her cup of tea on her thigh. She was at the farthest spot from Gordon in the room but no, he would not take it personally. Not yet.

"Last thing I need is to start drinking heavily while all this is going on."

"You'd be excused for it. It would be considered a sane response to events."

Yasmin gazed, moon faced, out at the street through the large window beside her. If she was going to take part in this conversation, she had not found a way in yet. Gordon resisted addressing her directly. He didn't trust her enough to make it easier for her.

"My friend Hisham is a little angry with both of you."

"Because I didn't tell him about the press conference," Garry Fry said softly, bringing his cup to his lips.

"He felt undermined. I'd say with reason."

"It was Henry's decision," Yasmin said. Though she was smiling, she was giving Gordon a cold-eyed stare. "I'm sure he never meant to make anyone angry. Anyone except the judge, the court..."

"I want to thank you again for coming here to London, senator. For what it's worth, it is my decision to include you in this effort we're taking to raise awareness about the obscenity of his sentencing."

"When you say we, are we talking about the three of us?"

"And Henry," Yasmin said, with a sudden lightness to her tone. "I've been spending as much time as I can there in Rabat. There's more I can do there."

Gordon recrossed his legs. The chair he was sitting in was probably worth thousands of pounds and there was virtually no way to sit in it that was comfortable. "I thank you for that."

Garry blinked, concealing his reaction with a quick pass of his hand across his mouth. The link on his French cuff was a silver death's head. "I thought it would be good to have Yasmin here as we plan this dinner and auction. She can speak to his current state of mind better than I can."

"I'll be returning there next week, senator," Yasmin said. "Henry needs help on the ground. I've been given a leave of absence from my articling."

"You're working with Hannah Eisenberg, aren't you?"

Yasmin nodded gravely. "I am. She's been wonderful through all this."

"This is an Amitas thing for you guys?"

"We've involved them, yes," Garry said. He was a man uncomfortable with losing the spotlight in the conversation. You could hear the annoyance in the way he'd upped the volume of his replies. "But they can only do so much. It is my network that must be mobilized."

"Hannah says she knew you in Vancouver, senator."

"That's correct. We went to the same high school."

Gordon looked out the window, pretending he was taking an interest in the construction crane on the horizon. It was a serviceable way of concealing his remembering. Hannah was the second woman he slept with. Smarter than he'd ever be. The first person who ever said "prurient" confidently in conversation with him (they were talking about Nixon's tapes at the time). The first woman who made the word willowy vivid for him. Her slender arms and legs so darkly tanned in those Vancouver summers. He remembered the wilder, hippie hideaway version of Kitsilano Beach where they walked together, the Spanish wine and the Gitanes she'd have in her giant purse. So much talking earnestly between cigarettes and sips before she'd allow him a kiss. Then Schubert's Impromptus playing in her attic bedroom. Hannah the 'dark eyed enigma' (his attempted poem, unwisely slipped as a bookmark in her copy of Crowds and Power) who found him boring after just a few weeks and told him so. She had made him a passable lover and then just walked away.

She was there that day in committee, representing Amitas, when he took the lead on filibustering the motion about the information on the detainees. It had been, what, fourteen or fifteen years since he had last seen her. Then it was at the film festival back home, that party in Yaletown. She and her husband had been involved in some way. There was one band of grey in her long, dark curls. She looked regal in the bar but he was in baggy, wrinkled chinos and walking shoes that explained he was divorced better than he could have, so he did not approach her. Then just two months ago, in the committee room, her hair completely grey and looking no less regal, she was sitting beside a guy Gordon recognized as being on the OLO's enemies list. It was the professor who came to his office a week and a half before, who said he had some "inside information" on what was happening to prisoners of war subjected to rendition. Mehdi someone... he was sitting there all composed in his collarless shirt, his clipped beard. Too smooth, this character, like someone who made millions peddling yoga pants. He was the deciding factor: once again Gordon did not approach Hannah. She and this man now were clearly adversaries, auditors, witnesses to his efforts at blocking any further discussion of what young Canadian men in uniform might have done abroad to ruin the lives of the innocent. Hannah must be working with him in some way... still trying to save the world.

Hannah had smiled for him when their eyes met before the vote on the motion. There was that elegant reserve he remembered. She mouthed a "hello Gordon." He wanted to speak to her then, find out how she'd been and what she was doing. Then her smile faded. She had looked away, shaking her head.

"Hannah and I were emailing this morning, senator," said Yasmin. "She says hello."

"I've got to tell you... being here in Spitalfields... I used to know this place... and you working with Hannah... it's like the world's getting so small. Or maybe I'm just getting old."

Garry furtively looked over to Yasmin before he cleared his throat, fixed Gordon with a sober, all-business look. "I'll tell you what we're planning," Garry said. "There's the auction and the dinner. We should have a hundred in the room. Some St. Petersburg money, some Shanghai... deep pockets."

"I'll try not to see the irony in that, given who's working closely with our favourite government."

Yasmin tittered, gave Gordon a thumbs-up.

"You say irony, sir. I just say complexity." Garry grinned and tapped his nails on the coffee table. "Anyway, I've spoken to my good friend Jay and we're working on a retrospective of Henry's work that will go up at White Cube. All proceeds to a fund set up in Henry's name."

"What do you think, Yasmin?" Gordon leaned back as he posed the question. She took note of his striped socks and could not quite conceal her frown of disapproval.

"I think it's wise to explore every option. I mean, I can sense there's momentum building on the ground back there but... look, there's a great deal of support for Henry's work among those who buy art. I get that."

"You know, I'm just going to float a notion for you both," Garry said, with both hands folded primly on top of his knee.

"These people who will buy Henry's work might actually care about him."

"Sure, they make it about him, they don't have to engage in politics," Yasmin said. "They can buy Henry's activism and hang it on their wall."

"You might say that. But the point is they do... buy."

"I don't think this can be solved with money. With just money, I should qualify."

"I'll agree with that," Gordon said. He was warming to Yasmin. It was her sharpness, her lack of sentimentality. He could see why his son might find her attractive.

"I completely agree," says Garry. "We have to do media. This is part of the strategy. Would you feel comfortable, senator, talking to the BBC? And if we made a couple of video clips and put them online..."

"Like YouTube?" Gordon could not help but scowl, partly because speaking of such twenty-first century realities made him feel like he was pronouncing another language badly.

"I don't think we can rule anything out in order to be effective."

"Sure. I'll give you that, Garry."

Gordon looked down at the caps of his polished brogues. Garry Fry would have been in fifth or sixth form when Gordon and Marithe were at that party in this neighbourhood. He would have been a little bespectacled nerd, no doubt—in a way Henry never was. As for Yasmin, she wasn't even conceived—her parents still in... did Marithe say Karachi? More and more every day, Gordon felt that the world belonged to those younger than him. And thank God for that.

"It would be ideal if you could say something as a representative of the Canadian government," Garry said. "Maybe if you had a statement from the Prime Minister or something, you know what I mean? That would carry some weight."

"I'm not sure that could be a thing. It's a Liberal government and I'm a Conservative senator."

Yasmin hardened her gaze on Gordon. He was not sure what he had done to earn her contempt but here it was revealed and it was palpable. "How do you work with these people?"

"I've been assured they're doing all they can behind the scenes."

"What does that mean?"

"Yasmin…" Garry sensed her anger and raised his hand as if, like a choirmaster, he could modulate her tone with just a gesture.

"I guess it means they've spent a long time working with the government there and know what will be effective."

"I think it means they're embarrassed by Henry's arrest because his work has exposed the Canadian government's involvement in the rendition of the detainees they put in places like that."

"You're saying guilt by association."

"Implication. At the very least."

"I don't think it's quite that simple."

"No? Listen, I'm an American citizen. I get it. I know what you're up against, senator."

"See, it's nothing like the American position at all. This is my point."

"No? How do you explain it to Henry?"

"I'm glad you asked that, really. We had a long conversation about this very thing. When we were in Venice."

"Not the Biennale…" Garry said, with a puzzled look.

"No, the what… the Counter-Biennale or something… Henry spoke to architecture students. Forensic architecture."

"Ah, yes," Garry said. "No sales."

"Point is Henry understands what our government is trying to do."

"Really?" Yasmin arched an eyebrow, looked over at Garry.

"And he understands my position."

"Your position's not helping anybody on the ground there. Anybody who actually cares about democracy."

"We'll have to disagree about that," Gordon said.

"Yes, I suppose we will."

"Anybody like a biscuit?" Garry asked. "I served the tea without even offering. I'm such a terrible host. I've got some cheese and actually some caviar in that little... I like to call it a fridgette. Fridgette in the kitchenette."

"Thank you, I'm fine," Gordon said. "I'll speak as a father who's missing his son. How about that? And only if the media asks. No video clips or any Skype two-handers that make it look like I'm a bloody hostage, okay?"

"I think that's fine, Gordon," Garry said. "I think we just appreciate you being here. I'm sure everyone will at the dinner and auction."

Yasmin was staring down at the floor, performing thoughtfulness. Everything about her earnestness seemed forced, and now she was aware of how much. And so she was retracting from their company, finding her footing, a position of greater seriousness.

Gordon turned and solely addressed Garry. "I should head back to my hotel, get some work done. I'll do whatever I can. Just not anything on record as the voice of the Canadian government, okay? My own party would find that, as the kids say, problematic."

Garry got to his feet at the same time as Gordon, ambling beside him at a courtly distance. "Understood. I'll be mindful of your time. We'll just set up a couple of interviews. We can arrange a videotaping here... less bloody stage business."

"That should be fine. I don't have to be back in Ottawa until next Tuesday."

Garry had gone into the small closet by the staircase and fetched the senator's coat and Trilby. It was a hat Gordon could only wear outside of Ottawa. He did not want to risk calling attention to himself, seeming eccentric. Henry already made him a man of questionable character among the Conservative caucus. And yet Gordon rarely felt more himself than when he was wearing this hat, walking foreign streets.

"I can't thank you enough for coming, Gordon."

"Oh you're welcome. Spitalfields... I've got memories here."

His gaze was focused on Yasmin's sensible black pumps, the way her black jeans fit so tightly around her ankles. She had not moved to follow him out and he disliked leaving any room where he knew he would be spoken of when he left. Yet there was nothing he could do. He knew she considered him feckless, not even a worthy adversary.

He decided to walk for a while, take in the London afternoon. The sun's rays bathed the townhouses in a pale light that erased the grit and the years of his remembering. There were two steel pails with ridiculously colourful bouquets of flowers outside a news agent's. Life surged on with all its rude energy and he couldn't stop time, couldn't stop his fears about his son.

He pulled out his phone and looked in his contact list for Hannah Eisenberg. She could tell him about Yasmin, be candid about her character. But no, he took her card but never put her contact information on his phone. Was it sub-conscious sabotage or self-preservation? Too early to say, perhaps.

But there was Marithe's number, of course. He resisted thinking too much about this: he just punched in her number, strode on, the ungainly foreigner, down the high street.

"Is that you, Gordon?"

"It is."

"Where are you? The reception is terrible."

"I'm in London. I met with Garry Fry."

"You have word on Henry? They're moving him, you know. Prison outside the city."

"This they told me. The ambassador said it would be better for him. But I haven't spoken to Henry this week yet. I mean I wish, but…"

"That's fine, Gordon."

The silence on the line was killing. It made him feel guilty, that he was somehow not thinking of his son.

"Marithe, I was just in Spitalfields. Remember that part of town?"

"Of course."

"Remember Roz DeCourcy?"

"I do, yes. Gordon, have you been drinking?"

"Not at all, I swear to God. Marithe, do you know what she's doing now?"

"You're serious."

"Of course I'm serious. I mean I was just in Spitalfields."

"I don't know why that matters. I have never understood what you find important."

"It's just I'm in Spitalfields and I wondered what happened to her."

Dead air. If Marithe hung up right now, it would be understandable. Maybe he should be drunk, all things considering.

"She's a district court judge in Woolongong, Gordon. Has been for twelve years."

"That's back in Australia, right?"

"That is, yes. Gordon?"

"Yes, Marithe."

"Our son. You and your government friends, bring him home safely, okay?"

Now it was his turn to pause. He slowed his pace, pinched his eyes to stop the tears. "I will do all I can."

"Safe travels back from London, Gordon."

"Good afternoon. I mean good morning."

The line went dead. He wondered how much of his last words to her that she had heard. But it didn't matter. What she asked of him was all he needed to know.

As he walked farther along the street, he sensed two men walking behind him. And he could sense them watching him. He stopped, looked in a boutique window and glimpsed their profiles in the reflection. Like bouncers dressed in their best suits for Sunday mass. History happens first as tragedy, then as farce… who said that? He sensed them slowing their pace, giving him just enough distance not to suspect anything.

Would CSIS actually care about him here? These men are podgy looking, ill dressed. Throw a brick down Sparks Street in Ottawa and you could hit more than a couple of these characters. Should he have turned and confronted them? Picked up his pace and attempted to lose them? No option was good at this point. And frankly, he was probably just being paranoid. All in his head.

He stepped in the door of the first pub he saw. The malty odour of spilled beer hit him first as his eyes adjusted to the cavernous room. He had to pretend he had a larger purpose in being here yet all he could muster was the furtive, haunted look of a stranger hiding for safety. He thought he had more dignity than this performance would suggest. Yet no one followed him in. They made their point, he supposed.

"You all right then, boss? We're serving in twelve minutes. Can I help you?"

The bartender's slender arms were covered in tattoos. He had a sharp ferret-like face, but he looked sincere, a man to be trusted.

"I'm not sure. I don't know who can help me, really."

Gordon could only laugh in surprise at the words that came from his lips. The most genuine thing he'd said today. It was hard to know what to feel about that. But it would come to him after the first drink. Or the second or third.

13.

If you were to ask Ashwin how things went this week, you would get a predictable response. "Well it's been shit, hasn't it?" He'd pose a question because he wanted to affirm one thing: if it wasn't shit for you, you weren't doing anything of consequence. If you were to challenge him, suggest there might be progress with what's known as "the Raeburn situation," you'd be worth his contempt.

His office door had been closed every day for the last six business days. He arrived at 7:50 most mornings, just a few minutes after Torquil Forsey. He would nod and grunt in Torquil's direction as he passed his desk. Torquil could smell the odour of metabolized gin and nicotine on him. It was familiar—he used to smell it on his mother before she quit drinking. But Torquil could do no wrong by her. With Khadilkar, he can do nothing right.

What concerned Torquil was that he was being left out of the conversations Ashwin was having. And this was Ashwin's doing. What ambassador would leave his charge-D out of all that must be done on such an important file? The message was clear: he thought Torquil was useless. There was no question in Torquil's mind that Ashwin was blaming him for how difficult the file was. It took everything Torquil could do to manage Raeburn's imminent move to a less dangerous prison and… nothing, not a word of thanks or commendation. Khadilkar was looking for a reason to have him demoted, sent back to Ottawa, consigned to a desk job in the bowels of Foreign Affairs for the rest of his working life.

It's him or me. That's where we are now. Torquil had known this was coming for the last six months. And he was ready. More than ready.

What else did Ashwin do behind his desk? Well, Torquil was no slouch when it came to covert activities; he's got enough information for a file of his own on Khadilkar. He paid Noureddine the janitor the equivalent of forty Canadian dollars a night to type in Ashwin's security password, go to "history" and print out the links Ashwin visited every day. Ashwin liked bespoke suit and shirt sites, especially those based in Hong Kong. He was also looking at cottage properties in the Gatineau Hills.

And oh yes, there were the online conversations with young men from this country who were most likely under-age. These conversations lasted, on average, about 30 minutes. Multiple visits to his excellency's favourite apps and sites every afternoon, beginning at around 3 pm. If Ashwin really wanted to make recommendations about Torquil Forsey, well, Torquil Forsey had a few recommendations for the Privy Council Office in return.

Still he needed allies. And he couldn't continue to pay Noureddine. This was a battle Torquil would lose in the long term if he didn't move quickly. It was 5:52 pm, closing in on eleven back in Ottawa. Four hours had passed since he had sent his own report on Ashwin's activities to an Associate Deputy Minister at International Trade, to a Senior Policy Advisor in the Minister's office and (surprise, Ashwin!) to the Clerk of the Privy Council, who considered Torquil's father the closest thing to a mentor that he had ever had.

But no one responded yet. The fuck was going on? Everyone he had emailed could be considered a friend of his. They had been at his condo in the Glebe, drunk his cocktails, enjoyed his suitably famous dinners with the wine pairings, the six courses that had highlighted what both he and one-time partner Alain did so well (before Alain left him for that ballet dancer half his age). If there was something Torquil had written in this report that these friends of his found objectionable, they would have license to tell him. Candour—and discretion—was implicit in correspondence of this nature. Only gmail addresses, only text messages. And, if urgency was warranted, only calls to personal cell numbers. This was how it worked, and yet, judging from his empty in-box, you would think everyone had forgotten who he was back home.

5:58 now: those observant of his work day would not respond until at least tomorrow morning. And everyone but a few stragglers downstairs in translation had gone for the day here.

At his desk, with the glass door of his office shut and Yo-Yo Ma's version of Bach's cello suites playing, he felt the old horrible anxieties begin to do their work on his nerves. Was his tone too dramatic? Read melodramatic. Was he too catty, too colloquial, too eager to show how clever he was in his editorializing about the "collateral damage" of Ashwin's "transactional failings?"

He'd been over here too long without a return home. Out of sight, out of mind. Why would anyone want to put their own political capital on the line and take action for him? He'd over-played his hand, assumed his political value was greater than it ever could be. Vanity and ego were evident in his every word, all dressed up in the righteousness of a senior bureaucrat who'd forgotten his place in the natural order.

You're a disgrace, Torquil. Just recalling the timbre of the old man's voice, imagining him in the sitting room of the family house on Lisgar Street, bellowing down the hall… it was enough to make Torquil's heart begin to pound. God he needed a drink and a cigarette.

He sent off two last emails concerning a delegation of Canadian geophysicists attending a conference in Rabat, and then he re-opened the draft of his email to Senator Gordon MacPhail. In it he was doing nothing more than thanking him for meeting, providing him with an update on what this government's Ministry of Foreign Affairs here had told him about the progress with the Canadian government regarding Henry Raeburn.

And yet he felt like he was being too obsequious. He was too eager to please. If he were a Conservative senator, he would find cause to be suspicious. Again it was his tone. It was all wrong— a mix of the too formal and the too familiar. It was as though he was a man who had forgotten his native tongue.

He stared at his reflection in the glass door in front of him: the so-called 'scholar's forehead,' the bags under his eyes. "Son, just try to do some good and don't break anything. But don't make your old man's mistakes—look after yourself because no one else will." This was his dad in the parlour of the old house on Lisgar, once he had found out the public service had hired Torquil. The old man's hands had trembled when he held a crystal tumbler of Dewar's and soda. Maybe he too, for all his successes, never felt like he knew the codes.

Being exiled in Boston as the Consul General once his career was over was their way of telling him they'd always viewed him as an alien. So the father, the son. ET phone home, Torquil.

The last movement of the second cello suite faded into silence, the gigue that veers so off course from the sarabande and the minuets. And yet, as a whole, it held together. As sombre as the suite is, there was still some passion, some wildness, something close to joy.

Joy? Damn your sentimentality. You want to impose a narrative to excuse all that is discordant. Bach is not life. Life is not life anymore.

He heard the door click two offices down. That was Ashwin, emerging from another afternoon of transactional banter with some young man, complemented with a half hour or so of lurking on Twitter in between emails to Ottawa. Torquil hardly needed Noureddine anymore to confirm all of this. The only questions he had concerned what Ashwin might be saying to his new friends in Astana, in Ankara and Sofia about deals he was working on for them; he couldn't get into those emails but he might have to try.

Friends in low places. He could faintly remember that was a country song or something. Torquil was just about to search his music library on his computer when… there was his Excellency approaching… with a lopsided pout, the foppish haircut he's too old for, pushed back high off his brow.

"Mr. Forsey! Wonderful to see you still here. First in, last out. You continue to amaze, sir."

Ashwin had stuffed his magenta tie in the pocket of his suit jacket. He had a sway to him that indicated he'd been at his tippling, swashbuckling best for a couple of hours.

"I'm just trying to send this last email to Senator MacPhail. It's hard because I don't really have anything to report."

"Really? You? Nothing to report? I find that hard to believe, Mr. Forsey." Ashwin seated himself in the one chair facing Torquil's desk, exhaled with a sigh.

Torquil could feel Ashwin's hard gaze on him. He could just make out in his periphery that familiar, self-satisfied look that spoke of secrets he was vain about keeping. If someone were to paint an honest portrait of Ashwin, this would be the expression that summed up the man's character. But Torquil didn't have the courage to take it in, to look at him directly. His fingers tapped out chattery nothing-words to Senator MacPhail, words he would assuredly erase when Ashwin finally left him in peace.

"I'm afraid that's the case. Unless you've heard otherwise from Al-Falah's office."

"I… have not. But you don't need to ask me, really, do you?"

"I'm sorry?" Torquil looked up from his screen, as if he'd been so absorbed in what he had been writing, and that he hadn't quite registered Ashwin's practiced air of menace. It was a bad performance.

"I said you don't need to ask whom I've been speaking with. You've been doing your intelligence gathering all on your own."

"If you mean I should been emailing the Justice Minister's office as well here… I mean, of course."

Ashwin laughed. It was a high pitched titter, soaked in as much ridicule as he could muster. He had considerable reserves. "No, I don't mean that at all, really. You know what I'm talking about."

Torquil felt that jolt of adrenaline caused by his fear. It came with the churn of his guts, the thumping of his heart in its brittle cage. For a brief moment it was almost invigorating, a reminder that he was still in the body he inhabited when this feeling was an almost-daily event. The bullied years at Lakefield—all those broad shouldered boys who never became the captains of industry their parents had hoped for. "I don't, sir."

"Sir? We're far too familiar for that tone now, don't you think, Torquil? I mean I know you're very careful to refer to me as the ambassador at all times. Very careful. Scrupulous in correspondence, I'd say."

"In correspondence?"

"Derek Kushner sent me your email. Derek, you see, Derek and I go back more than twenty years. At one time I asked him to help me in my campaign to be president of the Young Conservatives at Queen's. I lost that campaign. But I gained a good friend, Torquil. A very good friend. Two years ago, I was the one who pushed for him to go to International Trade."

Torquil stared blankly at Ashwin. "No, Derek has never mentioned you. You never came up."

"Ah but Gordon MacPhail did, yes? You should know the senator isn't really someone on the team. He didn't even join the party until three years ago. He is a bag man, Torquil. With a son who is a liability."

"Whom we have done little to help."

Ashwin let out a breathy, high pitched "hah!" He tossed his head back, put a hand on his hip, easing into his bullying swagger. He leaned over Torquil's desk and placed both hands on the edge. There was a pearly white half moon under each nail of his fingers. "Let me be as diplomatic as I can, Mr. Forsey. What you've done is a declaration of war. But you, sir, are like a small pathetic island in the middle of the ocean. And I'm a state with considerable resources. It will take just one air strike over an afternoon to settle things."

Torquil could only stare at him coldly now. He let his eyelids drop as if he'd just been tranquilized.

"It's coming, Mr. Forsey. If I were you, I would wait for the sound of the planes and then hide under this desk."

As Ashwin walked away, there were two pressing questions in Torquil's head. Was that it? Would he just show up for work tomorrow and both of them would pretend this didn't happen? He knew there was no point in speaking. And yet, despite himself, he called to Ashwin.

Ashwin did not turn around to acknowledge him. "Duck and cover, Mr. Forsey. Duck and cover." There was the faint sound of Ashwin's laughter as he shut his door.

And then silence. Just a klaxon from a fire truck or an ambulance out there in the darkening streets. But that was always there, like a greater world emergency. Torquil pressed cancel on his email to Senator MacPhail and then he opened up the tab to his gmail account.

It was likely that Ashwin would read what he was composing now. If not tomorrow, at some point in the near future. But there was nothing to lose anymore. He typed in the first three letters in the address line: M... E... H. And the computer did the rest to fill in the name of Mehdi Mekhounam.

i

14.

It was the day they were moving Henry and his nausea had returned. And this after he was sure he had finally gotten rid of it. For a little over two weeks he'd awoken to that feeling of his stomach churning, leaving him in his cot, fighting a fever, hoping that the one or two bananas he'd manage to take with him after his march to breakfast might stay down and that he'd sleep through the afternoon. He couldn't read or write for very long, words came as if they were received from a weak radio signal hundreds of miles away. The prison medic ruled out dysentery but there were times when he'd wake up in the middle of the night, sure that he was dying. Well, if it was going to happen, best wait a couple of days so it could happen in the prison where this government kept its favoured criminals. He could go out in style.

With his sandals neatly placed on the floor beside the cot, he was lying down, gathering his strength when he heard the rattle of the guard's baton on the bars of his cell, the low croak of the boy-man's French as he told Henry to get up, the van had arrived for his transfer. Henry shot up from his position, taking in one last smell of the damp wool of his blanket and that too made him want to vomit.

"I'm ready."

"Good. Put on your footwear and stand to attention."

Two guards that looked barely familiar from his first week walked into his cell. They were both older and heavier than most in here, bellies hanging over their thick leather belts. One was carrying forms with him on a clipboard.

"You are leaving here. And I have good news for you."

Henry nodded, his eyes on this man's polished toecaps. *Isn't that good news enough?* He resisted the urge to respond.

"Your camera… all your equipment… it can return to your country."

Henry looked up, trying to conceal his surprise and yes, his gratitude. "That's very good news."

"Sign these forms. Provide the name and the address where these items will be sent."

As Henry got to the name and the address, he hesitated. Everything could all be sent to Garry or his father. With either one or the other, that would be the simplest, logical thing to do. Yet there might be a better decision to be made here. He never really got a chance to speak with his mother, to thank her for the fact that she had come to this country, reclaimed her role in his life. This would allow him to reconnect with her, so their conversation could continue the way it had with his father for years. He felt such love for her in this moment, as he wrote her name and address down… the old address of his childhood home… that he had to squeeze his eyes shut to stop the tears. He'd write her, as soon as he got to his new cell, tell her about the package that would soon come to her.

"Good. Done." This guard slapped the steel cuffs on Henry's wrists while the other chained his ankles. They were almost gentle about it, like two ministering nurses, and yet it somehow felt more menacing, as if they were anticipating resistance so they could strike him.

The older one of the two stood squarely in front of Henry, inches from his face. There was a faint odour of coffee and some cheap cologne on him as he spoke.

"Listen to me. You're going to walk down the south corridor but you do not look up or say anything to the prisoners in the cells you will pass, you understand?"

Henry nodded but that was not satisfactory. The guard spat on the floor inches from Henry's feet.

"Do you understand?"

"I do."

"Good. Once you reach the courtyard you will stand at attention until the back door is opened. And then you will proceed and take your place on one of the two benches where you will sit until the van reaches its destination. Is that clear?"

"It is clear!" Just the effort to raise his voice caused his stomach to stir. Another somersault felt imminent. Yet thankfully there was nothing more to vomit from earlier this morning. He gritted his teeth and winced until the wave of nausea passed and he could feel the light prickle of perspiration at his temples.

"So good. Now walk."

For what seemed like just a few moments of light-headedness as he trudged forward, he made it through the corridors, the light from the late morning was just striped patches of golden warmth on the tiles. Two heavy steel doors opened, creaking like the gears of a ski lift he could picture. He closed his eyes, and he was on the job in a boxy blue parka, freezing as he worked the lift at Sunshine Village, the resort in Banff. He was just out of high school then, figuring out the rest of his life. The freedom, the innocence of those days hit him like the force of gravity in remembering and he felt something between a sigh and a weeping sound escape him.

"Take your seat at the back Henry-Raeburn." The guard said his name like it was all one word. "And quickly! Let's go!"

The flimsy rubber sandals he'd had from the very first day slapped heavily along the gravel as he trotted to the door. The sudden movement felt surprisingly good, like his stomach was settling. A little adrenaline was all he needed, the one real medicine this place had provided him.

He was the only one on the journey. The metal cage he was in smelled of a different disinfectant than the one he was used to, and there was a brownish smear on the floor that had to be blood. The swirling, darker lines of the stain were the pattern the cloth left when the blood had first pooled there. He would like to photograph it but he would need a really good lens—a Zeiss he didn't bring to this country. The prisoner who had caused the stain must have been severely beaten. He thought of the times he had passed a truck on the highway back in Canada, carrying row upon row of pigs, tightly packed, heading for the abattoir. This journey was the same process, just moving units of meat from one station of confinement to another. He felt alone with the ghosted souls of those who had suffered in the back of this van.

After what could have been a half hour or an hour, he heard the faint sound of car horns blaring, the low, chattering rumble of human traffic and storefront music as the van lurched and then idled, accelerated and decelerated in shorter intervals. They were in the city, where those passing must have wondered who was behind the blacked-out windows. The two guards in the cab of the van raised their voices. Maybe they were having an argument over which route was taken and how slow the traffic was moving. Take your time, gentleman, I'm in no rush. He felt the van suddenly veer to the left and then they were descending a hill.

The van blared its horn. The shouts of the guards... they were enraged by something. There was a popping sound, a tire punctured on a nearby car. But no, it was not a puncture at all... there was the sound again... it was gunfire. He could hear shouts on the street, the two guards no longer seemed in the cab of the van, there was no sound from there anymore.

He heard a woman's loud wail. She had to be keening over a fallen body. There was nothing else it could be, it was the death song.

There was a thump on the back door just a couple of feet from him, and he could feel himself rise off the bench reflexively. Then he heard the jangle of keys, one scrape on the door frame. The handle jerked upward and then the heavy door creaked open.

The figure that filled the doorframe was not someone who would be giving Henry a warm welcome into freedom. There was a piercing, black eyed gaze, the rest of the face concealed by a balaclava. And there was the assault rifle in his hands. The figure shouted, raised the butt of the rifle and... of course it was coming... he was helpless as it swung for the side of his head.

When he returned to consciousness, feeling a dull, throbbing pain along his jaw up to his temple, he could hear the tinkle of keys. He sensed someone's hands working at his ankles and then tugging at his wrists. He turned his head and took in the man in the balaclava, noisily huffing, breathing through his mouth, muttering curses in Arabic. Their eyes locked for a moment and it enraged the man. His eyes widened; he raised his hand and gave

Henry a sharp slap across the side of the face where he was just struck. All Henry could see was red as the pain was searing now.

The man roughly pulled him up and shouted for him to move. "Fast! Fast!" Henry nodded in recognition to the words in English as he felt the rifle poke him at his shoulder. He was out on a street he did not recognize. It was an intersection with stands of grapes and melons outside a small grocery store, a café with smeared windows. He glimpsed a minaret as he ran but that did not help him get his co-ordinates, he could have been anywhere in Rabat. The afternoon traffic had gone quiet as they moved until he heard the sound of rubber squeal on the pavement. Out of what looked like an apartment garage came a grey SUV. It looked like it was heading straight for him then veered and braked. He felt the sharp poke of the gun at his shoulder once again as another figure wearing a balaclava, in the back seat of the car, opened the door and yelled at them both in Arabic. He knew what this meant: in seconds he was in the back of the car and there was a hood placed over his head as he was shoved down into the seat. He felt the car accelerate but could make out nothing of the shouts of those in the car.

"Welcome to your freedom, American. We will make you thankful."

★

Three sleeps later, Henry's nausea had passed and the pain on the side of his face had begun to subside. He had managed to digest some rice, two small dry sausages, some figs. He had recovered enough to submit to what they have asked him to do.

Now that the hood was no longer over his eyes, he was able to discern that this place was once an auto mechanic's garage. It still smelled of thick black grease and spilt diesel. One cinder block wall was charred with a grey cloud. *Wabi-sabi,* so thickly inscribed with age. Henry would love to paint on it: a pastiche of the Civil War battle scenes he remembered so vividly from just a few minutes spent in the Park Avenue Armory. The figures would carry AK47s, haul anti-aircraft cannons. There would be

Mujahadeen advancing on Fisher's Hill, Virginia. Let it stand as his lost fresco. Garry Fry could book tours here when this was all over. If Henry died here, they'll call it his masterpiece.

The wall was his backdrop. They placed an orange chair of molded plastic, one identical to the ones he remembered from his high school cafeteria, squarely in front of the video camera on its tripod. Henry walked forward, closed his eyes. He rubbed his stubbled cheeks with both hands, as if he could wipe off his beard, erase his mask of imprisonment.

It was a banal observation, and yet Henry had never actually realized this until now: the camera is a gun. It came to him as soon as the man this group called Gato positioned himself in front of the tripod. *Point and shoot*, all the control, all the power was in the hands of the person looking through the viewfinder. What was captured could remain secret forever. The word exposure had all the resonance and ambiguity of detonation. Given all the years Henry tried to reflect on his chosen art form, he'd been living in denial of what the camera provided for him: just pure sublimated violence.

He knew the script. He'd memorized it over the last two days. His pronunciation of the group's name in Arabic as well as French was as close to flawless as his tongue could manage. How could he not treat this like a performance? One more serious than life itself.

"My name is Henry Raeburn and I have a message for the Canadian and the US governments... and for all of the nations that have profited from the conflicts here for so long. My freedom and my life is nothing in comparison to the millions of lives... the generations of these people... that have been sacrificed."

He realized how seldom he had ever uttered his own name with the surname he had chosen for himself. It had been years and it still felt like a stranger's on his tongue. Would this be a different video, would it even be possible for him to record it, if he had said his name was Henry MacPhail? This thought fluttered as he stared into the lens and... here was a gift for Gato and the three others... his eyes began to water. Tears came just as he said "I am pleading with you to consider..."

The camera clicked. Gato muttered a curse and then clicked it on once more. "Continuez!"

Father, I don't want to be this stranger… this prisoner… anymore.

"There are hundreds falsely and unjustly imprisoned right here in this country. No court, no trial, no hope for justice. Like those whose lives are taken in drone strikes every day on the battlefield, they have been erased as if their lives meant nothing. It is up to you to determine whether I will share their fate."

After Henry uttered the last paragraph. Gato made a circular, threading motion with his index finger to indicate Henry should say his final words, pleading to the camera for a peaceful, safe conclusion to this incident. He closed with "insh'allah."

Gato held up his hand as if to stop Henry from rising from the chair—as if to stop time for all those in the room. He couldn't be more than five and a half feet tall and looked barely out of his teenage years in his track jacket and fatigues. Until you saw the pale green eyes that gave him his name. They were the eyes of an old man, the source of his authority and power over all the others here. He was looking through the viewfinder in the camera, replaying the clip. It was Henry's tears that made him smile and nod in satisfaction. "Bon, good, Henry Raeburn."

Henry glimpsed, for a moment, the desert sky from a window. He used to be comforted by his belief it was the same scattering of stars over the Vancouver night sky. But no more. Everything's other, everything's made strange. Even his name.

"I've never understood why we think it's wise to plan your life but cowardly to plan your death." This is what his grandmother wrote all those years ago, in the letter the family kept hidden in a shoebox. Lizzie Raeburn, hated and erased, her paintings an embarrassment to the family. And the stigma of her self-portraits had its effect on him; not once had he ever put himself on camera. Until now.

Yet those words about her death, like all those images she painted of herself were with him now. More than ever.

He needed greater reserves of bravery to live in this state. Even if the voices came into his head, just as they did for Lizzie Raeburn. *You'll live through this, insh'allah.* But there was no guarantee it would matter for those who had the money required. If there was anything exposure to his father's new career had given him, it was the understanding of how expendable he was to the government. And the clock had started to run, with this video finally over. Let the reviews of his performance come in.

15

"No connection to Al Qaeda at all. Not to Daesh either. This was the challenge for the government. They had virtually no intelligence on them, aside from three of them being grad students. Upper middle class kids."

Hannah Eisenberg looked incredulous. She folded her arms and leant back in her chair. A plate shattered on the tiled floor, just behind the bar, and for a brief moment she flinched. She was already nervous enough sitting here. "Gordon, come on. You believe that?"

"Shouldn't I?"

She looked up at the ceiling, brushed back a few long strands of grey curls from her brow. "It would be unlikely. This is a surveillance state. It's like East Germany in 1985."

"I actually remember how that was." Gordon saw himself and Marithe in a dour café on Unter den Linden, drinking their third spiked coffee, trying to spend the East German marks they had in order to get through the border station at the Wall. They had just visited her grandfather. The old man had been a chemist but something happened... something he wouldn't talk about. He was close to destitute, living alone in a barracks-like apartment block. Had a budgie in a cage, a broken refrigerator with nothing in it but the rind of a sausage and a half-eaten tomato that had softened to pulp. Marithe, drunk from the horrible yellow liquor in the coffee, called her "opa" her hero. In that café Gordon had felt nothing but bloated, clinically detached, nursing a young fool's resentment that the drama of history had made Marithe legitimately serious (okay, humourless) and him a callow, North American cliché.

"I suppose you would. How is Marithe?"

"That's right, you met!"

"Yeah, it was on Davie. I remember because I was back for my mother's funeral."

"You remember her name. That's impressive. That's got to be decades ago."

"She's an economist with the government out there, isn't she?"

Gordon bit his bottom lip and looked down at the arrangement of cutlery on the table between them. The bar was a kind of French brasserie he thought she might like. Usually people would recognize him here, say hello, and he wanted Hannah to realize he was a man with some profile now. This despite his wiser self's recollection of how silly this was. Indeed he felt that he should display some world weariness as he paused to figure out how to tell her the state of his marriage.

The words were slow to come, because what he was remembering was that moment on the street when the two women he'd truly loved in his life had met. He remembered how Hannah took Marithe in, how she smiled as Gordon babbled on in the street. The fine wrinkle lines around her eyes. That she had remembered Marithe's name might mean that he was correct in what he was feeling in that moment: Hannah could be imagining what kind of woman she might have become if they had stayed together. Marithe offered her evidence of how free to be herself she could have been with him—and how true to his own better self he'd managed to be over the years. Maybe this was why it was difficult for him to speak in the present tense about Marithe, mumbling about her teaching position and then taking a breath before he could say "we're no longer together. We haven't been for some time."

"Gordon, I'm so sorry to hear that. I mean, you both seemed happy when I saw you that day."

Happy. That might have been true. He had his own well-worn summary of what had eventually happened, one that passed over his infidelity, speaking of cause rather than effect: there was too much change over two decades of anyone's life now and a marriage couldn't be sustained. But he stopped himself from trotting it out right now. Hannah would see it as him trying to impress her with his fake profundity. She'd had a finely tuned bullshit meter when she was a teenager. It must have the precision of an Atomic clock now. "We probably were when you saw us. And then I fucked it up by fucking around."

Hannah allowed herself a smile, her gaze going to some spot on the floor behind him as she selected her words. "Things like that happen for a reason. I mean, it did when I was with Isaac."

"You're no longer together?"

"He passed away five years ago."

"I'm sorry…"

"There was twenty-two years between us, Gordon. When you're twenty-four, you don't think that's going to matter. And then it does. We spent the last five years apart but I console myself that I was there for him at the end."

"Cancer."

She nodded, looked at the back of her hands as if he'd reminded her to check her freckles. "It got to his pancreas and ripped through him. I wasn't going to let him go through that alone."

"He taught law, yes?"

"Constitutional. He always encouraged me to teach. He said I was too idealistic to practice. He was probably right."

And yes, Gordon remembered again that one time he had seen her and Isaac together. He was at a party in a Yaletown bar during the Vancouver Film Festival. There was a feature film premiering that one of his clients had funded, about a murder on a First Nations reserve. It was well meaning, well-acted, and by his second glass of Chardonnay he could hardly recall a thing about it. But he was a bachelor in his forties and one went to these things. As he left one dead-end conversation with an actress and headed to the bar, he saw Hannah with a thickset old man she towered over in her heels. Guy looked like he could have boxed once: his thick nose was a touch out of joint and he had a combative, wide-legged strut in his ill-fitting, banker's suit. And he had the basilisk eyes of some old Caesar; you could tell he would be ruthless in the courtroom. Hannah had tucked her hand into the crook of his elbow as they made their way into the private back room where sundry activists and film people were celebrating. That was where he was supposed to be as well, but as soon as he saw Hannah he had decided against it. Too much time had passed and he had thought about her with unwarranted regret. That husband of hers would read it all on his face immediately, creating drama he didn't need after his misadventures with infidelity.

"I don't know. You seem in a good place now."

"A good place?" She gave him a quizzical look. She was not going to let him off with cheap clichés.

"I mean you're doing important work. You've got kids like Yasmin inspired."

"I'm sure there are many things your party would call the work we're doing. But I don't think important is one of them."

"Why do you say that?"

She eyed the sliced baguette in the folds of the red gingham serviette in the basket. She pulled her hair back from the nape of her neck, then plucked a piece of bread to tear in her long fingers. She'd ignored his question, made it rhetorical.

"Can you answer me one thing, Gordon? When was the moment you decided you could be one of them?"

"One of who?"

"Gordon, the younger you would have never done what you did in that committee meeting in May. I mean I watched you, from the cheap seats."

"The younger me lived in a world where fourteen year-old boys weren't shown porn in madrasas to convince them of the decadence of the west and the evil of women who will not wear veils to cover their bodies." He got this all out in a low monotone, his gaze fixed on the plastic stir stick in his gin and tonic.

"I'd call that a unique perspective on a whole religion."

"You know it's more than anecdotal. It's indicative."

"I don't know what it has to do with you trying to silence a crucial conversation. One about what we have done to contravene the Geneva convention."

"I guess I can't forget we're still at war right now. And now it's just as much in Paris as it is Syria. Has Trump made things worse? Probably. But in the long run he probably doesn't matter. Our government doesn't matter. You know what I mean? And what goes public about Islamic State becomes valuable information. I mean, that's my take on it."

"Your son's art must cause you great embarrassment, I'm guessing."

She took a long sip from her glass and squinted slightly as she looked him in the eye. She was not going to wear her glasses for this lunch, and he wondered if it was important for her that he not see her untouched by any frailty caused by age. Such a thought betrayed more of his vanity than hers, he decided, while he tried to find words to respond to her.

"You know I've met Henry? He came to our offices. Yasmin introduced me."

"He never told me that."

"Perhaps he still might, once he's free."

"I'm going to keep on believing that will happen. Thank you for sounding so hopeful, Hannah."

"Haven't they set the ransom?"

"They have, yes. Henry read it from a script in the last video they sent. Five million dollars. Our government has made it clear they're not going to pay a cent of it."

"Do you have any way of paying it?"

"Marithe does. My former father-in-law is a Heinemann. Of Heinemann AG. She and I will be in Hamburg next week. But it's not going to be an easy conversation. Neither Marithe nor Henry's grandfather have spoken to Henry for a decade. It's complicated."

"Heinemann AG? I'd say that's more than complicated, considering their clients."

"Marithe has never wanted anything to do with the family business either. I mean she's made her peace with it now, but with Henry, I know that old man blames her for the road he's taken."

"And what about you, Gordon? You didn't answer my question. Henry's choice of subject matter can't make things easy for you either."

"You mean the black sites. Well…" He allowed a tight little smile to form as his gaze went above her head. It was as if he was visualizing his son's photographs, recalling their details. "I understand his intention. I guess this is what artists must do. I mean I wouldn't want to live in a country where he wasn't allowed to take those photographs."

"But how are photographs of these sites any different in principle than those reports on what happened with those detainees in Kandahar?"

"You know you can't compare—"

"No? I'd say the Moroccan government actually has, Gordon. They made the same calculation you and your government did that day in committee."

"Calculation?"

"They're presuming no one is going to care about some Canadian artist. They could defend their actions in the name of protecting their country, right? And now that he's been abducted, why give his captors any media attention? That's what these so-called terrorists want. And why commit any extra resources to their arrest and the return of your son to custody? In one way Henry's captors are solving a problem for them. It takes the spotlight off their own human rights record. I see Henry's predicament as very similar to those detainees, all the suspected Islamists who have been subject to rendition for more than a decade now, and who are in that black site Henry was photographing. I'm sorry, Gordon. I want to be optimistic but I don't see the political argument for Morocco to act effectively."

He wished they were in a booth so he could recline a little, cushioned from her logic. The intelligence that attracted him as a teenager had sharpened and refined within her. Like an ageing ballet dancer who has reduced her range of movement to the few, deft, deeply expressive gestures employed for maximum effect, there was a calm, easy grace to her that she couldn't quite summon as a young woman. Now it was here right in front of him, and it hit him as the highest form of beauty she'd attained.

"So-called. You question whether the people that abducted my son are terrorists."

"I do, yes."

"What is it, semantics or something? I would never imagine you making such a distinction."

She reached out across the table but stopped before her hand touched his. "I'm sorry… I mean yes… given they've committed an act of violence… this abduction… in order to work against the police state. Yes, then. Terrorists. But they're not the people the state and our government are making them out to be."

"You know this. How do you know this?"

"Yasmin is emailing me. She's there, trying to get your son free."

"And you trust her."

"She was the best student I've ever had articling with us. I do trust her, yes. Why wouldn't I? Or maybe I should ask why wouldn't you?"

"Forgive me if I'm a little confused about who to trust right now."

"What do you mean?"

"I've got the charge-D over there. This guy's telling me our ambassador is lying to me, telling me he's doing all he can while in reality he's just caving in to his friends in Rabat. And maybe other strange bedfellows."

"That charge-D might be right."

"I've got Henry's art dealer, trying to turn this into an international campaign. And of course he'll benefit when the prices for Henry's work go up. Everybody's got a goddamn agenda."

Hannah tilted her head. It was as if she were reframing him, taking him in a different way. Her smile was different, warmer. "Do I have an agenda, Gordon?"

He shook his head. "I guess we've known each other too long."

"I guess we have."

"Even though…"

She patted his hand. It was a way to stop him from going on. And it worked. He could respect her wish not to sentimentalize their past in this moment.

"Mehdi Mekhounam. You remember him at committee?"

"Of course."

"You should speak with him. He knows far more about all this than I do, Gordon."

"I'm not sure he's going to be receptive to an overture from me. He came to my office. He was looking for an ally before he appeared at committee. He told me what he had heard from former detainees, showed me the transcripts. I mean I listened to him, told him he had a case."

"Then how did what he went through... with his access to information requests... with that theatre of the absurd at committee... how did you let that happen?"

"I was one of the last appointees when my party was in government, Hannah."

"But you're one of them. You have some say, Gordon."

"You serious? Hannah, my political capital is negligible. One of these kids working over at the OLO, with his Star Wars action figures on his desk, he called me in one day. He put it best: I was appointed because I was the least worst option for them in BC."

"I'm wondering what you would have to lose then."

"I guess I'm telling you I made my choice. That day in committee... I can't walk it back. I mean I'm sorry about what happened to Mekhounam. He's got a case. He wants the story on what happened to those detainees in Kandahar. Okay. But I made my choice."

He felt her gaze on him, but he couldn't look up, look into her eyes. All he could focus on were his hands as he willed them to stop trembling. They were an old man's now. She must see that. How unattractive he must have become to her. This suddenly mattered more than he could have ever imagined. He wanted to tell her he regretted raising his voice but that would only make it worse.

"I'll speak to Mehdi. How's that?"

"You'll speak to him?"

"I can talk to him and see if he'll still meet with you. He's got the network on the ground. People trust him. He's your best chance to understand what's really going on."

"You honestly think it will help?"

"If it's as bad as it sounds with our embassy... and it probably is that bad... you've got Mehdi and you've got Yasmin there now. It sounds like the ransom money is a long shot. I think you've got to take this into your own hands. Forget your precious political capital, Gordon."

"Can I ask you something?"

She refocused on him, brought her glass to her lips. "Of course."

"With all the work you're doing, with what I must represent to you now... why are we here in this restaurant together? I mean why did you agree to meet me?"

Hannah laughed, and it had the same lightness, the same music it did when she was seventeen. "I don't know, Gordon. I wake up some mornings, look in the mirror and I think who is this old woman? I still feel seventeen inside. So I suppose I just figured there's that same version of you that I remember, still inside you."

He laughed in return. "I'm afraid there is."

She let her hand touch his. "Don't be afraid about that. Now let me get the bill. My expenses aren't public like yours."

"Far too public. That's true."

He rose from the table and took her hand in his. He kissed her fingers. He wanted her to see this as him being corny, making light of the intimacy they once had shared. He muttered his thanks to her and it would have all come off with the lightness he'd hoped for if it weren't for the fact that she was blushing. And in that flush on her cheeks was more than he should have known about her. Up flickered a sense of possibility that could compel him to think too much tonight, as he sat before the television screen in his condo, watching-not-watching the news with a tumbler of that Japanese whisky he'd come to like too much.

.

16.

The embassy staff was having a birthday party for Ghislaine Laurendeau, second in command on the fourth floor. She was forty-six today, five years younger than Torquil. At 11:30 am, Martha Bonnell and Nigel Barber had transformed the main lunch room with four long cords of sparkly lights and paper streamers. They'd arranged the small mound of wrapped gifts and cards on the kitchen counter. By noon it was as festive as it had been for the Christmas party.

Ghislaine's favourite Edith Piaf songs played from an iPod dock with two small speakers. Non, je ne regrette rien. Torquil loved the song as well but he stood at the back of the crowd that formed around Ghislaine with his arms folded, balled fists. He murmured the words of the song to himself without his lips moving, like a ventriloquist. No one needed to know how much the song affected him.

It was his job to get the cake for Ghislaine and he had over-delivered, as they say on the third floor (admin). He found a French bakery five blocks from the embassy, ordered a large vanilla creation with salted caramel in the icing. It would have been inconsiderate to put forty-six candles on the cake; he asked for just enough to crown the top tier. When Martha and Nigel brought it in from the photocopy room, Ghislaine turned and beamed at Torquil with all the fondness she'd developed for her sometime partner for mixed doubles over the last two summers. Only he knew of her love for salted caramel; he was her dear friend the thoughtful bachelor.

It was after Ghislaine had cut the cake herself and served everyone that Ashwin made his move. He had begged off a slice; he was content to have a sip of the Veuve Cliquot and that was all he needed, thank you, big dinner tonight for the Chinese

Infrastructure Minister. He left the flute glass three quarters full as he headed for where Torquil was standing, chatting with Nigel about the air conditioning on the first floor.

Torquil watched Ashwin from the corner of his eye as the ambassador glided through the small groups of his co-workers, a shark darting along the dappled shallows of a crowded beach. Torquil knew he was the prey.

"Mr. Forsey, could I have a couple of minutes with you?"

"Of course, Ambassador Khadilkar."

Ashwin motioned with a slight nod of his head for his office door. Torquil carefully placed his paper plate with his slice of cake on a corner of the counter for all to see. No matter what he was about to face, he hoped to come back and have his last two bites. It would allow him to approach Ghislaine, elaborate a little on what he had written for her birthday in the card he had chosen for her. Ashwin was striding quickly though, only pausing to wait for him to enter and then he firmly shut the door behind them.

"Have you been thinking at all about our last conversation, Torquil?"

"Of course I have, sir."

"Good. I certainly have too, as you can imagine. It must have taken a lot of guts. You knew what you were putting on the line, didn't you?" Ashwin leaned against his desk with his small hands gripping its edge, facing the divan and the chairs in front of him. He gestured to Torquil to sit.

"I know it was foolish. I know I've probably destroyed my career. I acted out of principle."

"You see there's the challenge. Because I've been acting out of principle too, my friend. Sit."

Torquil frowned, turned and approached the black leather divan. He slowly seated himself, conscious of the squeaking sound he made. It offended his sense of drama to recognize it, for he felt like he would remember this as a moment of high seriousness. It was clear, from Ashwin's dramatic pauses, that was how he wanted this moment to be remembered as well.

"Let me explain it for you, Torquil. Upon reflection, I realize I haven't done that enough while we were working together."

"You really don't need to explain yourself, Ambassador Khadilkar."

"Ashwin. You can call me Ashwin right now. It's just us."

"Okay. Ashwin."

"Okay. Torquil." Ashwin slowly blinked, with a solemnity that put Torquil off balance. "You believe I've been far too collegial with this government. I'm sure you think that these are the people that imprisoned Henry Raeburn in the first place. It's their oppressive disregard for free speech and human rights that has created all this—what did the Herald Tribune call it?—revolutionary ferment."

"It has been my experience that this is a difficult government to work with, amb... Ashwin."

"It certainly is. But I don't have any illusions about the government that could take its place, if you know what I mean. And they don't like our kind. We're corrupting their young men."

"I've heard as much, yes."

"You see, as far as I'm concerned, this government has very little interest in doing anything to find Henry Raeburn's captors. He brought this upon himself. He and his ridiculous English art dealer or personal manager... or whatever the hell he is..."

"Garry Fry."

"I mean, Jesus, Torquil. Dealing with that kind of operator... he's going to make millions off this whole episode."

"It is my sense that Senator MacPhail feels the same way."

"Senator MacPhail. Oh, God don't get me started." Ashwin shook his head, feigning weariness. "MacPhail and this Hisham Mahmoud. The dynamic duo."

"He's a father who wants his son home."

"He's a politician, whether he likes it or not. And he wouldn't be where he is without a few of my old friends. I know you hate us. I know you still can't get over how Canadians could have ever elected us."

"Ashwin, I did not do what I did... send that message... because of your politics."

Ashwin licked his bottom lip and smiled as if he were savouring a glass of his beloved Grand Cru. "I'm sure you didn't.

You sent it because of yours. But let's stick to the matter at hand. You think I'm fraternizing with our enemies or something."

"I guess I just don't see the utility in some of the relationships."

"Oh, you've been far more pointed than that in your correspondence. I believe you called them footmen for Russian oligarchs, did you not?"

Torquil felt his heart begin to pound in his chest, the adrenalin… his old friend from his teenage years of being bullied… had started to flow.

"I might have…"

"Right. You're not the only one who's managed to hack into emails, friend. You know there's a steel plant in Ramsay, Quebec. You ever been to Ramsay?"

"I have not, no."

"You haven't missed anything. Maybe thirty thousand people. Most of them work in that plant. It was shuttered for eight months last year until Korzakon acquired its assets. Korzakon could have gone to Braddock, Pennsylvania. Trump and his team are very close with them. Or Eisenhüttenstadt. Possibly the ugliest city in the Germany. There were big incentives on the table, know what I mean?"

"I think so."

"They decided on Ramsay. These people I meet with, they may not be to your taste, Torquil, but they do business here. I know it offends your old Laurentian sensibility."

"It's what they trade in, if I may, Ashwin. It's the ties to the cartels, the human trafficking."

"Please! Stop! My virgin ears!" Ashwin put his hands on his temples, did his best damsel in distress. He did Hasty Pudding theatricals when he was at Harvard. It was one of the first things he had told Torquil about himself, back in the days when he was trying to bond with him. "You're not going to get the Townshend Family to invest in Ramsay anymore, Torquil. You're not even going to get Hud Bingeman, of the Scranton Bingemans, to fly up with his friends at Regent Capital, bag some pheasants and stay at the old Townshend lodge just a few miles out of town, yes? That's over."

In the silence that followed, Torquil folded his hands together in his lap, as if he were sitting for a photo, staying composed, giving nothing away. It was a tactic he had honed from his father's withering lectures three decades ago; Torquil learned to play defence well.

"I understand your position."

"Mr. Forsey, this is not positioning. You know, when I was a staffer, one of my first jobs was as a policy advisor for Dennis Flynn, when he was ag minister. I had no clue about ag. I'm a fucking North Toronto boy. But I went to my chief of staff. This was Peter Rosen, God rest his soul. I asked him for my full job description and he just laughed at me. He said your job is very simple, Ashwin—you make your minister look good at all costs and you... be... fucking... effective. Effective, Torquil."

Torquil nodded. Surrender. He had to accord Ashwin's diatribe the seriousness he was demanding.

"You remember this young woman who would show up in the courtroom with Garry Fry. Raza. Yasmin Raza."

"I do, yes."

"You know she's back in this country. She's got a work visa and a residence permit. She's a fucking American."

"I did not know that."

"Oh yes. She's at a legal clinic in the Youssoufia district. Has been for two weeks now. She'll get a nominal honorarium. I always wonder who actually supports these leftists when they're here. Is it mom and dad? Like, a mosque or something? I mean, we know where that money comes from."

Torquil could not quite give Ashwin a sense that they could speak as colleagues once again. It was likely to be used against him. No, best be wary. "She may be on paid leave. I think she was articling..."

"You see, this is what I had hoped... you know her. You had a few conversations with her."

"I did, yes."

"I am quite convinced she knows more about this group that abducted Henry Raeburn than anyone."

"I'm sure she hopes she can find him. They were in a relationship."

"You could find that out quite easily, Torquil. I know you could."

"I'm not completely sure what you're suggesting."

"It's intel gathering. It's being effective."

"I see." Torquil crossed his legs, his gaze going to the window behind Ashwin. The dusty bronze light poured in from the garden with its squat palm trees, its long shallow pool. He'd miss the languorous afternoons here. It was here he had realized more than half his life was over. There would be no prizes for his public service, no rising through the ranks. Better hold as fiercely to beauty as possible… or at least an ideal of it.

"The opportunity for a second chance with one's career… I think you know it is exceedingly rare, Torquil. Now, you could raise an objection. You could say it's a serious thing to spy on an American citizen. Found out, you could face a trial, never mind dismissal. And all the details would be available to the media through access to information. But I think we've already crossed that particular Rubicon, haven't we?"

Ashwin turned from Torquil and moved with quick, graceful strides to take his seat behind the large mahogany desk. Once he had seated himself he brought his hands together in a pose suggestive of an office portrait. He nodded to indicate Torquil could take his exit.

"I guess you'll need an answer on this soon."

"I will, yes. Time is of the essence. We have a Canadian held hostage right now."

"I'll let you know tomorrow."

"Good! I hope I haven't taken too much of your time. And that no one's eaten your slice of cake. That was very thoughtful of you, Torquil. Ghislaine would miss you. They all would miss you."

Torquil could only bow curtly before he hurried, with as much dignity he could muster, out of Khadilkar's office.

17.

Since 1856, a Heinemann son has run the family firm, Rolf said. He is eighty-two and looks like he can take a few sets of tennis off a man half his age. He had proudly announced, over coffee after lunch, that he was still filling out this suit he had made for himself in Milan ten years ago. He looked out along the glass wall of the penthouse condo and pointed to where the company's shipyards once were. "We went from five hundred working there to two thousand, during the last war. And then... pfft... mit the bombing."

"You remember it?" Gordon asked.

"Of course! Papa, he wouldn't leave the city until Bremen was hit. Our family home was near Hammerbrook... just over there... now there's really nothing left of those old neighbourhoods. Just shipping firms there, I suppose... the foreign ones."

Marithe was still on the phone in the kitchen. She'd been thinking about changing her flight ever since lunch downtown with Rolf and Lotte, and she was not going to wait until she got back to her laptop in her hotel. Of course Rolf didn't have one here. He could barely use his phone for anything more than an alarm clock for his insulin shots. She needed two more days; Lotte's Alzheimers had gotten much worse than Rolf had let on over the last year. And maybe that extra time would be necessary for the Henry situation, given how evasive Rolf was being right now.

"They're revitalizing the whole port area, aren't they?" Gordon sounded genuinely inquisitive. It seemed like a safe question, one that wouldn't cause Rolf to get testy. It's been, what, twenty-four years now, since Marithe had first told Rolf her marriage was over and she was moving out on her own. The long silences in the conversation with Gordon and Rolf made it seem like the divorce happened just last week.

"Of course! They are doing what they can to rewrite history. They rebuilt the emigration halls on Veddel Island there. I'm sure they would like to say we were all eager to leave during the war. My father wasn't. He was never making more money in his life."

"Marithe always told me that he hated the government. He thought they were clowns and thugs, she said."

Rolf looked over at the kitchen area and regarded the figure of Marithe pacing and muttering on the phone. Maybe he was trying to make out what she was saying. If so, the effort frustrated him. He resurfaced from his reverie and remembered he was still in a conversation. He allowed himself a brief smile of surprise that he had recalled the thread of it. Like finding change in an over-coat for the old man. "I suppose he would tell his granddaughter that. It was important for him to be that kind of grandfather. It is harder to be that way when you're the father."

"Yes, I suppose you're right."

"Well, didn't you find it was that way with Henry? Your children know you too well. They can see all your faults. All the lies you tell yourself. And them."

"Henry and I, we're good. I remember what it was like to be his age."

"Es ist klar. You had a… prolonged adolescence, yes?"

"I'm sure that's the way it looked to Marithe."

"To all of us, my friend. But you are almost American. This is typical, from what I understand."

Gordon was not going to give the old man anything but a look of wistful contentment, as if he had long ago forgiven him-self. Yet anger surged within him, and it could only be directed at Marithe, still on the phone. The hell is keeping her? She was not going to save her mother. It was her job to save him from this conversation. There was too much at stake for him to get angry with Rolf. And yet the old man would probably come away with more respect for him if he did. Pity that this was not about his feelings.

"It definitely took me longer to grow up than it did Henry. I'm sure you had to grow up pretty fast too, once the war began."

Rolf seated himself in his favourite chair. It was a recliner upholstered in a shade of taupe that a depressed man would select. He waved off Gordon's overture as he slumped down. "I was a spoiled child. They sent me to Berlin to live with my Oma and Opa. I don't remember leaving the garden and the back lawn. That is when I learned to play tennis. I had a very good war for a boy of my age. Until the chocolate tasted like no candy bar I had ever eaten."

Marithe's muttering got louder as she sang a goodbye to her Mutti. It sounded like she was talking to a child. The daughter she'd always wanted. She gently placed the phone down on the white kitchen counter. It was glistening white marble from Ferrara, Rolf's favourite place in Italy. He had spent more time thinking about this condo than he ever thought about his grandson.

"I'm sorry that took some time." Marithe wrapped her long black cardigan closer to her body. Cool for September here—and Rolf kept the temperature in each room even cooler, as if he was preserving himself cryogenically.

"You take all the time you need, Marithe," Gordon said. "It sounds like she needs you."

Another wave of dismissal from Rolf. "Needs her? She can barely recognize her. She calls her day nurse Marithe half the time." He had his gaze fixed on a spot on the broadloom a few metres from his chair. Eye contact might have an impact on his resolve to battle through this meeting.

"Papa, I am going to stay on until Sunday. We must make additional arrangements."

Rolf shrugged. His creased and wrinkled face was more expressive than Gordon remembered. Like Buster Keaton in his final, alcoholic years. It was fitting that a man who manufactured armed vehicles should age like an old vaudevillian, given the existential comedy of deception the work required. "You stay as long as you like. This is still your home too, yes?"

"Yes, Papa."

"I'll have to get back to Ottawa. Committee returns on Monday."

"Of course, Gordon." There was a surprising gentleness in Marithe's tone with him. It had been this way since they arrived in Hamburg. If Gordon didn't know better, he might start to think she was willing to forgive him.

"I will probably meet with my new friends at CSIS. I don't know if he'll have any news on Henry but maybe he'll think of something to tell me that sounds promising."

Rolf turned his head as if he could strain to see Gordon from behind his chair. "Your government, do they know of Henry's criminal record? The drugs, the stealing."

"I'm sure, yes, Papa." Marithe seated herself on the couch, glancing up at Gordon to say it's okay, don't take the bait. They still had it, this language beyond words.

"Who knows. Maybe he assaulted one of their women. Of course they treat their own women horribly, these ones in their djellabas, more African than Arab. They rape them and force them to marry to cover for their sins. Aber when the white man does it. Ha!"

"Papa, your grandson did not sexually assault anyone. And his crimes were caused by his addiction. His illness."

Marithe gave Gordon a searching look. He felt something like gratitude warm within him for her valiant defence of their son with this bully. Gratitude and affection. Nothing sexual… no… his Hamburg was a port city where all ships have sailed.

"Maybe he is some artist now but Marithe, he was not ill. He was degenerated. Mit the drugs, the black clothes."

"Young men are allowed to be angry at the world," Gordon said. "But not all of them make something of that anger. He did."

"He put himself into this situation. And he is not a young man anymore, yes?"

"I went to Venice with Henry. He was invited there to show his work. Your grandson. Doing interviews in French."

Rolf took a paw swipe at the air and emitted a raspy groan of disgust. He then chuckled to himself, pleased that he would not take Gordon seriously.

"He took me to the Porta Magna, the old arsenal in the city where they made the naval ships… the guns. You ever been there, Rolf? Henry, he knew it all… the whole history. He said it was just like the family business. That's what he called it, Rolf."

"Warum… why are you telling me this?"

"Gordon's telling you your grandson is a serious person, Papa."

Gordon peered out the window of the view of the port, taking in the few blackened church spires that survived as ruins, the old warehouses in brick of faded ochre, like little Monopoly houses. No get out of jail free for Henry.

"You know we have contracts mit this government, yes? Ten years ago, I was there. I met with their Minister of Defence. We had dinner together. The man, he took me for a beefsteak. He took his fork and knife, he cut the whole beefsteak in little pieces. Like he was going to serve it to a dog. Aber they don't like dogs. They think they're filthy. Ha!"

"Papa…"

"Once he cut it all up, he stabs each piece with his fork. Chews it with his mouth open. Savages. You think I want to deal with these people?"

"Rolf, it's not the government that's the problem, currently."

"Marithe, she tells me he's got a girlfriend who's one of these people."

"Papa, she's a good person. She's there, right now. She's trying to get him out like we all are."

Gordon leaned forward, as if he and Rolf were playing chess on the coffee table between them. Maybe they were really, and this bluster was the old man's gambit. "They've come back with a ransom amount."

"Ha! I'm sure they have."

"Rolf, I don't even think it would amount to a rounding error for one of your orders with their government."

"And wouldn't it be quite a victory for them! They could say they got the money from one of the government's arms suppliers."

"Papa, the victory is your grandson back home safe and alive."

"A grandson who has renounced all claim to being of this family. Whom you wouldn't talk to for six years."

"He is my son, Papa. He will always be my son. He sent me his camera, his things… I love my boy."

Rolf bolted from his chair, his hand immediately going to his suit jacket. Concealing his belly. No, nothing soft with this man. "And your father, Marithe? Your family here? When you go to England for your school, then to Canada with this… this politician? You try to hide us from your life now. You fill your son's head with English leftist nonsense. This… this is what happens. There are consequences!"

Gordon stood up as well. He wouldn't let this man tower over him, domineer them. "What are the consequences if you let your grandson die a hostage? That's got to be a branding challenge for the firm, yeah? I don't know, you're the businessman… I don't expect you to feel anything about what Henry's going through."

"He changed his name. Raeburn. Ha! He doesn't care about you, Marithe. He doesn't care about his family. The consequence for him? I'm sure his photos… his art, he calls it… ha!… I'm sure he will make lots of money."

"Raeburn is my mother's family name. She was a painter. She was his grandmother. Just like Lotte." Gordon turned from Rolf and Marithe and slowly walked toward the front hallway, headed for the closet where he hung his overcoat. But he turned to regard the old man and his daughter one last time. "Thank you for the lunch, Rolf. And your hospitality." And then he was out the door and down the corridor to the elevator. He could faintly hear Marithe, speaking in German, in the calm, conciliatory tone she'd default to with Henry when he was a child. She would have to try to reason with her father on her own; he couldn't be in the old man's company anymore. Rage was on his eyelids when he exhaled, blinking as his heart raced.

18.

Verisimo Coffee is on a stretch of Dalhousie that Anne Forsey, Torquil's mother, once referred to as "troubled." She used to volunteer at the women's shelter around the corner. Dear mother the ideal mandarin's wife, Westmount raised, New Brunswick Anglican, lapsed believer and recovering alcoholic, offering cups of coffee and soft biscuits of sympathy to the ladies of the evening who used to work this neighbourhood and had nowhere else to go after a bad date. *Down at the butt end of Dal-whoor-sie,* Tommy Robichaud called it, Torquil's first crush. Tommy had his first apartment around here, when he was waiting on tables at some long gone, forgettable, fake Irish pub. Had nothing in his place but a hot plate, a hide-a-bed and a ghetto blaster with two CDs— Madonna and Maria Callas—so Tommy would often take Torquil here for their first drinks of the evening. That was when Verisimo Coffee was a diner, and its liquor license and five dollar bottles of beer made it a popular late night dive for the security guards, janitors and ex-cons who never made it out of Lowertown, working ladies who studiously avoided them—and the more adventurous, misunderstood kids with fake IDs and thrift shop clothes. Now Verisimo was gentrified, with an espresso machine that had the lines and polished chrome of an old Italian sports car, small, spiky-but-whimsical paintings of wildlife scenes over each booth and the smell of freshly baked muffins throughout the day. For Torquil, this was a perfect place for him and Mehdi Mekhounam to meet; there was no chance anybody from Foreign Affairs—or anybody working on the Hill for that matter—would walk into the place.

Torquil had been back home for close to two weeks now. He'd been staying in his mother's condo, and she was the only one he'd told of his decision to leave the public service. He explained to her that it was not like it was when she and

Torquil's father were EX-01s. The prospect of golden hand-cuffs—the pension, the benefits, the decent income that was everything an educated, ambitious, kid could hope for, coming from a part of the country where memories of the depression were still vivid enough, well that was no longer the attractive proposition it once was for a bachelor well into middle age. Here he was, with three languages, more than twenty years in postings around the world; he was an ideal prospect for a global public affairs consultancy firm, where he would probably make double or triple his salary. Now was the time to make the leap.

"Well, Torquil, I admire your courage."

Oh mother, you don't know the half of it.

It took a great deal of courage to call Mehdi Mekhounam. It took him a while. He had spent these vacation days on long walks through the city, taking in the autumn colours, feeling the freshness of the morning air. That sharp October light cutting through a corridor of pines near Rockcliffe Park was like nowhere else in the world for him. So many memories… of his teenage years when Ottawa was a city to escape, a place to forget. There was no sophistication, no glamour, no real *bohemian ideal* (his term that he had scrawled in capital letters in his diary when he was fifteen). He should have realized, given how much of his past still felt unresolved, that this was where he would end up once again, a failure at escaping the misconceptions of his thwarted ambition. Now he had nothing of his own—no startling artistic creation, no great romance, not even any real adventure to claim from all his time abroad. All he had were terrible secrets—and they weren't even his own—and all he could do was give them away to someone like Mehdi.

"If it is more comfortable for you to just send what you have to my private email account, that would also be fine."

"No, I cannot take such a chance, Mr. Mekhounam."

"Mehdi. Call me Mehdi."

"Mehdi, I wish this was only about risking my job."

A silence on the phone. Then the faint sound of a television blaring broadcast news.

"I understand, Mr. Forsey."

There was no need to say *please call me Torquil*. Formality actually made their meeting less of a betrayal.

★

"Are you still following the issue of the detainees, Mr. Mekhounam?"

Mehdi arched his thick, greying eyebrows, looking incredulous for a moment. "You think I would forget about it? These thugs at CSIS, they've gone after me. They're feeding stories to Fife the knife and Steven Chase about who was funding my research down at Princeton."

"Well who was funding your research there?"

"I received one small grant for a project that was with an NGO for stateless people. But the NGO also got money from a Palestinian organization."

"Ah." Torquil smiled as if he were familiar with these kinds of conversations. He poured some cream in his coffee and stirred it a bit too vigorously. "So you're really on their shitlist."

"I don't care. I filed three more ATIPs last week. I'm getting intel on the ground."

"About the renditions?"

Mehdi nodded, his thick fingers ripping into one, then two packets of sugar, as he poured them into the swirl he was creating with his spoon. He looked down into his cup as if he was expecting some transformation to become visible. "Have you heard about the catacombs?"

"Pardon? In Paris?"

Mehdi smiled, looked up past Torquil, as if he was about to launch into a reverie. "No, not the catacombs in Paris, I'm afraid. You know, over there, the Prime Minister is sensitive to criticism. About three years ago he suggested that UN officials come tour this so-called black site, see for themselves. He could make that claim because there was a series of underground tunnels and cells where the real work is done. There's an entrance in the ground a few hundred metres from the outside perimeter. That's where they ship the bodies out."

"You know this?"

"There are photos taken from a drone plane. Photos this government knows about. But I haven't seen them. No, I have only heard from those who have managed to communicate with those inside."

"You'll never get those photos by ATIP, my friend."

"True. But with what I know, I can sharpen my asks. They can't redact everything."

"You're speaking with Yasmin Raza."

Mehdi's hands went flat on the table, as if he was steadying himself through a small rumble beneath the floor. "You know her."

Torquil cast a glance from side to side, but there was no one here in Verisimo but a young woman with dyed pink hair at a stool near the front. She had just come in, and she seemed oblivious to them. She'd been absorbed in whomever she was texting, breaking into these muted titters that only called attention to her.

"I was asked by our esteemed ambassador to watch her and report on her activities. Nothing formalized, of course… nothing traceable. No, I would be doing the work of CSIS without CSIS having to be told… or doing anything that could be reported."

"This is Khadilkar, yes?"

"It is."

"He's dirty. Really dirty. I'm hearing he's taking payments from a natural gas firm based in one of the 'Stans."

Torquil shook his head, chuckled in his lowest register. "This would not surprise me."

"So what did you tell him?"

"Who, Khadilkar?"

"Yes. What did you say when he asked you to spy on Yasmin?"

Torquil reached into the soft, battered leather briefcase that was his father's when he was at the Privy Council. It was one of the few items he'd asked for when the old man died. He pulled out the sealed yellow envelope and put it on the stretch of table between them.

"I am here, sitting with you. And I have this. That should answer your question."

Mehdi leaned back from the table, his gaze sharpened. He looked into Torquil's eyes for any possible sign of deception. But all he was getting back was Torquil's glare, fixed and grave.

"Is this what I think it is?"

Torquil nodded. "All of it. Unredacted. The names of every rendition. Details on their detention."

"Interrogation?"

"The means of interrogation, yes. Duration and intensity."

Mehdi took the envelope and removed one, then two pages. He reached into his breast pocket and pulled out a pair of cheap drugstore reading glasses—square, plastic frames that might have been fashionable in Canada a few years ago—and put them on to scan the pages. "How did you get this?"

"How did I get it?" Torquil allowed himself a small laugh. "I stole it. I went in to the files at the embassy and took them out."

"This is the original? You didn't photocopy these pages or anything…"

"Why would I take that chance? I mean I had to disable the security camera for ten minutes or else I never would have made it out of the embassy. If there are copies of these pages, they are only here in Ottawa, where a great deal would no doubt be redacted."

Mehdi scanned a paragraph of the page before him. He inhaled sharply and shook his head at a passage. Torquil could read it upside down but there was no need, he knew the passage that caused this reaction. "This is stolen property. Classified."

"Yes it is."

"You can go to prison for the possession of these documents."

"That is true. But I'm sure my experience there will be nothing like what you're reading."

Mehdi exhaled deeply and took off his glasses, placing them back in his breast pocket. His gaze went up to the corners of the ceiling. Perhaps he imagined that Torquil was dumb enough to ask him to meet in a place with cameras. No, sir. "The theft of them is one felony. Possession is the other."

"That sounds about right, yes."

"I can't take these documents, Mr. Forsey. I've been given classified material before…"

"Nothing like this," Torquil said, a bit too sharply. His nerves. Imagine them betraying him now.

"No, nothing like this. The other time was when I was down at Princeton. CIA docs. But the charge is the same. And this government would, shall we say, take an interest in my trial."

"As they would mine."

"Yes. Yes, I suppose that's true, Mr. Forsey." Mehdi cast a searching look out the window behind what Torquil could take in peripherally. But what was out there, really? Nothing but passing cars, the sleepy, mid-day emptiness of the unloved streets of Ottawa. "But I've had to make this calculation before. I have a son. He's with my ex-wife. They're in Vancouver now. I'm not a rich man, I can't afford another trial."

"I don't suppose there's a lot of money in your work, no."

"It pains me to say this, Mr. Forsey, but I can't take this envelope."

Torquil leaned into the table. It looked as if he was going to fold his hands but no, at the last moment he reached out, pulled the envelope across the formica with his outstretched fingers. His mother's too-small hands, that was what he inherited from her. "I understand. But here's the thing. I will not keep these pages either."

"Pardon?" Mehdi put his coffee cup down before he could bring it to his lips. Perhaps he was expecting Torquil to be motivated by frustration at the limitations that have emerged with his career, his hostility with Ashwin Khadilkar. And maybe he imagined that Torquil even lied to himself about this, that he had undergone that parody of a religious conversion that marked the whistle blower out from his colleagues: *we are complicit with governments run by gangsters and something must be done!* Torquil will be the martyr for a progressive movement he has finally embraced after decades of tortured compromise and self-loathing—with or without Mehdi's help and involvement. Well it was not quite that simple, Mr. Mekhounam.

"I don't see the need to keep them for myself. I'm leaving the public service. I have, as they say, no dog in this fight. If you don't want what's here, I could just…"

"You're going to destroy these pages? I don't see why that would be necessary. You could just put all of this in a brown envelope, make sure Fife got it. Happens all the time in this town."

"Oh I've gone the brown envelope route before, trust me. This was when I returned from Syria. All I will tell you from that ordeal is that you cannot trust a reporter to do the work anymore. Maybe I chose the wrong person, but she came back to me and said the publisher of the paper shut the story down. But with you…"

"You'll trust me. I suppose I should be flattered."

"You and no one else. Take it for what it's worth. I'm staying at my mother's condo here in town. Doesn't that seem ridiculous? Anyway, I thought she might have kept my father's paper shredder. You know he was once the Clerk of the Privy Council."

"I did not know that…" A nervous titter from Mr. Mekhounam. A little bit of a scramble to get his bearings again. That was mildly entertaining for Torquil.

"Oh yes. And my grandfather ran the Federal District Commission. That became the National Capital Commission under Mike Pearson. A fine tradition of public service, you'd think. Well I've cut that run short. Ha!"

"I don't see why you would destroy them."

"Oh I do. They're stolen, for God's sake. Anyway I think burning them is probably best."

"You're giving me an ultimatum. Either I take these documents or they will be turned into the usual blacked out pages once I ask for them."

Torquil looked out over the head of Mehdi, in serene reflection. "I hadn't seen it that way but I suppose you're right, yes."

Mehdi tried on a polite smile but it soon evaporated. It was Torquil's flippancy that pissed him off, Torquil could tell from the way he wouldn't meet his gaze.

"You're putting me in difficult position, Mr. Forsey."

"Yes, I suppose I am."

"Could you at least give me a couple of days to think this over before you torch these pages?"

Torquil leaned forward once again, trying to project genuine warmth. "I could, yes. I understand this is not a decision to take lightly."

"This would be helpful."

"I'd understand if you wanted to contact somebody still on the ground over there, see if you could score evidence like this from some other source. Contact somebody like Yasmin."

"I may speak with her, yes."

"Don't think she's going to be that helpful, unfortunately."

"I have a broader network."

"I'm sure you do."

Mehdi reached for the nylon ski jacket he'd left in a slump beside him. As he pulled his arm through one sleeve he made a show of checking the time on his watch. "I've got a class to teach."

Torquil put the envelope back in the leather briefcase with sharp, crisp movements. A file he'd snapped away in his mind. "I thank you for your time with this."

"No, no, it is I who should thank you, Mr. Forsey. I just have to think this through."

"Of course. If something's free, it's probably you who's become the commodity, right?"

"Something like that. The risks."

"The risks, exactly."

★

The meeting ended sooner than Torquil thought it would; he had time before his appointment at the bank this afternoon to walk across town. He could cut across at the Chateau Laurier, steering clear of the old man's office, avoid the monument where that soldier was shot. That occurred the last time he was in Canada for an extended period, when he still had some semblance of a life here, and the shooting had allowed him to reflect on how his old city rhapsodized about safety and security. Comfortable illusions. The wilderness of private despair and its promise of violence was unloosed everywhere now. He would choose his routes carefully.

As he began to walk along Dalhousie he spied, in his periphery, the dyed pink hair of the young woman in Verisimo. She had crossed to the other side of the street and was walking at a careful, measured distance behind him. When the traffic lulled he could hear her footsteps, scuffling the leaves on the sidewalk. He passed Guigues Avenue and wondered should he turn up one of these side streets, test if he was being followed? No, he was being ridiculous and paranoid.

And yet she was still right behind him, still keeping him in her sights, a quiet stalking presence he would be crazy to deny. Whatever crazy might mean now.

19

This morning Henry woke up on the floor of an office, stared up at the ceiling and took, as he wrote on the notepad he'd been allowed, his "personal co-ordinates," the state of his head. It was the constant moving that was contributing to his feeling of disorientation, messing with his sleeping patterns. Each set of rooms his captors have camped in looked recently abandoned. From glimpses of quick transactions he knew they were aided and abetted by a network of those who are either desperate for the handfuls of bank notes or those who quietly supported his captors—or maybe it's a combination of both motives. They were middle-aged men who've come down from the status they once had in this country and are now caretakers, taxi drivers, security guards. City guys, *haratin*… not of the villages. And they all looked the other way when Henry was spirited out of the old grocery van that had become this group's latest vehicle. It was as if any eye contact with Henry would cause them to reconsider their decision to help those whom, after all, have already killed at least two policemen—and maybe others Henry doesn't know about. He feels like he's already fallen off a high wire and landed in a tangle of netting.

The small measure of freedom he'd been allowed had hardly made things easier. His captors simply did not have the space or the resources to isolate him beyond keeping him in a separate room, taking shifts to monitor him at gunpoint. They had allowed him to eat with them, to take the grapes, the figs, the good, fresh bread from the same table. He knew their names: Gato, Achraf, Fayçal and Karima, and they had, over the last three days, decided they will speak in English and French to him. So, in communication there was reason to be hopeful, all things considered.

And yet he was their bargaining chip, one they were clearly capable of killing if he was no longer of value. The hope he found in living each day right now was, he wrote, "like a dog's hope for scraps at a table." It was not meaningful because he had no control over his fate. This he had to change.

Throughout this period as their captive he felt Gato's eyes on him, watching him carefully as he spoke to Fayçal and Karima. They are a couple; it was obvious in the way they left the table together after meals, the communicating they did only with their eyes and furtive smiles. Karima, who looked a few years younger than Fayçal, still the middle class student in her expensive running shoes and jeans, was the one who had the authority, who cast a critical eye on how open Fayçal could be. Gato put himself above such criticism. As slender as a runner and dour in his self-imposed hours of solitude, at the table he picked at his food and said little, as if this was all an anthropological experiment and he was committed to his fieldwork.

Achraf could either be Gato's younger brother or a friend who had given all his loyalty to Gato from years of deference to his intelligence. He was not attractive; it looked like he broke his nose when he was younger and it never healed properly, and his halitosis was powerful. The business of living without calling attention to his unattractiveness must have been made easier by standing in the shadows for his more charismatic friend.

Fayçal, as bearish and imposing as he could appear in contrast, seemed to be genuinely remorseful about the recurring headaches and the tooth Henry lost from the blow he had taken to the side of his face when he was abducted. "You understand there was no other way to subdue you and to have you obey orders in the time we had that morning?"

"I suppose that is true," Henry said. "But it is a sad fact of the situation here that we are enemies. And that you all feel that you cannot trust me."

It was this exchange over dinner that finally provoked Gato to weigh in. He sighed, plucked two grapes from the plate, spat out their seeds in his fingers and then pointed at Henry, poised to scold him. "Your friends, the woman from Canada and the man from England, they have shown us no reason to trust them. So why should we trust you?"

"You know Yasmin and Garry?"

Gato shook his head, as if he had wished to forget it. "They spoke of 'raising awareness' about this government and those detained... like my cousin. The woman, she spoke of millions that were possible. She kept saying the international community. What the fuck is the international community? We have been living like we're the ones in prison for four weeks now."

"I am sorry there is not more help. Or that the money hasn't come to you. I understand why you need it, that you need resources to free those detainees, then create a real opposition to this government once you get to Europe." At this Achraf could not conceal his look of surprise. He turned to Gato, as if he could offer some explanation why the foreigner knew so much about their plans. "I know a little Arabic. I think you know we are on the same side."

"Are we? I know a little English," Gato said. "I learned the word for you: you're a misery tourist, Henry Raeburn. You sell your photographs and you make millions of dollars."

"Not millions, sir."

"You stay here for just long enough to get your photos, and then you leave those who continue to suffer and you fuck off back to America."

"But that's not the whole story," Henry said.

"Then tell us more."

"I don't make art to make money."

"No? Then you're a fool." Gato allowed himself a brief moment of levity as both Achraf and Fayçal giggled. "You should know you're running out of time. You think we need you to get money? You're just plan A, Mr. Raeburn."

Gato's chair scraped along the floor as he shot up from the table and left them. When he opened the door to what was his private quarters, Henry glimpsed rows of folded chairs in plush red velveteen stacked near a sleeping bag spread out on the floor, the gutted remains of an industrial size popcorn machine. An enemy of the state plotting his revolution in an abandoned movie house.

Achraf looked at his watch, motioned to Henry to rise from the table and return to the room where he was kept. All Henry had there was a three day old El Pais, his journal and pen and an old book called Tristes Tropiques that Karima had allowed him to take from a bookshelf at their last location. He could understand about half of it, he was still at the part where the author's on the journey from Petain's France to Brazil. When it was Karima's turn to watch him, she had helped him with the vocabulary, but when faced with a grim four hours of Achraf's company last night, he had little to lose by putting the book down and attempting to get information from the weakest link of the group, the one most in thrall to Gato's authority.

"He said I'm running out of time. You know how long I have?"

Achraf sighed, recrossed his legs as he sat on the one swiveling office chair in the bare room. The carpeting, some approximation of sea foam green, smelled like an old closet where the clothes of a dead person hung. "Only your government can answer that."

"If I could send another message to them, maybe that would help."

"No. No using video and internet in this place. Too dangerous. They can geo-locate us. Maybe you know a little about that."

"What's the plan B, Achraf?"

"The what?"

"Gato said I was just plan A. If you kill me, what is next?"

"It won't matter to you, will it? You'll be dead."

"What if I want to help you?"

Achraf steadied himself as his chair squeaked and swiveled. "We don't need your help. You... you're just money, understand?"

And so Henry slept on that. From the simplest minds, sometimes the clearest words were spoken.

Karima woke him about twenty minutes later with a poke of the rifle at his hip. As he was writing she told him it was late, that if he wanted to eat he had to rise. She carried a gun with the most confidence of all of them. If he did finally face his day of execution, they should give her the responsibility.

"I want to say something this morning. Will that be all right?"

"I'll ask Gato. Come."

At the table Gato had already finished his plastic cup of yogourt, picked at the harsha and honey he'd left on a paper plate. He sipped his espresso while Karima told him, in Arabic, that the foreigner needed to speak. Gato looked Henry up and down as he stood, waiting to take a seat. He looked amused as he nodded, then shook his head in disgust as Henry sat.

"Each day it looks worse, I know. There's no money for my release. I'm sure it's harder to stay... undiscovered." Henry reached into the pocket of the baggy trousers they had given him to wear, pulled out the piece of paper he'd ripped from the notepad. "This is a change for my will. If you must kill me, I can give all I can earn from my art... all I have... you can tell me the organization that will get you my money, and it will be yours."

Silence. Gato looked amused rather than challenged by the offer. But Henry knew it had surprised him. Gato's eyes darted from Achraf, to Karima to Fayçal. This was a test of his leadership and resolve, he had to know his expression only made that more obvious.

"You want to show your solidarity, we'll give you your chance, Henry Raeburn. But no one here is going to reward your vanity. You listen too much. Achraf, you take him back, he can have his meals alone again. Like a dog. The more you accept that's what you are to us, the easier it's going to be for you."

Achraf reached for the assault rifle he'd leaned on the wall beside him. He pumped it for the click of the magazine, glaring at Henry. Then Henry was escorted back to his solitude.

20.

When Torquil was a small boy, he was terrified of heights. He experienced vertigo for the first time when his father took him to the Crow's Reach in the Gatineau Hills. His father had the best of intentions, of course. He wanted to instill a sense of wonder in his son. The majesty of an old forest, viewed from an elevated plane, would also give him the best perspective on all that was there before that improbable capital on the other side of the river. Maybe he even hoped that Torquil would have his first experience of the sublime. Yet as his father gripped his shoulders tightly, a few safe metres from the precipice, it was all too much and Torquil began weeping, ashamed of his fear. For at least a decade after he would not approach any balcony or take a window seat on a plane.

And then, at some point during his late adolescence, his fear just evaporated. Torquil the precocious aesthete went, with his two best friends (the nerd club) to see Hitchcock's Vertigo at the Mayfair repertory cinema. He found the drama overwrought. James Stewart's character did not seem implausible as much as unable to transcend his past. Torquil was at that age when he believed he could outgrow anything from his childhood. He was in a hurry to be an adult. And Kim Novak did nothing for him. The final scene in the bell tower left him unmoved. To prove it to his friends, he walked across the Billings Bridge on the railing, with the Rideau Canal five stories below him, as if it were a tightrope.

But now, as he looked down eighteen floors from the balcony of his mother's condo, he had to admit to himself that the old terror was returning. He had yet to leap up on the railing, but just the cold, whistling blast of wind and the marble-like surface of the Rideau River assured him of how quickly he would be swept away—a carcass of shattered bones and gristly bits of flesh, seconds after his descent, unrecognizeable to all that once knew him.

He took off his father's watch, gently placed it on the railing. He couldn't have it break. Let it belong to his mother now. He could only hope it reminded her of her happiest years with her husband rather than the last years of her son.

He wishes he didn't have to leave a body at all... now that would be an ideal death. He remembered the black and white photo of a Buddhist monk who had set himself on fire during the Vietnam War. To believe in anything that much. Yet from all he had read and heard, there was nothing more painful than burning to death. Nope, sorry, he had too low a pain threshold for that kind of suffering.

And here came that wind again. It already carried the chill of some Arctic cloud, a knife-like sharpness to its bite on bare flesh. Still, apparently the least painful way to die was to freeze to death. You fell into a deep sleep. Of course, you'd have to go through an ordeal of all-too-vivid agony to get there. You'd have to take an overdose of painkillers and curl up on a park bench in December in this town to manage it effectively, and Torquil couldn't wait that long.

The leap off this balcony remained the best option. It ensured his mother didn't have to discover him. That would make her occupying this place in the years she has left too painful. She'd convince herself he was a ghost that haunted these two rooms.

Who knows? Maybe he would be that ghost. He couldn't imagine why though; he'd always hated her choice in decor. So many better places to haunt from his past. He wished there was something left of the East Village he remembered but alas... everybody knows that the war is over, everybody knows that the good guys lost.

And who won? Let's concede at least one victory to Ashwin Khadilkar. Though he probably didn't feel like he was winning, if the drunken message he'd left on Torquil's phone is any indication. "That little bitch Yasmin Raza has disappeared and I bet you she is working with these fucking terrorists. She and her boyfriend. I had given you, as they say, one job, Forsey. There's nothing I can do for you from here on in." This was all too true.

But then Torquil decided he'd had his own job to complete (well, aside from this current challenge). He had always been a self-starter when the job at hand aligned to higher ideals. In the end, of all the virtues, one should at least strive for that kind of nobility.

Torquil steadied himself on the flimsy deck chair and put one foot on the railing. It was best to leap out from here; it was like a threshold that afforded no view of what was below. One fluid movement and then… airborne. He would probably suffer a heart attack before he landed, wasn't that what was supposed to happen? Should have Googled it… how was that for an epitaph? His mother would not be quite that creative with what she came up with, and irony had never been her strong suit.

The world that I hoped to live in, the one I hoped to love, both have never been found, no matter where I traveled to, no matter how hard I looked. And I know there is no chance of me stumbling upon them at this point in my life. That's the best he could do. Too bad he shredded that note. Up to others to make of what he'd left behind something better, he had graced them with that final gift.

Self-pity, like regret, was a useless emotion. To be truly creative is to live in the moment. And yes, to be ultimately destructive as well. Let the moment rule the mind.

And the body. Leap at last. One… two… and three…

21

About a week ago, Karima took Henry back to his room and, once Henry was on his patch of prayer carpet where he reads, she shut the door behind them. He wasn't sure what was happening when she removed her hijab. But then she reached into the inner pocket of her nylon running jacket and took out a pack of Marlboros. "You smoke, Henry Raeburn? Fayçal will not let me." She placed the swivel chair by the window that looked out on an alley wall, opened it and then lit up. Henry took her up on the cigarette. With her long black hair free, the furtive glances she cast on his chest and arms as he smoked, he could feel the old tension of attraction, one that neither of them clearly knew what to do with. The cigarettes together had continued, always after dinner, just before she finished her shift watching him each night. They would speak of his life back in Canada and America, his photographs. She told him nothing of her life at all, even though he'd tried to ask. But tonight she was no longer an interrogator. No, she finally had a secret to share.

"Your friend Yasmin. You know she's still here in this country."

Henry closed his eyes, smiling, bringing his hands together to mime a prayer—one that had been answered. It caused Karima to frown.

"I had hoped she was still here. How do you know?"

"Gato said she emailed him. She told him she had officially disappeared herself. She left her work doing legal aid and is living with a woman she was helping, one whose husband was in the same prison you were in."

"This does not surprise me."

"This might. She asked Gato to meet."

"What did he say?"

"He said he asked her if she had the money for your release."

"And?"

"She did not answer." Karima blew a long stream of smoke out the opening of the window.

"She must have it. This is it!" Henry flicked his butt out into the alley. All the violence in him from his last few weeks was concentrated in the power of his fingers. "When will he meet with her? Did he say?"

"Gato said that Yasmin did not mention any money. But he did say something I think you should know." Karima crossed her legs as she swiveled the chair to face him directly. "She said she missed talking with him and that she hoped they could meet alone first. He called her a dumb American girl who was probably just going to cause problems."

Henry took his bowed head in both hands, as if he could massage away the confusion. "Can you do something for me, Karima?"

"I already give you cigarettes. Isn't that enough?" When he didn't laugh, she laughed for him. "What is it?"

Henry opened his copy of Tristes Tropiques, produced the piece of paper that had to suffice as the amendment to his last will and testament. "Can you see that she gets this? You can talk to Gato. He won't take it from me."

"What makes you think he will take it from me?"

"Please. Can you try?"

Karima exhaled into a slouch, folded her arms in her lap. "Out of all the places we've stayed, I hate this place the most."

"Karima, I know you're a good person. Could you try?"

She snatched the pack of Marlboros, concealed them under the waistband of her jeans and then wrapped the hijab around her long hair. She watched Henry take her in and allowed herself a smile. "We help each other kill ourselves. Slowly or quickly, I suppose."

He whispered thank you as she left him, shutting the door behind her.

22

"He was an odd guy. Nervous as hell but I suppose that was understandable. He was in the middle of something he couldn't control. It's just… it's just incredibly sad." Mehdi shook his head, looked out through the grey light pouring in from the balcony. LeBreton Flats looked as barren as an airfield, the river darkened in the first autumn chill to a thick slate blue line. "How's your coffee, can I get you some more?"

"I'm fine, thanks. This is really good." Hannah brought the mug to her lips. She felt compelled to demonstrate to Mehdi how much she liked it and the tone of her voice felt all wrong. Too cheery. He had put out a plate of store-bought muffins and mis-shapen croissants drenched in icing sugar, but he was not pushing them on her. Bachelor hospitality. Mehdi and Hannah were friends but not close enough that to be in this man's apartment at eleven on a Saturday morning didn't feel a bit too intimate. Yet Mehdi's awkward courtliness was reassuring; he seemed on the verge of apologizing that he had asked her to come here when she'd called him to meet. "You know I saw the story about the death in the Citizen but because it was in that home, I just thought it was an older person."

"A part of me wonders if it was suicide."

"You think someone would want to get rid of him?"

Mehdi was doing a fair impression of being nervous himself. He was up on his feet, moving with a lumbering, heavy tread to fill up his own mug with more coffee. It was easier for him to continue this conversation if he could avoid addressing her directly. "I read that Citizen story on him carefully, for any indi-cation there was reasonable cause to doubt."

"Who would want to get rid of him?"

"You kidding? You seen how this government works?"

"We're not talking Putin's Kremlin here, Mehdi."

"No, but what are we talking about then?"

"I think paranoia's lazy, Mehdi. Lazy thinking." As he glared at her, she put her hand to her mouth, as if she could stuff the words back in, and then she faked a cough. "I'm not saying you're paranoid. I mean I'm talking about my own thinking."

"Well I don't think it's paranoia, okay? You know the crowd our government has decided to run with. You don't think they're capable? I'd say there's a calculus at work."

"A calculus? Mehdi, I was a terrible math student, so help me here."

"I'm just saying they could have weighed the risks. This charge-D, he was more expendable than those who'd lose his position because of a story on this black site, out there in the press… our press."

"I guess I just can't see the beige kind of Canadians we're dealing with as that nefarious, know what I mean? Too banal."

"Do you know about Ashwin Khadilkar, the one they stuck in that embassy?"

"Of course I know of…"

"I guess I'd just say it's a different kind of banality."

"Mission creep banality," she arched her eyebrows, in the hope he'd lose a little of his strident tone.

"Sure. Something like that. You're better with words than I."

With the distance between them her gaze had gone to the window. She was formulating her thoughts but slowly. And there was too much silence. Yet she couldn't quite speak.

"Hannah, I see a guy like Khadilkar in Rabat, I know he's ambitious. I know the friends he's made. I just think he might be enabling some bad behaviour."

"Gordon MacPhail had the same feeling about this guy."

"The senator? You talked to him?"

"I talk to everybody." She stopped herself from saying anymore. No, she didn't need to justify herself to him.

Mehdi walked back into the living room, regarding the cream coloured walls with unease. The condo had the look of a once-stylish hotel room. Only the splashes of primary colours in the framed photos of some Iraqi market square lightened the gloom. He stirred his coffee a touch too aggressively. The spoon tinged against the inside of his mug like an alarm in an old watch. "My point is… these people like Khadilkar, this government… for them we are an obstruction at best. We're sentimentalists."

"Yes. I'm made aware of that every day."

"More than ever, yes? They think we have a vision of how the world works, and it's like… it's like a child's. We're determined to remain innocent. And they, only they have the guts and the courage to accept the realpolitik, yes?"

Hannah laughed. She didn't find any of this funny but Mehdi was too earnest on this point, too angry for someone who could remain detached and objective about the necessary transactions with this government. He was clearly not fulfilled by providing his students with little lectures on hard truths. He'd give them away to people like Hannah for free.

"So just give me a chance to state my case. I believe this Torquil Forsey became such an obstruction. I think I can tell you why."

"You're not going to put yourself in jeopardy by what you're telling me."

"Probably. But it needs to be out there. I just can't be connected to it."

Hannah raised her free hand to halt him. "I'm just saying be careful."

"I know. But I know of no one else I can trust, Hannah."

"I don't believe that."

"I'm serious. If you hadn't called me, I was going to call you."

She looked down at her fingernails, bit the tip of her thumb as she took him in, considering whether she should believe him. But of course she would. She had no choice now, she had to say why she was really in this room with him. "Mehdi, I've lost Yasmin. And I want to bring her back."

"You make it sound like she's your daughter."

"No, not my daughter. But my friend? Yes? Someone I still hope to mentor in some way? Yes."

"And you're sure I can help you."

"I'm not. I wouldn't be that presumptuous."

"Because I don't know anything about what happened to this senator's son."

"That was not something I had even considered."

He sat up in his chair, composed himself more formally. "Except that it proves that karma exists. I think of his father, that day in committee."

"It was a travesty."

She looked up to see if the word registered strongly with him. He gave her a solemn nod in agreement but it didn't ease the tension, it just added to how wooden she felt. She'd sensed that any perceived familiarity that she had with Gordon might jeopardize how honest Mehdi was about to be with her, how much he felt he could trust her.

Mehdi's cold detachment about Gordon's son irritated her though. Mehdi was younger than Gordon. He had never had to question his own politics, it seemed. The way he stroked this beard, he liked to wear his wisdom with too much self-regard. She could handle vanity in herself, she didn't like it in men.

"Mehdi, with your contacts in Rabat, would you be comfortable finding out what you can about Yasmin? No one I have spoken to feels they can help. Or maybe they're just telling me that because they're scared of what the army over there will do to them if they try."

Mehdi tilted his head as he was conceding the greater validity to what she was speculating. But his silence suggested he was weighing this up carefully. The worst thing she could do was fill the empty air with more words. So she waited. He seemed to like the gravity the silence provided him. "I can understand why she would do this. The Moroccan government is losing support from its military. You probably know this. There are at least three generals who speak about how they could run the country better than the prime minister. It would be very surprising if you didn't have a faction who sympathized with the group that took Henry Raeburn. I imagine she's decided they have history on their side."

"This is my thought too."

He walked over to his kitchen table where there was a blue file folder with a document inside it. He approached her, handed it to her with a stern look. "You read something like this, about the atrocities they commit, you realize Henry's captors have just cause to hate the prime minister's way of governing. He sacrifices men who are his brothers for what his foreign masters ask of him."

Within the first few sentences on the second page, she knew what he had in this document was what she had feared. All the details of the "conditions of incarceration." One blunt declarative after another. "Periods of enhanced interrogation" compelled her to pause with a sharp intake of breath.

"Hannah, Torquil Forsey asked me to meet. He offered this to me over a cup of coffee, the idiot... but I said no, no... and then..."

"And then yes."

Mehdi nodded as he took his seat once more. "A couple days later, I gave him a call. I'll give him this, he read me well."

"You sure it's real?"

"As much as I can be sure, yes. I believe he stole it. He had become, as my friends in Gaza say, full kamikaze. He must have figured he'd pass this off and then go out with valor or some such thing."

"But it is just such a thing."

"Sure. And here I am with it. I mean, what else can I do now? I have to make sure it gets out there."

Hannah looked up from the page and then closed the file folder as if it were a prayer book. "I hate this part of work, Mehdi. Hate it."

"This girl Yasmin..."

"She's not a girl."

"I'll do what I can for you. I'll make some phone calls tonight. But will you do what needs to be done with this document? You know it's not just for me."

Hannah exhaled and took in the view of the flats from the balcony. Yet the blankness was not what was holding her attention. It was the series of blurry photos she could still see in her mind's eye, plates from the book "Sites Noirs." The work of Henry Raeburn. She recalled the feeling of her last embrace of Gordon after their dinner together. It angered her that he'd made her feel something for him, and that she couldn't deny it.

"Of course I will, Mehdi. I'll do what I can."

Mehdi closed his eyes, brought the palms of his hands together in some trite prayer-like pose that filled her with a surge of disdain she masked with a tight smile.

"Thank you, Hannah. It is all I ask."

23.

Ashwin detested the Hotel Delcassé. Yes, it was expensive, the work of two very rigorous Dutch architects and a designer who had worked for Macron. Yes, the restaurant had a chef who'd trained at El Bulli. It was all so beautiful but it was not a hotel for serious people. Just look at who stayed there: French and Spanish trust-fund kids who spent their days surfing and their nights doing coke in the restrooms on the terrace, British admen and their third wives who'd finally outgrown Ibiza and then, of course, the Russians. It was these ageing gangsters from the Vory, the Gulag-spawned mafia, that kept the Delcassé in croissants and Bordeaux flown in daily from Paris. They traveled in packs, stuffed like fat Merguez sausages in crayon coloured tennis shirts and five hundred dollar jeans, their bull necks weighed down in thick gold chains, tattooed arms sporting more gold bling and outsized, complicated wristwatches. Ashwin had heard of at least two murders that had occurred in the hotel over the last year: one was a Ukrainian flayed and left hanging on the balcony of his room, the other was a prostitute, from Riga by way of Dubai, found floating in the pool on Valentine's Day morning. She was whisked off to the morgue before anyone could ascertain if she'd been raped before drowning. So much bad karma, and yes, Ashwin liked to say he had a special understanding of that word, debased by ex-hippies. Yet here he was, because "Tony" Osipov didn't want to stray too far for their meeting and hey, they've got Mamont vodka behind the bar.

Ashwin had already ordered his Pisco Sour as he waited for Osipov. He was dressed down deliberately in a steel blue suit he got on Kowloon Road, with a white shirt and a slate grey tie. The more he could play the faceless bureaucrat, the starker the contrast he'd make to the Russian. It was essential his new friend did not presume any kind of kinship, did not believe Ashwin could be corrupted by his love of luxury. No, everything about their conversation would be staid and transactional, thank you very much. Tony had helped with the Astana potash deal, and he'd played a background role in the initial meetings with the Novgorod steel company looking to buy Stelwin's two mills in Manitoba. All of these future investments for Tony had helped in laundering the millions he'd obtained from the Vory's more traditional sources of income. So, there was always a win-win proposition in play. Still the risks of associating in public with a Tony Osipov involved the presumption of vulgarity by association, and that required Ashwin taking the edge off or else he'd present as diffident and a touch too effete for this company.

"Thought I saw you there. I been in the restaurant." Ashwin felt Tony's large hand on his shoulder as the big man glided past and took his seat opposite. "My fault. I forgot the cocktail section."

"No problem at all, Tony!" Ashwin wanted to wince visibly at his response. He could never find the right register for men like this.

"I came in early anyway. Made some calls and had that fucking hamburger they do here. With the truffle oil. You had that?"

"I have not, no."

"Fucking champion. Michelin gold star! I know you'd like the menu in this place, Mr. Khadilkar." Tony pointed a thick, nicotine-stained finger at Ashwin. "You, you've got your Alberta beef in your country. You guys got standards."

"Ha! I'll take your compliment, sir."

This was a touch too friendly, given all that had happened with Torquil Forsey's death and the possible leak of crucial security information. As Osipov ordered himself a triple of Mamont, neat, Ashwin was already bracing himself for what his British and German diplomat friends called the Russian specialty: the love sandwich. In between the pleasantries at the start and the end of meeting was the threat, the clarifying realization that violence was no longer just an option as part of a plan, it was a serious consideration. And no one was excluded—not even a helpful

Canadian diplomat. The love sandwich allowed you to leave the table on a positive note, before you spent a sleepless night trying to figure out ways in which you could bring a crisis situation back under control. "You see the Russians have something we don't have in our foreign service," said Nigel Crittenden, "absolutely no limitations on criminal activity, with nothing but a nod and then a look the other way from the Kremlin." Ashwin wished he could levitate, have an out-of-body experience, watch this all play out from somewhere near the small, star shaped chandeliers above them, coasting along a constellation made of tin.

"Good. 'Cause I like you. You remind me of the Indians I deal with in Mumbai. Square dealers. I trust your eyes. I like you, Mr. Canada, but we got some serious shit to talk about. You know what I mean."

"I think I do. Yes. It's just as serious for me, believe me."

"I don't know about that, friend." The waiter gently placed the cut glass crystal tumbler of vodka in front of Osipov. He raised it like a pint glass of draught beer, mumbled "Na Zdorovie."

"I know you're worried about your friends and their intentions to invest in Stelwin. I am also."

"Worried? No. We're not worried, Mr. Canada. We put... what... 60 million down? We make no profit in six quarters, we still pull out, no matter what you guys do. No, it's our investments here in Morocco we need to talk about."

Ashwin looked down at the backs of his hands, splayed out on the dark wood. He was ageing quickly in this posting. "The security investments for the army here."

"Da. Yes. They've been secret. We need to keep them that way."

"They will be."

"Anybody finds out we been helping this government take care of these fucking Jihadis, nobody wins, you understand what I'm saying?"

"Would we say Jihadis, really?"

"You know what I'm talking about. We run the risk of leak right now. Information highly classified."

"It's a manageable situation."

Osipov grinned like a fed wolf. Yet the smile wouldn't take, it was like a taxidermist's afterthought. "You think so?"

"We'll ensure nobody close to you is at risk. Anyway, I think the Americans will have a tougher time with any leak than your friends."

"We don't see it that way, you understand?"

Ashwin loosened his tie, spoke lower over the smooth dance club muzak playing. "We've got skin in this game too, Tony. Nobody in Canada wants to see such a story go anywhere." He took a deep swallow of his cocktail. It tasted like more, the only thing that would get him through this conversation.

"Skin in game, sure," Osipov was reflecting on this, turning the outer ring on his diving watch with his thick fingers. "So what you going to do to… control the situation?"

"We've got all of Forsey's emails before he died. We know who he was talking to. Our CSIS… if he tried to sell information to anyone, we'd know."

"Really? Interesting."

"Why is that interesting?"

Osipov drained his tumbler, waved to the waiter and then pointed to his glass, like he was in some beer hall in Moscow. "We finished a drink and you haven't mentioned this Mehdi Mekhounam."

"The university professor? I haven't mentioned him because he's nothing but an irritant. Our government investigated him long ago. He's written a couple of op eds… sorry, pieces in newspapers… about the movement here. Why would you even care about him?"

"Because Forsey gave Mekhounam a thick fucking file before he killed himself. You see we weren't going to depend on your government to watch where the ball was going. We did it ourselves."

"You mean the Russian embassy in Ottawa?"

"And some friends, yes."

"You're sure about this."

"Mr. Canada, if we depended on you guys to tell us anything, we'd all be fucked." The waiter brusquely placed the next tumbler of Mamont in front of Osipov. Osipov hummed a little song of approval. He got along better with the people here than Ashwin ever could, merely through a tacit understanding of mutual contempt.

"I'll need to verify this. I'm sure they've been watching him."

"You're sure, are you? How come you know nothing?"

Ashwin could feel the scream form at the back of his throat. If he let it out, it would still the air, make the bar go silent. He was enraged that he was at this man's mercy—that Osipov was far better and smarter playing at this level than Ashwin knew he'd ever be. "I'll find out everything. We'll put a stop to whatever Mekhounam's up to. He can be arrested if he has any documents. Possession of stolen property, at the very least."

"Da. That's good to hear. Because if you don't put a stop to it, we'll do it our way, understand?"

"I understand."

"And you don't want that. Very embarrassing. We don't give a fuck. I mean, do a little research. I can give you the names of some peoples who became problems."

"I trust you."

Osipov smiled. More convincing this time. Here came the love again, but definitely without the truffle oil.

"Good! And I trust you, Mr. Khadilkar. You look me in the eye when we talking. You got balls."

"We'll put a stop to this. Like tomorrow."

"No, no..." Osipov swallowed his second vodka at the table in one draught. "You supposed to say yesterday."

"Yesterday it is."

"Best to live like there is no tomorrow, am I right, my friend?"

Ashwin started to flinch as Osipov's hand reached for his bicep, but then he stopped himself, managed to smile uneasily. Just a friendly squeeze from our Russian friend, that was all. But Ashwin could feel the force behind it. The seriousness.

"I should go. See if I can get to the office and find out what I can before the day's end."

"I appreciate you hard working guy."

"Next time, we'll lunch. I'll do that burger with you, see how it compares to Alberta beef."

"See? You're all right, Mr. Canada. Just like my guys in Mumbai."

"Oh, better than that, Tony. I promise you." Ashwin fastened the top button of his suit jacket, discreetly concealed the monogram on the cuff of his shirt. "Have a good day, sir."

He hurried out of the bar, with quick, darting glances at the tables for anyone who might have recognized him. But no, it appeared this meeting would remain completely private. Even deniable, worst case scenario.

And that was the only scenario with a high degree of probability now. He hurried along the sidewalk past the bleached white confusion of office buildings that surrounded the hotel, scanning the roadway for a taxi. Much to do before the day ended.

24.

Gordon first saw the video when he was at Heathrow, waiting for his connecting flight to Ottawa.

It happened while he was contemplating another cognac, taking in the golden light of the afternoon at a table to himself with a Herald Tribune in front of him, feeling good about the last 48 hours. The dinner and auction of Henry's work had gone off as planned. A million in the bank, Garry Fry said, in the email. Gordon's speech was "top shelf." So good. Sure, they were still at least two million away from raising the ransom money, but "it's about the awareness," Garry assured him, and who knows, he might be right. As for Yasmin's disappearance, Garry was philosophical. "She is an idealist, just like Henry. They'll both survive." Yes, well, Gordon would drink to that.

There was a family all set to leave on vacation, camped at a table nearby—mother, father, their adult son and daughter—turned out like the royal family on a tour of one of the old colonies, all navy and khaki linen. They spoke in clipped, quiet phrases to one another, the tone of detente as they suffered through their flight delay. The daughter was scrolling through messages on her phone, the son was doing a crossword puzzle. And the faint aroma of lavender cologne emanated from that side of the room. No matter how dysfunctional things were at the end of their marriage, Gordon and Marithe would have never had this kind of a nuclear unit.

The bartender eyed them cautiously as he polished wine glasses. Waiting for the next bellowed order from the father. Churchill, reimagined as an estate agent.

"'Scuse me, lad. Can you get the BBC on?" He made a screen shape with his small, doughy hands.

"He speaks English, dear," the mother said. She tugged at the pink ribbon that held back her greying blonde hair in a pony tail. A little too girlish for her daughter, never mind her.

The bartender turned with the remote in his hand to flick through the channels. And there it was: BBC World News. Something of business interest was being reported on from Dubai.

Gordon returned to his Herald Tribune. He had read the same paragraph of the story on the poisoned Russian journalist twice now. It was all very straightforward, short declarative sentences. But his shredded concentration from his lack of sleep had turned the words into groups of letters that faded to white.

Then the BBC newscast switched abruptly to a grainy video image, taken from a CCTV camera in a shopping mall. Darkly clad figures with AK47s ran into a bank. One of the figures gestured with his gun to a teller, and the teller hurried over to the switch to make the steel-reinforced doors come together.

"And now, a development in the abduction of the American artist Henry Raeburn. Footage has been obtained which shows the artist taking part in a bank robbery, reportedly carried out by his captors in broad daylight. The criminal group, with reported ties to Al Qaeda, abducted the artist during his transfer and have been in hiding for more than five weeks."

Gordon was up on his feet, barely conscious of his movements as he approached the bar. He was focussed on obtaining the remote control from the bartender. The family watched him approach, wide eyed and unsure of him.

But Gordon's gaze was fixed on the figure alleged to be Henry. He had to know it was him. And as he got closer to the screen, the slow motion, blurred sequence of the bank robbery, with all its points of focus, did reveal that the man the BBC producers had hit pause on, though he was bearded and more slender than Gordon remembered, was indeed Henry. He looked so much like his grandfather now.

"Could I have that remote please?"

The bartender moved cautiously towards Gordon with the remote in hand. Perhaps he feared Gordon might become violent. And in any confrontation, he'd likely lose his job if he attempted to calm a man down in this state. No one would believe he didn't escalate things unnecessarily. Gordon held out his hand for the remote with all the polished empathy he could muster.

It was in this moment that he realized he could not rewind what was playing out. It was all he wanted to do—to press pause, study the blurred image of Henry. Maybe he could will it to transform into someone else.

"Thank you." He fidgeted with the buttons on the remote, but he knew that all he could really do was increase the volume. And so he did. And then he turned to the family. "My apologies."

"Y'all right, man?" The son looked genuinely concerned. The mother whispered the son's name—Corin—with a scolding look that clearly had no impact on the young man, for he remained focused on Gordon.

"I'm… him, there… in that bank… that's my son."

Now it was not just the family but the bartender as well who was staring at him as if he was possibly unbalanced. The threat of sudden violence from him seemed all too real to them. The father eyed his phone on the table in front of him as if he wondered what would happen to him if he picked it up. Maybe this crazy man would also produce a gun and threaten him.

"He's a good man. This… this is wrong! I'm a senator. We're Canadian. This… he's Canadian, he's not American!"

He turned and pointed to the screen with the remote but the newscast had moved on to a story about a police crackdown on drug traffic in the Philippines. He gently handed the remote back to the bartender, murmuring "I'm sorry… I'm sorry…"

"Not at all, sir. I am sorry."

He moved toward the bartender. It was all impulse, he suddenly felt he needed to embrace him. But then he thought better of it. Steady, Gordon, you have a public role. He nodded his head solemnly. "Thank you, sir. Thank you. May I get my bill?"

Once he returned to his seat he picked up his phone. And surprise, there was a new voicemail message, the same 613 number calling three times. It had to be one of those kids tasked with managing him in the OLO. What was he going to tell him that the video hadn't already? But there was also a 44—London area code. Garry Fry. He was probably hoping Gordon could tell him something more than the BBC could. Now the reconvening had to start: Marithe, Hisham…but the only person he really needed to talk to was there on the screen. Henry, his only boy in the world.

And then into the emails. Yes, of course, here was a message from a Dennis Wilson from CSIS. And then… how reassuring… six emails from international.gc.ca addresses. As he scrolled down further though, there was a surprise: y.raza. Now that was worthy of clicking on first.

> Dad,
>
> I'm writing you from Yasmin's account because I need-ed you to read this. I could not send you anything from my old addresses. They no longer exist. Yasmin has decided of her own free will to come with us, so there is no point in trying to reply to this address either. She too will be disappeared by those who enforce the law and decide what is just, and who is worthy of being rec-ognized as a citizen with all the rights, freedoms and obligations such status provides.
>
> This is not about money now—if it ever was. This is about freeing those prisoners that have been locked away in a black site, here in this country, without a trial, without basic human rights, without hope for release. The living hell they are going through made my brief stay in prison here like a vacation in comparison. My duty to act is so much bigger than my narcissistic pursuit of artistic success. There must be justice before there can be peace, and I have no interest in being an artist of war.
>
> I will try to continue our correspondence now that this has happened. You have always stood by me, espe-cially when it seemed that no one else would. I am no longer alone though. I am grateful to have found

support from Yasmin. And I have found, in those that rescued me from prison, new friends and companions in this struggle who inspire me and earn my respect and loyalty every day. I am safe and I am fine. I miss you but I know you understand.

Please tell Mom I will try to find a way to send her messages too. I only had time for one but I promise to stay connected to you both, in whatever way I can, in the days, weeks and maybe months ahead.

You once told me that it was not enough to be intelligent. One had to be serious, and that if I truly cared about what is good and what is just—and acted accordingly—I couldn't help but find my purpose, and also find love and happiness. How right you were, Dad.

I hope I still make you proud.

Talk soon again (I promise),

Henry

Before Gordon could contact anyone, even Marithe, he needed to take a walk. This was not his son's voice. He would get in a train, wander around downtown London if he had to. Nothing was more important than solitude now, and yet he had never felt this alone. His mother, his father, even his love of Marithe—these were losses he could accommodate. They seemed inevitable over the course of time. The loss of Henry was different. And now, for the first time, it felt real.

25.

"Clutter is not the sign of a disordered mind, but of creativity, apparently. So… there you are, I'm a frustrated artist, Gordon."

Hannah cleared away a spot on her huge steel desk so Gordon could put his coffee cup down somewhere. It was impressively unattractive, an industrial pale green raft of papers and books surrounding an old PC that hummed like it was going to crash soon. Three… four… five pairs of glasses… she was probably misplacing them so often among this mess that she just kept buying new ones. Or perhaps they were an indulgence to a vanity she kept concealed in her working life—at least she did when they last met. Was there always a little bit of vanity with her? He'd known her for thirty-five years but really, he didn't know her at all.

"I feel a little frustrated myself. I just don't know what to believe."

"You've met with CSIS."

"Twice now. They said I should stop hoping for any further communication from Henry. I can't accept that." Gordon was wrestling with the notion that everyone knew more than he did, and he couldn't quite take the anger out of his voice. Only three hours of sleep the night before.

"And I'm thinking to myself am I just blaming everyone but him? Am I blaming Yasmin?"

"Gordon, I've met with CSIS too, now that she's disappeared. I've given them access to all our emails. I think this is complicated. I don't think either of them planned for things to go this way."

"But she knew this group of men before the abduction."

"Not just men. There was at least one other woman, if CSIS is correct. They're going from intelligence files they received from that government, mostly."

"You don't seem convinced."

"I don't think we get the best information from that government. And I don't think our ambassador is effective there."

Ashwin Khadilkar. Gordon thought of all that Torquil Forsey told him about the ambassador's shady dealings, his bullying and threats that kept him immune from any investigation of his little outpost of the empire. What a traditional figure the man was. Tradition was probably his highest aspiration.

"Yasmin told you nothing about these people before she left?"

"No, we spoke of them. Especially after your son was abducted. She knew two people involved. And only two to my knowledge."

"This Nabil Aguerd. The leader. He's also called Gato. Apparently he spent some time in Italy. He's got a PhD in Chemistry."

"And Fayçal Belhanda. A law student. I discovered that Fayçal was involved in the exchange program Yasmin did."

"Spoiled kids. They're educated. I'll bet they've all been abroad. See, this isn't Al Qaeda, right?"

Hannah folded her arms in her lap. Gordon sensed his anger was causing her to retract. "They're capable of violence. And now they've committed crimes they could be imprisoned for… as they say call it in Moroccan law… perpetual confinement. Don't you think they had to be pretty desperate to throw away their futures like this?"

"Desperate, yes. And this is why I just can't accept that Henry's become one of them. That it was his choice. And not just him, I suppose. Henry and Yasmin."

"How about I tell you what I know rather than what I think, Gordon. Because we're probably going to disagree about the motives of this group. And neither of us really knows."

"I just don't see what they would want… what would be worth throwing their lives away for…"

"Henry has been photographing black sites for some years now, hasn't he?"

"Four. I'm told the series has made his career."

"You're told."

"By his English art dealer Garry Fry."

"Yes, Fry. That name's familiar. Yasmin spoke about him."

"What did she say? I imagine she was impressed."

"She said she wasn't sure about him, actually. But she was going to give him the benefit of the doubt."

"What benefit?"

"That he had your son's best interests at heart."

"And she would know?"

Gordon crossed his legs and reclined in the chair as if he was inching away from the conversation. He was disappointed by how professional, how dispassionate and clear Hannah was being. She was affirming they were really strangers, despite how long they'd known each other. It was harder to bear when there was every possibility Henry was a stranger to him—and had been for some time. He had come here in the hope of something more than information; he had come for understanding from someone who once truly knew him. The past seems to be past. If he had to, he'd be combative, test her reserves of compassion. He hated how his loneliness drove him to need. Just push him further out on the ice floe.

"Gordon, I was speaking about your son. He's been working on this interest of his, these black sites that are in fact worthy of outrage, don't you think? Don't you think it all might have affected him?"

"By asking me this, Hannah, I think you're asking me if I'm outraged. And I'm starting to think this is less about Henry than the power I might have to address this."

She slowly batted her long eyelashes. It was a parody of coquettishness. "I think I have a realistic perspective about your power to do anything, Gordon. I'm trying to help you. Because you're someone I consider an old friend."

"An old friend who has gone over to the dark side or something."

"No. We both know where the dark side is. Your son and Yasmin have crossed over. I want to help you bring them back."

And he unfolded, leaned forward. He looked down and he saw that his hands were trembling and he flushed in embarrassment. Her smile was warmer and despite himself all he wanted to do was embrace her.

"You read that email he sent me. That's not his voice, Hannah. I know my boy."

"He sounds converted."

"No, it's positioning. Like a bad politician."

"Funny, that."

"I just think they've made him a ventriloquist's dummy to lure the government in, to raise the stakes, get more attention, get the story in the newspapers here."

"Gordon, you've asked me for my perspective. I think it's possible that your son is not even sure if he's sincere. He may feel that he wants to be capable of a heroic act. I say this because of Yasmin's silence."

"Her silence?"

"Maybe I flatter myself, but I like to think she looked to me as a mentor. That we were close. I keep thinking I'll hear from her. Through some means... but nothing."

"I'm resisting thinking of her as someone capable of great duplicity. I mean, that's a thing, isn't it? That you can justify pretending to be secular if it furthers a radical agenda."

"This is something you discussed with Dennis Wilson, your new friend in CSIS, I guess."

"No, with Hisham. Hisham Mahmoud. Remember him?"

"From Langley?"

"The same."

She laughed, brushed her curls back from her brow. Such warmth in her voice. Why couldn't they just talk about the past? It would probably be just as productive.

"God, he used to be so funny."

"I'm sure he still can be. I hired him for Henry's case. We weren't kibitzing."

"That's good, you two have stayed in touch."

"I trust him. I've always trusted him. Hannah, he took a dim view of the people around Henry. There was a press conference after the court decision there. You should have seen it. It was a circus. And Garry Fry, with Yasmin... it was their doing. It is Hisham's belief we would have had a strong chance of getting Henry off if the case wasn't publicized, if they didn't attempt to embarrass the government."

"He might be right."

"I thought to myself that's also why it attracted the attention of this group. Garry Fry spoke to the media about how Henry was a famous artist, his work selling for so much... that there would be an international outcry. I mean, if I'm looking for a prize abduction, for maximum leverage, there it is."

"I believe that's also right, Gordon."

"And yet you're telling me Yasmin knew of these people well before the abduction."

"Knew of them. But she did not know them as friends or peers. At least she did not tell me this."

"You think she would?"

She squinted as if she was sharpening her focus on him. Gordon had stumbled into a private place with her and he wished he could walk backward, retrace his steps. "I suppose I don't know, Gordon. I suppose I'm a little angry. I thought we were close."

"Are you close enough with her to speak to her family? Her parents are here, yes?"

"They're American, living in Philadelphia. They came from Lahore over thirty-five years ago. She was so proud of them, she told me. Her father was an engineer, her mother has a PhD in mathematics from Bristol. They were proud of all they had achieved, Gordon, sent three daughters to university. When she said she wanted to study in Canada, it broke their hearts that she could live so far from them. I'm saying these are accomplished people. This is an accomplished family."

"I want to contact them."

"I'm not sure if that's a good idea. I tried to call them but... nothing. Maybe they think that Yasmin was brainwashed."

"They could be right, yes?"

"I mean by me."

"Okay, I understand." Gordon was speaking in a lower register. He wanted her to know that he'd never suggest she was a bad influence on anyone. But he stopped himself from saying it. There was something about Hannah that still made him feel dumb, made him want to be better. "Hannah, I feel like every door I try to open is locked. You know what I mean?"

"I do." She reached across her desk and he took her hand in his. Wonder of wonders.

"Would we maybe go out for a drink again, sometime? Try to talk about other things?"

"We could do that, Gordon. I'd like that."

"Me too." And he let her fingers fall from his, tried to figure out how to make a graceful exit.

As he made to leave, she followed. She was going to walk with him to the elevators. *My heart swelled up…* that's what his sixteen-year-old self had written about the first time they walked on the beach together. It was the same feeling now.

"Gordon, I haven't forgotten about Mehdi Mekhounam.."

"Well thanks. But I know… I don't think he would have any interest in speaking with me."

"That's probably true. But he… um… he has good information. And he is discreet."

As he got to the elevator he turned to her. He had the courage to look deeply into her eyes. But as he started to speak it was she who looked away, pulled him close in an embrace.

"It was good to see you, Gordon. Good that you came."

This was not the time to say anything more, this he knew. He turned, stepped in the elevator and resolved not to think too much about this, not to think about her all the time.

26

Henry sat on the plastic slide, in the one spot of shade in the back yard. He was examining the burner phone Gato had given him. It was from China, apparently. He'd never heard of this brand. He was looking for any evidence that it had been tampered with already. He didn't trust Gato. He was not sure if he even trusted Yasmin anymore. But this was all he had, and he couldn't back out now.

"You should not overestimate your worth to us, Mr. Raeburn," Gato said. They were having an argument about the need for the weekly change of location. It was Henry's view that a group of men and women who move in to a building and then out again—even when the building is hundreds of kilometres from the capital—attracts more interest than if they were to stay in one place for a number of weeks. Henry was so obviously a foreigner that even a glimpse of him in a backyard could prompt a neighbour to pry further into, say, who was occupying one of the apartments in the building beside his house (this did happen). "If you do something that jeopardizes our safety, you'll put us into a very difficult position, do you understand me?"

What he remembered most was the look on Yasmin's face. Stern, drained of any affection for him. He confronted her about it later but she denied anything had changed between them. "This is all just so stressful, Henry. It's not you, it's… the living together, the lack of sleep." It was the lack of sex, too, he wanted to say, but he was afraid how she would respond. She might have said she didn't want to be with him that way anymore.

He heard the squeak of a clothes line being pulled through an old metal wheel. It was just next door to this abandoned daycare centre. There was a woman who was home most mornings. He'd heard her scold her children as they got ready for school.

This had to be her once again, collecting the clothes off the line. She was not visible because of the high concrete wall between them but surely… if he could hear her, she could hear them. Maybe Gato was right after all.

It was all this waiting now. And there was still more than two weeks to go before they could put the final plan in action. Gato said the delays were unavoidable. It was about what kind of safety they could all get once they made it to Spain: a location, supplies… so much logistics to work through. But he couldn't help feeling this was a test of Henry's commitment, if he could get the kind of money he had promised them. Even Yasmin seemed doubtful about Garry coming through, now that he had the images from the SD card. Suddenly all he represented was a source of money. He wondered why he had crossed over, more and more every day.

Well there was nothing he could do to change it now. *The resolve is all… the resolve to make this call.* His mind made rhymes of every small thing; he worried it was a sign he was losing his sanity.

When he repeated Garry's number in his head he closed his eyes, saw it written down in his address book, back there in Vancouver. "Henry has no disability, he's just a visual learner," his mother had said in a teacher's meeting a hundred years ago. That was from a time when she still defended him, still fought fiercely for his right to be different. Try as he might, he couldn't remember her number now. He dialed Garry's personal line— the one he gave out to no one—and heard what sounded like the ocean in a shell, and then the long beeps of a British dial tone.

"This is Garry."

"Garry, it's Henry."

"Henry? Henry, where the hell are you?"

He could hear a faint ruffling of papers, Garry shutting a door.

"I don't know, really. But I'm all right."

"We'll get you out. I promise. The photos from Yasmin… the new work… it's very strong. We're mounting them just like the Bucharest series. I don't think I need to tell you there will be serious interest."

"Thank you, Garry. For all you're doing. Did you get the package this morning?"

"What package?"

"A courier's package."

"That would be downstairs. Lise receives them. I haven't checked."

"There will be a brown envelope. In it is my new will."

"You know I'll have to report this to the police."

"Sure, of course. I thought if not you, my father. You'll have to get in touch with him and tell him the changes I've made."

A crow alighted from the tree above Henry. He watched its wings flap once, twice, then it landed on top of the concrete fence, where shards of glass were embedded, glistening in the sun.

"What changes might these be, Henry?"

"I had left my estate, including my catalogue to him. That's no longer the case. It's all to you, including the new work. It's time to auction it off, if you can. But let's do privately. To your network."

"Henry, I don't know how we can do this privately."

"You've done it before. Apparently you just made quite a bit of money from my work."

"Things are different now."

"Yes. Yes, they are."

"Henry, are you all right? They haven't harmed you, have they?"

"Garry, you're my friend."

"Yes, I am."

"Please just do this. A short time from now, I'm going to need that money."

"You've sent me your will. Henry, this worries me about what you're planning."

Henry laughed. Despite himself, he was thinking of Garry. It was odd, the habits of a mind. "Well, if you weren't worried enough before."

"I was."

"Please, just do this."

He wanted to tell him it would be all right, that there was a plan. He would be safe in Algeciras by the end of the month, safe from any possible threat of extradition. This money would buy his seclusion, his safety, a life with Yasmin apart from all of this madness at last. And maybe at some point, not too far in the future, he would be able to return to the world Gato and all of them here just call "the west." But the worst of it was none of this could be said. He couldn't trust that Garry wouldn't tell someone. Like, say, Henry's father—who'd get the goddamned Canadian government involved and fuck up everything.

"I'll do what I can."

"Good. And I promise, I will be in touch again very soon. And then we can meet."

"I'll go anywhere. Just let me know."

"I will, Garry." He checked his big black digital watch, the one Karima gave him, right off her wrist. It had been more than two minutes. He knew he was being watched from those inside there, the ones he was supposed to call his friends. They were probably listening too. He looked up and the crow was gone. "And you, how are things? You keeping well?"

"I'm fine, Henry. Don't worry about me. Worry about you."

"Love to my father and mother, Garry. Please tell them."

"I will."

"Goodbye for now."

The word goodbye caused his eyes to water. He looked down at the watch again and read SUN over the time digits. This was the day he used to call his father every week, just after he poured that first glass of wine as he made dinner in his place— more often than not for friends. What a charmed, lucky man he had become, his life better than he'd ever imagined it would be. He couldn't stop the tears from coming now. Maybe he never felt he deserved it all, deep down. He had to test it was real by throwing it all away.

But enough. The resolve was all now. He got to his feet, wiped away his tears with his dirty hand. He'd compose himself once again for those whose judgment he despises now.

Yes, even Yasmin's judgment, he realized.

27

Anne Forsey sounded frail on the phone. It was understandable. She was still grieving, no doubt. She told Gordon that she hadn't slept much the night before, she was attending to all the loose ends of her son's estate. If Gordon had known her, even casually, he would have taken that as an overture to mention all he was trying to manage, given Henry's new will. But no, should the conversation take that turn when they met in person, so be it. Tuesday afternoon was best, she played bridge on Tuesday mornings at the Rideau Racquet Club but she would be home after lunch. Just a visit for condolences, Gordon said. "Your son was a fine public servant, Mrs. Forsey, you should be very proud of the work he accomplished over the course of his career."

"That's very kind of you to say. It's more than I've heard from Ambassador Khadilkar."

He could have said more but it was best to be tactful. He called it a "lapse in protocol." Anne Forsey said she knew all about protocol, thank you very much, this was a question of human decency. Far be it for the senator to answer for the ambassador on that front.

"The Clerk of the Privy Council sent me a card though. I suppose I should be grateful. But to be honest, I think that's more because of my husband than my boy."

"Your son was very helpful to me. You should know that."

"Thank you, Senator MacPhail."

He said he looked forward to seeing her on Tuesday and could tell, from the cautiously genial tone of her reply, that she wasn't quite sure if she should look forward to seeing him in turn. He'd bring her roses, he decided, that would help put her at ease.

Yet what he had to speak about with her would not provide her with any comfort. It certainly wasn't giving him any peace of mind. Henry had spoken about his "preoccupation" (Gordon's diplomatic term) with black sites when they were in Venice. They had been in Harry's Bar, drinking Bellinis. Henry used to make a variation of the cocktail with ginger and maple syrup back in his bartending days, said he was curious about how it compared to the original. They sat at a corner table, pleasantly surprised by how rich and complex the cocktail was, "not a slice of tourist cheesecake at all," Henry had said, while he went into detail about all he had heard about six-hour waterboarding sessions, blaring white noise, a German Shepherd loosed on on exercise field while a terrified detainee ran for his life. It was a calm and pointed rebuke to Gordon's incuriousness, his insistence on speaking, "in broad strokes," about NATO commitments and Red Cross reports on human rights violations. They didn't argue, no, Henry had been as determined to make Venice a holiday as much as Gordon was. The conversation just petered out as they flipped through the glossy calendar that listed all the installations and exhibitions they had still to see.

Why had he not pushed the issue, been more curious, ask Henry why the black sites had become such an obsession for him? He was afraid the information shared would change both of their lives, and no change would be for the better.

And then, late on Monday night, there was Hannah at his dinner table in Ottawa, calmly placing the pages of evidence before him. Her cheeks were flushed from dashing from her car in the thunder shower and she looked so elegant in her simple black blouse and jeans. She struck him as so perfectly put together, with such a pure force of goodness coursing through her, that she was ageless. Yet there was nothing humourless or stolid in her ways. She laughed gently about the state of her wet hair, raised that first glass of wine to his with a shy smile, a soft light in her dark eyes. He turned the pages before him, and in the moment when he had read enough, he just looked up and nodded, and she took his hand in hers.

"This is probably all wrong… I never got the meanings right… but I'm hearing that poem you loved, when we were kids. Here there is no place that does not see you."

She nodded, smiled, squeezed his hand. "You must change your life."

"That poem was about the power of beauty, wasn't it? Not anything like this. See what I mean? Wrong…"

"Beauty is truth… truth, beauty. That's another school poem. Even when the truth is so horrible you want to look away from the page."

"No. I don't want to look away anymore. Not here. And not with you. You're still so beautiful."

And as he kissed her, it was she who pulled him closer. Once, so many years ago, she had consented to be loved. And only for a time. But now, in this return, there was something more powerful, strengthened by the force of time. This connection was no longer fragile. It was something real.

Now he was far more nervous about the truth while he anticipated the visit with Anne Forsey. Maybe it was because he was not just visiting a grieving mother, but he was going to the place—the very room—where Torquil Forsey took his own life. He had pictured a woman broken by grief; it all seemed too much like a premonition waiting to happen. He could do without any more signs and symbols, thank you very much.

She opened the door with a soft, musical hello. Her silver hair was stylishly clipped into a bob. Maybe she had gone to the hairdressers after bridge. She had dressed up her cream-coloured turtleneck sweater with a necklace of chunky pieces of turquoise. Gordon said his hello and remarked on her jewelry to put her at ease.

"Oh this…" she fingered the leather cord with a look of concern. "Torquil brought this home for me from Turkey. That was his second assignment. These roses are beautiful, senator. I'll just put them in a vase. Please, make yourself at home." She gestured to a fragile looking love seat.

He settled himself gently, mindful of the creak of the wooden legs. They were painted a pale green that his stepmother Ruth Ellen would have loved, called "classy." He heard Anne Forsey's tap run in her kitchenette as she dropped the roses in a vase. The room smelled of Lemon Pledge furniture polish—that, too, a Ruth Ellen favourite.

"You've got a lovely place here."

"Oh I've downsized considerably, senator. That was difficult, let me tell you. You tell yourself they're just things. But they take on so many memories over time. We gave a lot of pieces to Torquil. They're in storage right now. I can't… I just can't yet."

She was just about to settle into a white leather club chair when she brought the palms of her hands up and lightly tapped her forehead. "Where's your head, Anne? I haven't offered you anything. Can I get you a cup of coffee or some tea? I've got some lovely Darjeeling."

"I'm fine, ma'am."

"Some bourbon. It's past noon, that might be more your speed, eh? It wasn't that long ago when Bobby and I had friends on the Hill. But I can't touch any of that anymore."

He considered it for a moment, mainly because the prospect of pouring him a drink caused her to grin mischievously, put her at ease. But no, he needed to affirm the gravity of his visit, given what he had to tell her. He shook his head, declined with little more than a whisper.

"I suppose you don't have much time."

"Committee, this afternoon, yes. But this is important. I thank you for seeing me."

"I know of all that has happened with your son. I'm sure both of us have got a lot on our minds."

"That's true, no question. Mrs. Forsey, you probably know that over the years, my son has taken an interest in art of a more… political nature."

She sipped her tea and nodded. "Your son has a strong social conscience. I say good for him. Torquil, he was the same. He would give thousands of dollars a year to St. Christopher House in Toronto."

"He must have lost someone."

"He did, yes. I sometimes think he never recovered. He was living like a monk overseas, he told me."

"I found him very professional. Very conscientious. He came to my son's trial almost every day."

"Do you think he still enjoyed his work? You know the last ambassador he worked for in Turkey... that's where he got me this..." She bit her bottom lip. "This Ambassador Corrigan, I think, I can't remember..."

"Cadogan."

"Yes, Cadogan. She came up to me at a Christmas party and said Torquil did remarkable work. She said he was as talented as his father. Bobby had passed away by then. It's a shame. I wanted him to hear that."

"I think Ambassador Khadilkar is a very different person."

"How diplomatic of you, senator. You're in the wrong job."

They laughed together but Anne Forsey's voice soon faded as she stared out the window, awaiting the visit of a ghost.

"Mrs. Forsey, I want to tell you something about a document your son left behind. A couple of days before he decided to take his life, he met with a gentleman called Mehdi Mekhounam."

"Never heard of him."

"No. I suppose your son wouldn't want to talk about his meeting. You see, Torquil stole a document with highly sensitive information from the files near his office back in his last posting."

"Oh Lord." Anne Forsey put her hand to her chest, gently touched the pieces of turquoise. Her new worry beads. "What was in this document?"

"It's distressing information. It's about what this government knows. Sorry, let me be clear... it's about detainees, citizens taken in for suspected terrorist activity over there."

"You know, senator, it's interesting. About a week before he died, he got very angry with me. He accused me of searching through his belongings when I went in to the spare room where he was sleeping. I just went in to get his laundry, I had told him I was happy to do that for him."

"He probably had it hidden in a sock drawer."

"Or something. Anyway, he apologized afterward. And he said Mom, you don't understand, I feel like I'm being followed."

"He might have been."

"I asked him why and he just tried to laugh it off. He said he was still such a drama queen, just like me."

"You don't strike me as a very theatrical person, Mrs. Forsey. But then he didn't seem that way either. He was very level headed. Very serious. I mean… he had to be serious."

"Because of this document you mention."

"Yes, I've brought it there… in my briefcase by the door." He walked over to the entrance. He could feel her eyes on him. She'd leaned forward, her thin, liver-splotched hands folded together. All of this felt cruel but what else could he do, given what he had to tell her? As he returned to his seat, document in hand, she reached over, tapped his forearm as a gesture of solidarity… or maybe complicity.

"I want you to take a look at this because I feel I have no choice, Mrs. Forsey. I feel I have to make this public. And by doing so, your son's name may come up. It won't be from me, but that may not matter."

"No, it probably won't."

Her eyes went to the pages before her, but she was not really reading. She was too self-conscious. But what could he expect under the circumstances? She was dealing with her darker truth of grief, and there were no words for that on any page before her.

"I know I'm getting into something larger than myself."

"Senator MacPhail, I don't know a lot but I know enough about your line of work. If you do this, I can't see that new Leader you have or the people in your party taking it too well."

"I hope you understand… no, I think you understand… my son Henry, thank God, he's still alive. I need to do this for him."

Anne Forsey was quiet, her whispered "I do, senator" compelled him to look away from her. Was he being entirely truthful? Surely it was not only for Henry. He felt betrayed by the assurances of the kids in the OLO that there was "no there there" with the detainees story, duped like some hick backbencher they strung along with promises of position and influence, should they get back into government. So there was pride involved. But there was also this, looming larger than he could have imagined just days ago: he felt he had to do it for Hannah, to prove he was worthy of her love. Of course, exposing what he knew publicly might help make Henry connect with him. But there was more to this: there was his new love—and he felt like a bit of a fraud so nobly portraying himself for this grieving woman, a mother who did not have the luxury of hope for her son's return. No motive could ever be pure anymore; this he should have learned watching his father manage his self-loathing for forty years as a politician.

"I don't know how I'm going to make this public yet. But I know that even if I give it to a journalist, as an anonymous source, I have to come out and speak against this government. It just feels a bit too craven, too much of a performance to do so while any journalist would have to fight her own battle to keep her source secret."

"I can only tell you I think my son would have appreciated this." She turned back to the title page of the document. She didn't need to see any more of it. "And so do I."

"That is all I need to know, ma'am. Truly."

Why did he need to say truly? For himself. If he said the word out loud, he might come to believe it. She handed him the document as he rose from his chair and slowly crossed to the front hallway.

He felt weary. Now that he could do what needed to be done with a free conscience, all he wanted to do was sleep for hours until he could wake up with the energy and the force of his resolve. But there might never be enough dreaming to make that a reality anymore.

28.

It was Yasmin's suggestion that she and Henry walk the fence line at dusk. Back from the crumbling old *ksour* that they had taken over, the perimeter stretched right to the back acreage of the olive orchard. Here the sun-baked grass was shorn by the wind. The air smelled of eucalyptus and distant fires from the shepherds' camps where the roads faded into winding, nettled paths. Henry had come to love this landscape far from the city, the way its harshness had sculpted the trees to Giacometti-like figures that created snaky shadows, like the brush strokes of an old painter who could no longer steady his hands. Maybe that was the artist he would be some day, when he finally returned here, free and forgotten. He looked back as they moved together, took in the way their shadows joined, and he was longing for their bodies to do the same once again.

"I spoke with Garry."

"Did Gato have another phone for you?" Yasmin pursed her lips as she focused on the path. She was either annoyed or worried. Or both. It was a state she was often in with him now.

"No, Fayçal arranged it. Back in the city."

"Was it absolutely necessary right now, Henry? You know, every time you make a call, you put us at risk."

"It's been four weeks. I hadn't heard a thing from Mohsin, Gato's friend in London. The instructions were clear in the letter I wrote with the will, Garry was to check in with Mohsin after two."

"I just think we can't grow impatient. Maybe these things take time."

They came to a turn in the path and there were paw prints around a puddle of murky greenish water. The fennec foxes. Henry could hear them at night back in the workers' quarters of this farm. Their cries sounded desperate. Just as homesick and cast out as Gato's little pack, perhaps.

"Don't you think the risk also increases the longer we're waiting?"

"I don't know, Henry. We're in one place and I worry. Then we're in another, like here, and it seems we could be safe for months. There's nothing predictable about the danger increasing."

"I thought you were the one who was becoming impatient, Yasmin. I mean it's not just me."

"Why would you say that?"

"Why? You were the one who was getting frustrated with the way you and Karima are somehow just expected to do the cleaning, the cooking... like you're somebody's wives."

"Wives? Is that what wives are supposed to do, Henry? This must be an artistic tradition or something, yes?"

"No. Karima said it herself. When she and Fayçal were arguing."

"I did not hear that."

"That's where it was coming from. All I meant."

"Okay. I see."

"Anyway, Garry. I spoke to him. The news wasn't good. My dad, he's contesting the validity of the new will. He's got that lawyer he set me up with, this Hisham guy, involved. I'm sure he's convinced him."

"He was a vain man. Wearing those striped socks every day. Maybe he thought it was his trademark. He'd look at me like a perv."

"I didn't like him much either. Garry says he and my dad are meeting him in London. They're going to try to stop the auction of my new work, the shots you brought Garry. That can't happen."

Yasmin stopped, looked out at the hills past the orchard. "See that? It's not like a drone or something?"

Henry shook his head. "I think it's just the wing of a crow. The shine of the black. It caught the light."

"Uh huh."

"I think I've got to get in touch with him... my dad... we need that auction to happen. We'll need that money and soon if we're going to manage once we get to Tangier, deal with the characters that can get us to Algeciras."

"Uh huh." She was walking faster now, not looking back.

"I think he means well, my dad. He just doesn't know. And maybe he won't believe Garry."

"I guess not."

"Yasmin, have I done something to upset you?" He gently tugged at her sleeve and she turned to him. He looked into her eyes but she looked away, out into the rows of olive trees that lined the fields like a regiment in wait.

"I guess I just can't focus as much on your life right now, Henry. It's your estate, your funds, your parents' obligations. It's exhausting. You don't want money for our freedom, after this is all over. You want it for yourself."

"Haven't I proven how much I'd do for Gato, for all of them back there? I've earned it." He wanted to say he had done more than she had, that she conveniently chose to contact them after the robbery. But he couldn't bear her being any more distant from him. "I'm sorry. I just... I'm trying to think of how it's going to be when this is over. This is hard. Harder than I ever imagined."

"You're not the only one who thinks about home."

"We can make a home wherever we are when this is done."

She stopped now. She pulled her pale green scarf closer to her face as if to shield herself from the wind. But the air was still. "I don't believe that, Henry."

"What do you mean you don't believe it? It's everything now."

"No... no, I don't believe it is."

"It's not a question of unbelieving anymore."

"Henry, me and Gato... we've slept together. It's not as if I planned it... I mean obviously... it just happened."

He could only stand, stock-still, his eyes fixed on hers, as his lips tried to form words. But the rage and the puzzlement stole his clarity of thought. His voice. *Show me your tears for this.* But she was not crying. There were rings of golden brown that encircled her irises. How many times had he looked into her eyes and yet this was the first time he'd seen them.

"Yasmin, you can't…"

"Henry, I don't know what this means. Really, I never knew what we meant either."

"What we mean. How can you talk in past tense?"

"It's not the past tense that confuses me. It's the future."

"What, you're going to stay with him when this is over? When we get to Spain? This is not over for him. This is his life."

"Henry, I don't know what's over or what's just beginning. But I know it's not us." She reached out and gently touched his shoulder but he stiffened, retracted from her fingertips. "I'm so sorry."

He tried to smile but he felt his expression was frozen in the rictus of a mannequin. You try to bend the world to your will and it's you who's going to break. "No, don't be sorry. Have the courage of your confusion. Better now than before we carry it out."

And now she cried. But her tears were of self-pity and he could not share them.

"I'm a terrible person. I'm so sorry."

"You're a scared person. And so am I. But maybe fear clarifies. I guess I thank you for being honest."

He turned and began to retrace his steps, back to their encampment. She called his name as he went, but her voice was so soft and broken it seemed she really didn't want him to stop and turn to look at her. No… just go on. Nothing to be done but start to live with this new solitude as the truth.

29.

Ashwin had come to the realization that he hated the bloody Group of Seven. The later work of Harris, especially. All these mountains coated in layers of soft vanilla ice cream, the stark, sculpted lines of the rock face, bathed in sunlight. Not a sign of human life, never mind civilization on these barren peaks. Bow to this pristine, eternal magnificence, the sublime does not require anything of you but your reverence. And as his guest the major nodded with a moon-faced reverence at the painting and turned to the ambassador, he said "it is like the beauty of the desert, yes?" Ashwin fought the urge to bark out a laugh. *Fuck your precious desert and its tedious fucking heaps of slag you call your mountains.* Ashwin struggled to stifle his inside voice more than ever these days.

"I have yet to see much of the beauty of your desert, major."

"Well you must. While you are here, mister ambassador, sir."

"I expect to be in this posting quite some time."

The major leaned back in the Memphis chair. The leather squeaked as he let his right foot jiggle on the cap of his left knee. His army issue, black Oxfords were polished to a spotless shine. He took a sip of the Napoleon cognac in his snifter and kept his gaze on the Harris painting before them. "I think we all hope you are too, sir."

"Have you ever been to Canada, major?"

"I have not, no. But at Cambridge I shared a room with a young gentleman from Prince Edward Island. Eddie White. He was a Rhodes Scholar. Can you imagine being a scholar with a name like Eddie?"

Ashwin smiled. "I suppose it's very Canadian."

"I suppose. I think he decided I was not a serious person. And he thought me inferior, of course. You must have experienced this as well, yes?"

"From time to time." Ashwin gazed down at the crease lines on his trousers and slowly blinked. He'd be keeping such memories to himself.

"We had a large window that looked out on the courtyard of our residence. Every day I took it upon myself, while Eddie White was at breakfast, to throw one item of his out the window. One day a pencil, the next his toothpaste. It drove him mad and yet he never mentioned it to me. Not so much as a word while we shared that room. I believe he was scared of a conflict with me."

"Or perhaps he never would have imagined you would do such a thing."

The major laughed, glanced at his chunky steel watch. "Of course he imagined it. He was just frightened of me. As he should have been."

"Perhaps."

"Mister ambassador, what has happened with the case of your Head of the Political Section and our file of concern?"

"Mr. Forsey is no longer with us, major."

"Ah! Good then. And the document with the information on the detainment centre is returned, yes? Problem solved."

"Not really."

The major smiled, held what was left of his cognac up to the light of the lamp beside him. "What are you telling me, ambassador?"

"I'm saying he met with someone, back in Canada, who may have received the file. And who may be preparing to release it to the public."

The major took a deep breath, stared up at the ceiling. It seemed he was counting to ten to control his anger. "Can you explain to me why you Canadians are so bad at controlling these situations? If you embarrass our government about our facility, this… this is not good." He put a closed fist up to his mouth and stifled his quickening rage in a cough. It was beneath him to let Ashwin have such an effect on dwindling reserves of collegiality. "You jeopardize our relations with our Russian friends. And that will jeopardize the interests you have with our friend Adilbek, sir. I will have no choice but to exercise some leverage."

"We can get it under control. I know who this person is... the one Forsey spoke to about the file. He's an academic. I can find out what I can."

The major looked up at the Harris once again, tracing the horizon of the landscape with his gaze. Right to left, as if he was reading another language. "Yes, that would be good. I don't want to make this a diplomatic issue."

"I'm not sure what that means."

"There are Canadians here we are watching. One or two we might have grounds to arrest on espionage charges."

"This doesn't need to escalate."

"I'm glad you feel that way, mister ambassador, sir."

"Ashwin. Please call me Ashwin."

The Major shrugged, drained his glass. "So Ashwin. Maybe it escalates, maybe it doesn't. We'll see." As he got to his feet he stuffed his hands in the front pockets of his trousers, staring into the carpet as he pulled out his car keys. No driver, no security: the major would not humour anyone who'd suggest the threat level had risen in Rabat. "Do find out what you can, sir... Ashwin, sir. I give you until Friday? Then we can meet again."

"That's only two days."

"Should I not see this as urgent? At least as urgent as finding your Henry Raeburn and Yasmin Raza, is it not?"

"Yes, I suppose, major."

"You see? Quid pro quo, mister ambassador. I was told you have a talent for transactions. I think you understand."

"I do, yes."

"Good. Because we know about your extracurricular activities, mister ambassador. I imagine you'll want to keep those transactions to yourself. Good night, sir."

He'd love to tell the major he could not care less. Forsey already tried that avenue, thank you very much. But there was no point. Give this little man the victory of the moment. He'd dine tonight with the mistress he believed no one knew about, the young thing from the Jordanian embassy, and he'd recount it all—how he put the foolish Canadian in his place and took control of the situation. Ashwin would take second place among the major's list of feckless idiots from Canada, just behind Eddie White the Rhodes scholar.

At some point, hopefully soon, Henry Raeburn and Yasmin Raza would be added to that list as well. Ashwin watched the major strut like a pimp down the hall to the elevator. He laughed to himself as he poured another cognac. Must find that Harris painting another place to hang in the embassy as soon as possible.

30.

It was a short walk from Gordon's East Block office down to Queen Street and the offices in the OLO. Yet everything that occurred in that grey building felt so remote and distant from Gordon's day to day existence that it could have been miles away. Some nights, when he'd been working late, Gordon would walk down Sparks Street, glimpse the top floor and see that there were still lights on in some of the larger offices. He wondered who was up there and what they were scheming. It could be another country entirely.

Gordon used to enjoy that muted sense of exile from real power. Aside from the one committee meeting where the motion on the Red Cross report about detainees had to be managed, it was as though he didn't exist to the OLO. Sure, he had party responsibilities; it was a permanent campaign and somebody had to make sure there was money in the room when the Leader swung through Vancouver and said a few words at the Courtland Club. But that was second nature to Gordon. This was Dougie MacPhail's son. He had the charm, the connections—the history—that had made him indispensable from the time of his appointment. As long as he could be counted on to tap his network, he could make as much—or as little—noise he liked with committee studies, debates in the chamber. He was encouraged to travel, by all means meet with those who would never vote for the government and give them your ear. As long as the necessary legislation passed without delay or incident, you could be a stranger to the Chief of Staff and those who held all the power in the background, like Ginny McEwan. Yet all of that was before Henry and now that independence would not stand.

Was he provoked into this conflict? Whether he acted of his own free will seemed at best a minor concern right now. Events, dear boy. Did Macmillan ever really say that? Gordon felt like he used to know. In any event, it was true. He had suspected that he was being watched and followed. To some degree he had even sanctioned it. He was assured that CSIS was on the case. But of course there was no guarantee it was CSIS. Which led to darker speculations. He could still hear Hannah's husky laughter in the pale light of last Saturday morning, in her bed. "You will yourself into innocence, Gordon." He could only laugh in turn because it was so precise a diagnosis of his own failure of judgment. Such ruminations didn't even matter, given the destruction of Mehdi Mekhounam's office, the explosive device found under his car.

For months now he had been doing little but reacting with degrees of urgency. The threat of violence—done to Henry, done to others who would in turn increase the threat for Henry, for Yasmin, Henry's alleged romantic interest—had made time increasingly elastic. Stretching out, snapping back. The real, former ordinary life, he had just presumed it would always be there, like the muzak in airport lounges. He could imagine a continuous loop playing from interior to tastefully appointed interior throughout the greyest days of autumn. But with Hannah's call last Sunday, telling him what had happened to Mehdi, he hung up the phone and all he could feel was the silence. The RCMP now had Mehdi in hiding and in this Gordon felt a sense of kinship. The canned noise of his own former life couldn't play anymore.

Nobody had a clue who could have done such a thing, the police said. "Nobody seen nothing," the building manager said. But they were now convinced the courier the size of a linebacker, caught on video, timing his entrance to the building with the old woman and her dog, he was a suspect. Hannah had called Gordon this morning with an update on another video as well: there was a blurry image of a hunter green Range Rover, the official vehicle of the new international kleptocracy, angling into a parking space in the lot beside Mehdi's building at 4 am the night he had found his home office sacked. They must have come back to settle the matter with the explosive device. Two heavyset men wearing Canada Goose parkas (disguised as Canadians?), their hoods up, one toting what was most likely a tire iron, given how the heavy glass door to Mehdi's underground parking lot was shattered. Nothing else on video, the plates of the Range Rover mudded over, artfully.

Hannah said if she were in his position, she'd have no choice: send up the flare, scatter the predators. And she was right, as always. So he wrote the op ed, disclosed the evidence he had. She read it over, toned down his righteousness. "Let the facts of these crimes speak for themselves." 'Son, You Were Right All Along' was the hed he'd wanted to suggest, almost seriously, should the editor have asked.

He had made the mistake of sending his piece to the OLO and the party office prior to submitting it. He'd wanted to be the stand-up guy they had believed he was, didn't want to blindside anyone. Hannah had warned him that this was a bad idea. "Do you think they owe you anything, Gordon? They'll crush you." Perhaps she was used to such foolish martyrdom from others who had tried to justify their efforts as "acting in the best interest of all Canadians," as he had written in his concluding paragraph. "Think of the best interest for yourself," she had said, "even when a house is on fire, you save yourself first."

This particular fire lit up in seconds. He was summoned for his visit with his CSIS friend Dennis Wilson first, in that colourless boardroom Dennis seemed to like. Wilson, with his walrus moustache and grey shag, was determined to play Captain Kangaroo turned bad cop, demanding to know how Gordon had gotten the document without the necessary redactions. He wagged his finger and declared the government would lay criminal charges. "Have I got to tell you this? You're a goddamn lawyer." Wilson had read from his notepad in front of him. "This is information relating to investigative techniques or plans for specific lawful investigations. That's section 16.b of the Access to Information Act."

"I guess I have an issue with the term lawful investigations."

"You go out in public with this, it will not go well for you, senator."

"My son has been missing and presumed abducted for more than three months now. Exactly what about our situation is currently going well, Mr. Wilson?"

"Your son made some bad choices, senator. You seem to believe you must repeat his mistakes."

"My son believed this government was breaking the law. And destroying the lives of innocent people. Turns out he was right."

"Your son broke the law. And now you are too. Turns out that's wrong. And there are consequences. Tell me where you got the document."

Gordon had thanked him for his time, as if he had scheduled this interrogation. As Dennis Wilson scowled and nodded in return, Gordon had gotten up and left that boardroom. He was still surprised they let him walk out of the building.

But of course they did. Hisham had counseled that Gordon's defense of protecting a source was all he had needed to claim. And Wilson knew it too. He was the point guard who'd just been benched, all rounded shoulders and bowed head; he had spent all the menace he could afford.

Gordon exited through the East Block courtyard, hoping to catch the last of the evening light, but no, here it was just past 6:30 and it was already dark, already cold. Barely out of October and winter settled like an old grey blanket over the dollhouse parliament. It would be good to fly out of here soon.

And maybe sooner than he thought. Most days when he was here, the emails multiplied in the afternoons. But since Ginny McEwan had sent him an invitation to meet in the offices of her lobbying firm at ten this morning, he'd gotten hardly any emails at all. The heels of his brogues sounded louder on the pavement as he walked down to Metcalfe from the Hill. It was too quiet on the street, too empty of life.

A young woman met him in the lobby of the office tower. She was fair-haired and freckled, dressed all in black as if for his funeral. She could not quite conceal her curiosity as she took him in from the elevators. As she got closer she recomposed herself, put on a mask of dead eyed formality to nod to him. Yes, senator, I'm your escort to the guillotine.

"You might remember me. I'm Annie Baldwin from the intern program."

"Ah of course, Annie! How you getting on?" For the life of him he couldn't recall.

"I'm well, thank you. This has been a good year."

"Indeed it has, by and large." What the hell was he saying? "Good to see you landing well off the Hill."

He could be someone's kind uncle, just visiting from out of town. It was a far more comfortable role to play than the one he must now take on, the penitent who had gone rogue, who must bear the rage of a woman years younger than his son.

She ushered him in to the offices. "Just have a seat in here. Ginny's wrapping up a call. Take your coat?"

"I suppose that's wise. Not sure how long I'll be." He angled his shoulder out of his topcoat, discomforted by the serenity of Annie Baldwin's smile. She'd make a fine nurse, just the right amount of tact and seriousness as you awaited a grave diagnosis.

They sat in their places: she behind her small desk and he on an old desk chair. They scrolled the messages on their phones, reading what they'd already read because it was somehow more appropriate than interacting. For him to ask this young woman anything would feel like an admission of his anxiety. They were all of the tribe in Ginny's office, he knew how they worked, and he would not give them any indication that he cared if he was cast out from them.

Her phone finally vibrated in her hands. Two quick blurts. She nodded to her screen as if it were an animate object and rose from her desk. "I can bring you in now."

Ginny didn't look up from her work as Gordon entered. She was writing in a notebook, straining to concentrate on a final thought. The creak of Gordon's step on the Afghan carpet caused her to sigh. She looked up and did not smile. "Senator, please have a seat." The sober blue power suit matched her eyes. She could play a young Queen Victoria.

"Thank you, Ginny." He kept his hands clasped over his lap, ready to shield himself from a blow to the midsection.

"So this was a surprise."

"You mean the op ed."

"We'd been trying to manage this with some of our old contacts in government. Including Ambassador Khadilkar."

"I've appreciated that."

"Have you? You know we recently had Nick poll on issues like this, eh? Canadians really don't give a crap about what we're doing abroad. But they do care about special treatment for senators, you know what I mean?"

"I haven't asked for any special treatment."

"No? You've been traveling quite a bit, haven't you? I can't imagine that's economy class. You missed committee because you were in London, I'm told. That seems pretty far from where your son is."

"My son works with a gallery in London. They have his work. Should I be defending myself?"

Ginny pulled back, took him in with a raised eyebrow. He seemed to be entertaining. "Not to me, no. But you should know I've asked Rebecca in your office to get me your expenses over the last six months."

"She didn't tell me this."

"Because I told her not to. I mean, fire her if you like. We'll find something for her."

There was a hot surge of rage pressing against his eyelids. "I remember you, you know. This was around oh-six, the first few months of governing. You were staffing Fabian fucking Morris at a ports reception I had come out for. I watched you eat a shrimp and wipe your hand on your skirt. I remember thinking wow, this is quite a crew. You had no manners then. You have zero class now."

"I honestly don't give a fuck what you think, Gord."

"Gordon, please."

"I'm looking at your expenses and I'm seeing a story coming down the pike. A bad one. Your friends at the papers would run it too."

"I'm prepared to speak to anyone about how I manage my finances. And my office."

"It's not about what you're prepared to say, Gord. That's not how this works. It's the story and how it runs. And it's charges laid for possession of a classified document."

"No charges have been laid."

"Yet."

"I possess information, not the document."

"You think we don't know who gave it to you and that you do indeed have the document? Jesus Christ, Gord, I'm literally trying to protect you."

"I think you mean actually."

"And I actually don't give a fuck about you. I'm doing my job for the OLO and the party. And the last real PM in this country who put you in the Senate against his better judgment."

"Past tense, I think."

"That's good, you caught that. That's how this is going to play if you don't call that editor and request he does not run your op ed. We'll kick you out of caucus. Sure, you can join one of these independent groups but you know you'll have zero power and influence. We'll be done with you. And you will not be scheduling any press conference for tomorrow. I've told Rebecca to call that off."

He liked Rebecca. She had only been with him for five months but she was hard working. Cambridge graduated. Not the type of young woman who'd wipe shrimp sauce on her skirt. It would end in tears for her, no doubt. The party cut through soft souls like a hot knife through butter. The sooner they parted ways, the better.

"And yet she still works for me."

"She has higher loyalties. It's an admirable quality, don't you think?"

"Loyalties above family? Above your country?"

"You see I don't think you're serving any greater good, senator. A goddamn editorial. A press conference. You'll get your fifteen minutes of fame, sure. Whatevs, as the kids say."

He stared down at his brogues. There were faint outlines of salt stains around the toe caps. He did his best to rub out such corrosion. Now there was an epitaph for you. "You think I want that?"

"I don't think you realize what you'll lose." Ginny's small hands were gripping the edge of her desk. She could be the mistress of the waves, carved and mounted on the prow of a schooner. "You will not return to caucus. And we will do what is necessary to make sure that op ed doesn't run. We still have friends in the media… whatever's left of it."

He rose, sucked in his gut and then sharply exhaled through a brief moment of lightheadedness. *Must stop drinking so much wine.* Ah but not tonight. Not for a while, really. "Thank you for your time, Ginny."

She gently swiveled her chair towards her office window. She wouldn't dignify his last words with a response. He imagined she'd be gazing out at the Peace Tower after he shut the door behind him. She'd be reflecting on her power and how the less-than-mighty fall.

His was from not such a great height, all things considered.

★

He called Hannah at 1:30 am, after his fifth glass of the French Sauvignon Blanc that was hiding in the back of his refrigerator. It was finally morning where Hannah was—in Bruges at a conference on the rights of the stateless in Europe. She had emailed him about the bomb threat the first day, saying she had suffered a greater threat to her life from a cyclist while she was taking a photo on a bridge. On the growing list of reasons why he has fallen in love with her, her fearlessness was number four.

"Hannah, I need to do this press conference somewhere else. It won't happen here in Ottawa."

"I figured they would put a stop to that."

"They've put a stop to me in the Senate."

"Oh Gordon… I'm so sorry you have to live through this."

"As my executioner said to me this afternoon, whatevs."

"Come to Bruges. I mean it's beautiful. More bridges than Venice. We'll stay on for a couple of days after the conference."

"Will you come with me to find Henry? I know that's where I have to make this statement. Close to him. As close as possible."

He heard her exhale, the faint sound of cutlery on plates, the grey noise of other conversations near her café table. He took another sip. He needed no more suspense in his life, thank you very much.

"Yes. Yes, of course I will, Gordon. I miss you."

"I miss you, Hannah."

He stopped himself from saying the L word. She'd think it was the wine talking. But that's exactly what he felt as soon as she'd said she missed him. And there was no way back now. That was a last thought worth reflecting upon when he finally tried to sleep.

31

Hannah got lost easily. It was a trait she didn't have to think about, back in Ottawa or Vancouver. Which was just as well, because it had never fit with the conception she had of herself: intrepid, resourceful, independent. She only lost her bearings in cities she was unfamiliar with, and she was of that stubborn generation that would not depend on the GPS in her phone. She remained suspicious of technology, more than she was suspicious of her memory for markers at intersections. Here, in what they called the old Medina of Rabat, all she had was her Parisian French and an address she'd hurriedly written down when the call came from Yasmin to meet. 10 minutes before 2 pm, her breaths were coming shorter, her heart fluttering: she couldn't find the dress shop where Yasmin directed her to, couldn't even find the nearest bus stop that was her marker.

For the last two days, she'd gone over the last call with Yasmin in her head. It lasted no more than a minute, and Yasmin had sounded tired, with an Arab inflection in the rhythm of her English that seemed new. There was little said that gave Hannah any hope that the young lawyer she had once felt so close to was going to come back to her world—was going to be saved. Yes, saved. Call it presumptuous, culturally imperialist or whatever, but she believed Yasmin had fallen in with dangerous, violent people because she was misguided, impressionable—not because she was capable of violence herself. And nothing Yasmin had said on the call made her feel any differently.

"This is Hannah?"

"Hello? Yes! Yes, this is Hannah. This is Yasmin? Oh my God, Yasmin, where are you?"

"I am here in this country and I am fine. We are fine."

"Is Henry Raeburn there with you? Wait, just let me get Gordon, he's just—"

"No time. You can tell him Henry is doing well. We all saw the press conference from the courthouse press theatre. We saw it on television. We didn't know you would be here."

"Did Mehdi give you my number? Mehdi found you, didn't he?"

"It is not important. Listen, Hannah, we must meet. There are things I have to tell you. I can't do it by phone. I will give you an address where you will go for 2 pm tomorrow. It might be hard to find but that's necessary. You understand?"

"I understand. Yasmin, it will be all right. We can get you home. We can get you safe."

"You have a pen and paper?"

Hannah had emptied out her purse at the hotel bar, and everything poured out onto the tiled floor. There, a pen, there, a receipt from lunch with a client, there, one crystal earring she was never going to find the match for again. Lost and found: she wanted a broom to sweep away all this detritus of the life back home. Absolute focus on the present tense.

But she had managed, with the receipt and the pen to scribble down the Arabic street name. Was it correct? She wondered if Google Earth had not been updated to reflect new ownership of the shop she was supposed to be headed towards in the Medina. A dress shop? Could that really be where Yasmin had meant her to go? There was nothing but fruit and vegetable sellers and a couple of butchers along this side street. But that was all she had to go on, of course the number Hannah called from did not show up on her phone. Running blind to find a fugitive, she felt like a fugitive herself, one running from her better judgment.

And the side streets were open violations of noise and colour, chaos barely choreographed to observe some notional understanding of traffic rules, pedestrian safety. Women wrapped from head to toe in stifling robes of jet black, walking four abreast on the narrow sidewalks. And the sun bearing down—a shadowless, white-hot curtain of brassy light that glinted off the dusty windshields of the double parked trucks.

She stepped around crates of misshapen oranges, left on the corner where a halo of bluebottle flies orbited, humming with the menace of decay. She pulled her hijab closer to her nose so she could take in the scent of the perfume she had sprayed it with this morning—perfume that was a gift from Gordon. The faint smell of jasmine flower was no match for diesel smoke and lamb grilling on charcoal.

In a cavernous bar, men too young to be idle crowded the tables in flip-flops and polo shirts. They had passive, longing looks in their eyes as they stared up at a widescreen TV. They were watching a woman jog on a foreign beach, it was an ad for a fruit drink. The dance of the seven veils. Such a performance could hardly contend with the idleness, the futility of endless afternoons here for those without work. There was the source of your insurgency. Surely Yasmin must see this too, surely she needed to get out. If there were any sign she had suffered, Hannah swore she was going to make this a rescue mission.

A young woman approached and gave Hannah the smile of a fellow foreigner. There were gold bangles on her bronze coloured arms that caught the sunlight. She had the lean, hyper-exercised figure of a woman of expensive leisure and walked with all the confidence and fearlessness of an executive posted here by her company. She seemed immunized from the hungry eyes of the local men. If indeed she spoke French, she would know where Hannah must go to find this dress shop.

"Excusez moi."

"Pardon? Sorry, I'm American… Juh swee…"

"Oh, okay. I can speak English. I'm Canadian."

"Ah!" The American woman smiled, but it quickly evaporated with her wariness. "You look like you're lost. Where are you trying to go?"

Hannah handed her the scribbled address in her hand and the woman assured her that yes, it was not far now, just a hundred metres down to the next intersection. She seemed to know this neighbourhood like a native, and yet she offered no information about herself. Her sudden wariness was perhaps the moment she had recognized Hannah from the televised press conference. She could be CIA. As Gordon called them, Christians in action. Eyes everywhere.

She was hardly being paranoid, presuming this. The morning after the press conference, they were having breakfast on the balcony of their hotel room when Gordon had gotten a call from the States. A Virginia area code. It was a woman named Marci, and she said she was a friend of Henry's. And then Gordon remembered Henry mentioning her and her partner—Christians no longer in action.

"She says she got a call from Henry, Hannah. Late at night about a week ago."

"So he's okay."

"She said he was, yes. She also told me our press conference was picked up by the BBC and CNN. That's why she had to call. Got my number from Rebecca back in my office."

"What did Henry say?"

"He wanted to know if she could get him any information on the layout of the Temara interrogation centre Henry had last photographed. Like a blueprint for the prototype, floor plans... anything."

"Floor plans."

"They're going to do something. We have to get to them. I swear Hannah, I won't let him destroy his life like this."

She had stopped herself from saying that it was not just his life, it was Yasmin's too. She didn't want to admit to him that she cared more for her than Gordon's son. She questioned the authenticity of Henry's commitment. The more she learned about his art, the more skeptical she had become. Henry had found a way to be relevant and provocative, selling a kind of geopolitical porn to the wealthy who could feel edgy and politically aware with every purchase. It was really just a more astringent distillation of weltschmerz they were consuming. These were the same people tapped for political fundraisers, supporting the people in power who had no interest in doing anything about places like Henry's choice of subject matter. Young Mr. Raeburn was keeping the wheels of commerce and the empire-in-new-clothes going; he was more like his father than he would care to admit.

But then his father was capable of change, wasn't he? He was capable of great sacrifice. As he said to her the morning of the press conference, "I've just torched my career." And he did it in the most public of ways. It was an act she wasn't sure she could have done herself, given all that was on the line for Gordon. "I know the man I can be and how we could be together." And wasn't that worthy of her love?

Yes, no question. Here they were together. Yet the real foreign land, the real disorientation she felt was from suddenly being in this state of commitment. It was that language, not her rusty French, that she was trying to learn again, and everything was moving so fast.

Remember the landmarks, she told herself. It was a matter of taking precautions to keep the route back to the woman she was alone so clear in her mind.

★

This had to be the dress shop. There were pathetic approximations of Chanel suits hanging on mannequins in the cluttered window, along with an ancient suitcase, propped against the shin of one of them. The mannequin ladies were planning their own escape. Hannah entered the dimly lit space. There was an old TV on by a small counter, with a flickering image of a blonde newscaster, speaking Arabic. A woman emerged, serious, wrapped in a djellaba and flowing black robes. She nodded, silently beckoned for Hannah to follow her into the back of the shop where there was a card table and two chairs, concealed behind a long sheet as blue as the Mediterranean here. No series of addresses, no treasure hunt through these streets—it looked like this was it. Hannah was almost disappointed.

The woman in a djellaba briefly exited from a heavy steel door in the back of the shop. The noise of a truck engine idling was followed by a heavy click of steel on steel. Hannah took her seat at the card table and after just a quick few breaths there was the click of the door again. Only Yasmin's eyes were visible in her burqa but they were unmistakable, the flashing intelligence she had always loved about this young woman.

Hannah called her name and made to embrace her but Yasmin motioned for her to sit. There were creases at the corners of her eyes that suggested she couldn't help but smile.

"How are you? Are you eating okay? Listen to me, I sound like a mother."

"You do."

"I can't help it."

Yasmin's burqa carried a faint smell of cheap perfume. It was the making-strange of her for Hannah, affirming the distance between them now.

"You know I believe this was your decision alone. Yasmin, I understand it. Everyone who is close to this situation would understand."

"Thank you, Hannah. This is not permanent. You know that, yes? We're not going to be in hiding, just running forever."

"What can I do to help you? That's all I want."

"There is a blockchain art auction for Henry's last work. All the photos he shot here that he had given me while he was in prison. He gave Garry Fry the rights to it, and it should make up the difference of what we'll need. These works should, by rights, go to Henry's father. But this auction can't go ahead if the senator continues to contest the authenticity of Henry's correspondence, as he's contested the changes to Henry's will."

"He has to contest it. He's worried about Garry Fry exploiting Henry. He needs to file that court order."

Yasmin glared at her. The silence suddenly felt heavy between them. For the first time today, through all of the unknown turns she took to come to this place, Hannah sensed her own fear.

"You speak of this senator like he's your husband."

"I came here to help him. What he's revealed about that detention and interrogation centre is important. I came here—right here—to help you."

"That money is important. I need you to understand that, Hannah."

"Is this Henry? Are you speaking for him?"

You speak for him like he's your husband was what she wanted to say. Hannah felt an urge to slap Yasmin when she made her accusation. She was trying to let her anger dissipate now.

"I'm speaking for all of us. That money will mean we survive, it will get us to Algeciras, you understand? We need it very soon. You need to tell the senator this, okay?"

"I saw the video of that robbery. I mean the world saw that video."

"Yes. What are you asking me?"

"That was a criminal act. It was a violent act."

"You know the country you're in. You know who the criminals really are."

"I know you weren't involved in that but by joining this people you have crossed the Rubicon, Yasmin. This is what I fear for you."

"I ask you, as a friend, Hannah, to help us cross just a few miles of the Mediterranean, okay? I'll worry about the Rubicon."

Hannah nodded, bit her bottom lip. What was maddening about all this was that Yasmin was talking to her like she was an adolescent, one who had yet to realize the cost of her ideals.

"I wish I could see you fully, Yasmin."

"You are seeing me fully, Hannah. Maybe for the first time." She stood up, loomed over the card table. "Please give the senator our message, that is all I finally ask of you, okay? I must go."

She turned from Hannah and brusquely pushed open the back door. There was the hum of a car idling, a baby wailing from a nearby balcony, and then the door clicked shut again.

This was a land of ghosts, Mehdi had warned her. Spirits walk, take living shape, then revert to spirits in the blink of an eye. What's material can always slip through your hands, melt into the air. Now she realized how serious Mehdi was.

She walked back out into the streets and the land of the living. The storekeeper had disappeared, but maybe she was always just a figment of Hannah's imagination.

32

"I'm saying we can't guarantee your safety. We can't guarantee anyone's, especially foreign nationals."

Ashwin abandoned all pretense of grace and politeness when he approached Gordon in the hotel café and demanded they speak somewhere alone. He sported a bright red pocket square, flashing his rage like a toreador. Of course he knew who Hannah was but he did not even acknowledge her apart from a smirk and a glance. The two men stood in the small, carpeted alcove of the lobby, the whispering foreigners. Thank God the muzak blanketed over most of their conversation.

"So you're ordering us to leave."

"Not just you. Everyone."

"On the presumption that it's no longer safe? That's ridiculous. You know it is."

"You want to read the reports of rioting that I go through in the morning?"

"Rioting. They're demonstrations."

"Demonstrations sparked by calls for an inquiry into that site and a call for parliament to dissolve. There was a policeman killed in the old Medina yesterday. Father of two daughters. That man lost his life because of your publicity stunt." Ashwin jabbed his finger in the air as he spoke. A schoolmaster, dressing down a misbehaving child. Gordon resisted the urge to bat that finger away. "And there will be more casualties."

"If the people are angry here, don't blame the messenger, Ashwin." Gordon was so calm. He surprised himself. "I mean I thought you fancied yourself a bit of a politico. It's never the crime, it's the cover-up."

"You're in no position to lecture anyone on politics, senator. Or will we even call you senator anymore?"

"I don't know. It was never about the title for me, Ashwin. I guess that must seem strange to you. I was trying to serve."

"Of course you were. And I'm sure, just like Forsey, you told yourself you were from a better, vanished world. The proud old families, the selfless mandarins, yes? All of your vintage whose time is up."

"So you put yourself on the right side of history, is that it? You make deals with gangsters... you're the man of the future. The world's not quite Moscow yet. I know what you've been covering up too. Guys like you have always been around. You're part of the scenery."

Ashwin loomed closer, as if he was about to bump Gordon with his chest. His expression of outrage had hardened. He was prepared for a screenshot: portrait of the besieged. "I don't give a fuck about your history. It's not mine. I'm talking about now. You and your woman friend have forty-eight hours. Forty-eight, okay? And then they'll come for you."

"They can't come for us."

"No? Your press conference is now being investigated. The chief of police called me this morning. Two witnesses have come forward and presented stolen government documents. They're maids in your hotel, Gordon."

"You son of a bitch."

"I suggest you move quickly before I can't help you. Before they have grounds for an arrest." He took a half step back, regarded the cuffs of his shirt, poking out from the sleeves of his jacket now. "I came here because I wanted to help you. I took a personal interest. You should think about that, Mr. MacPhail. Something to remember, from your fifteen minutes of fame."

It was all that Gordon could do not to say a word. He just nodded wearily, squinting as he took one final measure of this man.

Ashwin gave him a small, courtly bow in return as he made for the lobby. But he couldn't resist looking back. "I hope they find your son alive, sir. But personally, I wouldn't bet on it. He's got what he wanted." He glided past the front desk like an impatient concierge, then weaved past a crowd at the front door.

★

Gordon met Hannah back in the hotel room. She was out on the balcony, sitting on one of the wrought-iron chairs, smoking a cigarette. From six floors up she could see the walls of the Kasbah, just past the old market streets. Directly below was a maze of gimcrack, boxy walk-up flats tottering on concrete storefronts, the narrow lanes clogged with delivery vans, scooters growling as they idled, waiting for an opening, a few metres of sidewalk to angle up and accelerate. Hannah stared out at this spectacle as if she were looking to find some pattern to the flow, some greater design.

"You're smoking."

"Yes. It happens every once in a while. My defences go down. It's when I need to think hard. I never think better than when I let myself do this."

"I could never really start."

"No, that's true, Gordon. I remember when you were trying. You were too pure then."

"Khadilkar came to tell us we had to get out. He's given us forty-eight hours."

"You're not going to leave, are you?"

"Hannah, I can't. It's my son. If I leave now, I'll never get him back. But I don't expect you to stay."

"What do you think you can do? I mean seriously, Gordon."

"I don't know yet but I tell you… with your conversation with Yasmin, with Garry Fry back in London, even with those Americans who once worked for the CIA, they can all speak to what Henry wants, what Henry's going to do. I don't know who's telling the truth. If he's able to speak to them all, why hasn't he spoken to me?"

"Do you not think he fears his location will be discovered if he contacts you?"

"He fears it? Or they fear it, this Gato and his group. From the moment he was captured, there's no evidence of Henry doing what he's done of his own volition. None to me."

"I don't know what to tell you, Gordon. I can only say that what Yasmin explained to me felt true. There's no extradition treaty with Spain, should they get there. It all makes sense."

"For them. They get Henry's money. They get their freedom. Who's to say that at that point, they no longer need him and murder my son? You think they're not capable of it?"

"No. Not the Yasmin I know."

"You sure you know who she is?"

She primly stubbed out her cigarette on the underside of her seat and neatly placed the butt in the saucer by her espresso cup. All had to be composed with her thoughts. "How do I say this… I mean it's true that when I saw Yasmin, I felt that she had become another person. If I was younger, maybe I would think I saw the real her now. But I don't believe in such notions anymore."

"She's changed. Of course she has. There's just no way I know if Henry's changed too. And I couldn't forgive myself if I simply arranged the conditions for his murder. I have to stay here."

"How?"

"Somehow, Hannah."

She came to him, took his hands in hers. So gently. They could have been exchanging wedding vows, the way they stood together.

"I can't take this any farther. I'm sorry, Gordon."

He looked out past the walls of the Kasbah, to the rusted, battered fishing boats shored along the curve of the river. Maybe it would be a vessel like that Henry and Yasmin would be depending on for their escape. Tangier to Algeciras, the drug runners the Moroccan police quietly tolerated. "I would never expect you to."

"There is my life back there. My work. For you, what we said in that press conference marked an ending. For me everything's just begun."

"I know. You can only be where people need you."

"But you have to think of yourself first. Sometimes I feel like it's the only thing I've learned in thirty years. Gordon, there's nothing you can do to stop this now."

"You know I can't believe that."

He had always felt like the one to embrace her first, that she just consented to be loved. But not now, not anymore. She pulled him close and kissed him. "I'm so sorry."

Once she pulled away from him, she returned to the room to collect her things and pack. He resisted his impulse to follow her in. He could have reassured her that he'd follow her soon, that they would meet back in Ottawa in a matter of days.

But he would have had to believe that. And he was stripped of such delusions now.

33

Marithe arrived in Rabat four hours before the Canadian embassy had issued its advisory for all government personnel and nationals. Slipped through that net, she was traveling with her EU passport and Germany had yet to issue its own travel ban. She had a feeling it was all going to get this serious. Yet it was the state of Gordon that surprised her. She realized how bad it had become. The beard did not seem a vanity project, and he must have slept in his tennis shirt. He gave her the address of the restaurant where they could meet in an email and said it was two doors down from an internet café in the Medina. The state of him, it was clear he sent the email from that very café.

"You're staying on?"

"As long as I can. I think they might be looking for me." He laughed weakly, shook his head. She noticed the dirt under his fingernails as he cradled his glass of water. Homeless, that was what he looked like. He gave off a faint odour of cheap soap.

"But they can't compel you to leave."

"Oh yes. They've found a way. I've got a room in this district. It's the only one where the police have less of a presence, if you know what I mean."

She reached for his hand across the table. He regarded it with a puzzled look at first. He briefly touched her hand too.

"I'm so sorry that it's gone this far, Gordon. All that's happened to you."

"All that's happened to me?"

"I'm amazed at all you've sacrificed. At all you've done."

"It's our son, Marithe. Did you think I wouldn't have it in me or something?"

She shifted in her seat, propped her elbows on the paper tablecloth as if she was arranging her thoughts to make a deal. It was not a posture that came naturally to her.

"Gordon, I was in London. With Garry Fry."

"I can only imagine what that was like."

"You know he's managed to communicate with Henry."

"Allegedly."

"No, it's real, Gordon."

"How do you know?"

"I've seen the notes he's received. The police have investigated. They know the mosque where these are being relayed."

Gordon waved the premise of her argument away. "You know I was going to sue. Hisham said I would have won too. This group he's with…"

"Gordon, I'm here to tell you it's over. You can go home."

He pulled back in his chair and gave her a look as if he was refocussing, trying to recognize her again. Then he realized he was mimicking the expression on his father's face, that glare after his last stroke, how the old man had to concentrate on the most familiar. Wouldn't that be fitting, if Gordon were to go out like him? Should he live that long.

"I don't think that's an option, Marithe."

"It is, it is, trust me."

There was a sudden roar of men's voices, coming from the TV behind him. Gordon turned, expecting to see some scene from the main square. It was a soccer game, a goal. He turned back to take in Marithe again, just staring into the faded checkerboard pattern on the tablecloth.

"This what Garry Fry told you?"

"I'm telling you. There were photos in Henry's camera. It was all work not mentioned in his will… either version. I had them appraised with Garry Fry's help. And then I sold them. Along with the funds Garry Fry held in trust, there was enough. These people can get their ransom now."

"No, this is not…"

"My father bought them all. Every last piece of Henry's work. And Garry Fry honoured his commitment to Henry. All of the money, in American bills, every cent this group has asked for, I have it with me."

Now it was his turn to reach for her hand. He could feel it trembling. It was all he could do to say her name. *Marithe*, she who was his wife one time.

"He is my son too, Gordon. You don't think I was going to do all I could?"

"Your father said he never wanted to see Henry again."

"I told him he needed to consider this a part of my inheritance. Take it from the total amount. That's exactly what he has done."

"That's noble. Truly. That's the word."

"Well…" she shrugged, laughed to herself. All of this has aged her. The lines around her eyes. "I believe my mother, in her moments when she's lucid, may have helped."

"Marithe, if it's not safe for me, it's only worse for you. Especially now. Where is this?"

She tapped on a satchel on the chair beside her. "It goes everywhere with me."

"That's crazy."

For the first time since they had sat down, she smiled. "I suppose you'd know. Look, there's nothing I can do but wait for word from Garry as to how this can get to them. It is the only way this transaction can occur. American dollars. Even the Russians prefer it now, apparently."

"Marithe, I know what their plans are. Believe me."

"How would you know?"

"I've got my own source back in Ottawa. The one who gave me everything I needed to know about this country. Things have gotten very bad. And Marithe, believe me, if you leave this city, head out to where the protests are raging, no one can guarantee you'll make it back. And with this…" He nodded to the satchel, with a wary look at the waiter behind her. "Marithe, you can't."

"Gordon, what do you expect me to do? Just get on a plane, take this home with me? Seriously."

"No. Give it to me."

"Give it to you?"

"Marithe, you can't risk your life for this. The forces against the government are gaining strength. In numbers. These are young men who see western women on videos and hate you. Hate the power you have. You know how that hate will express itself."

"Henry is my son too!" Marithe slapped the table and allowed her voice to rise, conscious of drawing attention to both of them in this cafe. She pulled her shoulders back, already withdrawing from the theatrical, the force of her resolve. "I have come this far. I'm not going to fail."

"No, you're not failing in this. Marithe, after months of trying, I've finally got intelligence on what is happening and where this group might be. This Mehdi Mehkounam, back in Ottawa, he's arranging for who will get me a car, where I can be safe."

She nodded, looking at him too intently. He knew he was being theatrical himself, telling her too much information. He mentioned Mehdi because the mere sound of his name gave him greater credibility, he figured. It was like he learned something from all his filibustering. Yet this was the only way he could withhold the information he could not share with her: how vital Hannah was in this, and how tomorrow, following Mehdi's instructions, he would go to an undisclosed location and purchase a gun—one he hoped, from distant memory, he'd know how to use. As he was speaking he was aware this didn't feel like an argument, it was already a prelude to a surrender.

"And if you get there, wherever Henry is, how will you both get back?"

"We'll make it to Algeciras, Marithe. Across to Spain and then home."

She could only look into his eyes now. It was her silent plea that he was telling her the truth. And yet the fact she could no longer trust him was the very thing that drove them apart, years ago.

"Marithe, we're in a different world."

She nodded, looking down at the glossy sheen of the linoleum floor. And then she reached over, handed him the satchel. "Tell me I'm doing the right thing."

"You're doing the only thing. I promise, you'll see us both back home very soon."

And as he took her hands in his, they folded together as if in prayer. If only such a gesture would conjure his faith now.

34.

Senator,

I'm hearing they're going to strike the site where Henry was arrested—and soon. Their group received intelligence from a few friends in the forces and they know where the border will be vulnerable, the route where they can make their escape. They could get the detainees and themselves across to freedom if they can hold off those who will make up the government's response. This could be a matter of a couple of days or just a few hours. I hope to get more information soon, but I would suggest that if you want to save your son, now's the time.

Good luck and be safe, sir.

M.

He appreciated the sentiment from Mehdi, but it was hard to imagine what safe might mean now. Was safe filling two jerrycans of gas and two of water and putting them in the back of this rented van? Was safe packing the money from Marithe, old Zeiss field glasses, a flare, flat tire kit, Coleman stove, sleeping bag, and crappy little pup tent? No, the only real measure of safety he could count on was the Walther PPK that Mehdi's contact Essaid finally came through with last night. Essaid, lean as a greyhound, still breathless from running from two makeshift checkpoints, pulled the gun out from the waistband of his briefs and grinned at the American dollars in his hand like he'd received a blessing. Gordon gently placed the pistol in the glove compartment. There was no safety here. No, there was only the maximum reduction of risk.

The pistol: he could not head into the desert without assuring himself he could still use one of these. Out past the soccer field in this suburb, there was the ruin of an Orthodox Church. Razed just last year, apparently, no one was sure what happened to the Christians who had a community here. Exiled? Scattered, made refugees? This was the country of so many variations on erasure. Gordon rose before the sun came up in the morning, tucked the pistol in the inside pocket of his track jacket, walked out to the church and broke in through a window. The walls were whitened like charred bone in places, and there were flourishes of graffiti in English, French and Arabic. The eyes of the icons were gouged out, bleeding chalk dust. Gordon put an empty plastic bottle on the pulpit (cheap vodka—Russians here too?) took aim from twenty rows back and pulled a trigger for the first time in more than forty years. It was reassuring, how familiar the jolt was. But it was less reassuring to see the plastic bottle still in place, a votive offering to the blackened, blurred image of Saint Basil painted on the wall behind the altar.

He emptied out two magazines before a bullet grazed the edge of the bottle, sending it somersaulting off the pulpit. The flat bang from the pistol was disappointing too. He remembered the sound as deeper and more powerful when he was young. The tricks of memory were predictable; there was always less felt in the present, never more. Still it was satisfying to know he wasn't completely inept, that with a little luck, he might be able to defend himself.

The silence after he had fired had the depth of the formerly real. He was sure someone must have heard the shots but of course who would investigate further? Nothing good would come from satisfying your curiosity about those sounds in this neighbourhood.

When he re-emerged from the church the sky had lightened, and in a distant field he could see two goats sauntering near a fence line. Their matted, rust-coloured coats offered poor camouflage against the sun baked grass and shale. Maybe they would be the last tenants on this land when the fighting was finally done. He was going to miss this country; for all its self-inflicted wounds, it bled real.

★

It was no surprise when Gato brought everyone together; it had to be time. He sat at the head of the table in this house (why have they become more palatial?), still in his black exercise clothes from the morning's sit-ups and push-ups. Hundreds and hundreds of repetitions every morning. Exercise was the one thing he did where you could accuse him of being a religious fanatic. That was his line, he always laughed the hardest at his own attempts at humour.

"We have studied. We have prepared. We have overcome our challenges in communicating to each other. Most important, I'm proud of how close we have become. The feeling of brotherhood and of sisterhood in this room. That has been our greatest achievement. That has been the key to our survival. I thank you for everything."

Henry sat in a chair at the corner of the table, nodding, his gaze not lifting from the grain of the wood. He could feel Yasmin's eyes on him. Even a hint of a smile from him would be proof of his detachment, his inability to abandon irony. They had made their peace now. He had shelved his anger at her infidelity, his humiliation about losing her to Gato. That his feelings for her so quickly dissolved into indifference provoked a reaction that still surprised him: she was angry and watchful, looking for any sign of cynicism from him. She'd say it was a product of his privilege, his fellow traveling. It was all so tiring now.

There was no way to explain his own sense of commitment to what was about to be done. There was no way to return to how he had felt in love just a few weeks ago. He couldn't care about Gato or her or Karima, he didn't care about any of them now. He tried, in the quiet moments before sleep, to position this operation as a thought experiment, perhaps the ultimate conceptual piece. He had always said his work was compelled by his politics, his desire to expose what was concealed. Of course one created as open a "text" as possible, but that was really about increasing the throw weight of the work. The feeling his photographs detonated in the viewer was supposed to lead to action, ultimately, to the liberation of those suffering unjustly. Collapse the trajectory from means to ends in the most radical of ways. Take out the openness of interpretation, if you will, and here was the artist in question with gun in hand. When I hear the world culture I no longer reach for my camera. Yes, that was his story and he was sticking to it—despite his own doubts about its veracity.

There was indeed an irony he would not reveal to anyone: it was his own liberation that consumed him. In his mind, it was as if the prisoners had already been freed in this operation. He was actually grateful for what had happened with Yasmin and Gato, because this sociopath felt duty bound to be good to his word: yes, Henry could go free if they finally got to Spain. Yasmin's infidelity was such a defining act of her character in Gato's mind—proof that all women are incapable of being trust-worthy, they're ruled by their desire (whereas with men, by justice!)—that letting Henry go free would be proof of his nobil-ity, his empathy for the cuckolded man.

"Now you all have your assignments once we get through the last set of doors in sector G. You should anticipate confusion and fear from some of the detainees, especially those in the south corridor. We know these are the ones that have done solitary. They have lived through the worst of the interrogations."

"What if they're violent with us?" From the quavering in Karima's voice, she was already consumed by fear. Yasmin gave her a stern look. As if it were her responsibility to control her now. Yes, there is such a feeling of sisterhood that's developed, Gato. Testament to your leadership.

"You stay close with Fayçal. He's your partner. Do not enter a cell alone, okay?"

Karima nodded solemnly, her gaze darting to Yasmin for approval.

"What you must keep in mind is that we have eight minutes, maximum, to get all of them in that truck." Gato pointed to the kitchen wall, as if they could see the second vehicle on the other side of it, in the garage. He seemed to think in blueprints all the time now. "It's not the guards who are our biggest concern. It's the time it takes the army to get there, once the alarms go off.

Eight minutes. That's our guarantee we can get that truck out through the west exit and onto the border road."

"Our van too," Fayçal offered.

"If it takes us longer, well… we fight it out. Our first priority is to get those eight in the truck. Eight brothers free. Don't lose sight of our objective now."

Fayçal nodded, his eyes fixed on his scuffed boots. He was ashamed he'd come off selfish. Since they'd been in hiding he'd gained about ten kilograms, grown his beard thick and long. He was willing a transformation of his identity—something Henry has given up on now.

"We'll have between twelve and fifteen minutes to get to the border from there. That is our window of opportunity.

"If our brothers are working the crossing, insh'allah," Fayçal said.

"Our brothers have been well paid for their support, we won't need to depend on prayer."

Henry couldn't let this pass. He raised his hand as if he had to ask permission to speak. "That rises to… sorry…" He shifted from his rudimentary Arabic to French. He had to be clear with what he was about to say. "That raises a question for me. Are we absolutely sure about the money from my work making it to this camp you mentioned over the border? I've heard no more about this for a week now."

Gato smiled. He allowed himself a warm look into Yasmin's eyes. But she looked away. There were limits to her detachment with Henry's humiliation. "You don't have to worry, Henry Raeburn. The last I heard, it was your mother herself who will be there with our money. She can take you home just like a boy from school."

"Thank you, Gato. It will be good to see her. I hope the money will help you all in the months after I'm gone."

"The money? That will go soon enough. The money is not important, Henry Raeburn, not to the rest of us here. We're prepared to be stateless. To live like refugees. We know that's just like human garbage in your part of the world, but for us the work has just begun. For you, you go back to your life. Your artist work. Maybe you'll write a book about your great adventure, yes? Make a million American dollars. How about you send us that money when you make it? Will you do that for us? No? I didn't think so."

Henry could only glare at Gato, with a smile that betrayed his contempt. He had never felt such hatred for one man before. Even when he had fantasized about taking out the torturers with this AK47 he carried now, that impulse for violence paled in comparison to what was coursing through his veins, that only denial would consign to adrenalin. He'd never been good with denial, really.

"Oh I don't know, Gato. I might surprise you."

"That's true, I suppose. Anything is possible, insh'allah."

Henry took one last look at Yasmin, and no, she could not look away. "Yes, anything, unfortunately."

★

It was not far to the black site, less than a half hour through the wilderness, but all Gordon had were directions he took down over the phone from Marci in Virginia. On the call he was hoping she'd cast some doubt on the likelihood of the raid going ahead. But no, she told him that Mehdi's contact was probably correct. She'd worked her old "spook sources" for all she could find out about Henry's abductors; all of them had done their military service before university. Why wouldn't they carry this out? Gordon did not offer a reply, the question was rhetorical, really. The better question he could only ask himself was this: why did he still believe that somehow there was not going to be violent conflict out there? Ever since the demonstrations erupted, the eerie silence in the streets of this neighbourhood offered the best indication of what was soon to follow: the raids, the skirmishes, the shop windows smashed, the police cars set on fire. It was there in the news footage every morning, on the TV in the café. The commentators were searching for similes behind their news desks and he was sure he heard "tsunami." He had folded the piece of paper with his directions in four as he walked down the corridor in the cramped rooming house, then he had taken the back stairs to the lot where his rented van was, to his relief, untouched.

He had waited until the morning rush here as he left Rabat because the sheer volume of the traffic would give him cover. People still had to work here, still had to get paid. He would be in one van among many in the clotted arterial streets. He pulled out into the flow of trucks and taxis that were heading in the direction of the airport, not the city centre, and all the noises of traffic idling—the radio voices, the engines revving, the wailing vocals of *rai*—it was all consoling. Until the traffic thinned, and he was one of the outliers headed the wrong way. Roads to the outback were for fool's errands or worse now.

There was no way he could get this van near the site, he realized. Yet it was absurd to imagine he could park it concealed from view. There were just stunted olive trees wilting in rows, little crowns of garrigue shooting up from the earth, stubbornly clinging to life. Gordon had checked the elapsed time on his black rubber watch he used to run with (just, what, eleven days ago? How quaint his middle-aged man's vanity already seemed). He had to pull over somewhere close, and as a six turned to seven on the odometer, he glimpsed a service road just over a small hill. Lucky seven, he'd take this turn, it was all he had to go on.

He doubted that any of his efforts at stealth were going to matter though. Surely he had already been tracked. Khadilkar had made sure his friends in the military were well resourced with Canadian drones. World leaders in innovation now, Team Canada. All he could do was hope the armed forces viewed the drone footage later, consider this curious traveler in the old white van as a low priority. Given what was supposed to occur at the site—or what might already be happening—he could be right. He pulled over after two minutes along the service road near a break in a fence line of rusted wire. He waved at the clouds like a shipwrecked man, taunting his invisible watchers. Yes, there was more than a touch of madness in this gesture but his reserves of rational thought were riding the red line.

He packed what he needed, including the pistol in a pocket of his backpack and attempted a shuffling jog, heading toward a hill about a half kilometer in the distance. He could walk and preserve his stamina, maybe that would be wise, but the quickened pace helped to block out his darkening anxiety. As the tempo of his breaths increased, he closed his eyes, and all he saw were the familiar pulsing red squares against the black of his eyelids. He was off the map now, like an ancient hermit disappeared from the capital of the faithless. For the first time in his life, he did not know where he would be when night fell.

He felt a wave of relief with his uncertainty when he crested the hill, however. There, about a kilometer away, he could see the site. Just three long, black rectangular buildings, penned off in silvery electrified fence. The parking lot was half-full with government trucks and vans, a few Japanese and Korean compact cars. Nothing about this vista suggested an imminent siege.

Yet it had to be today. This was the clear message he had gotten from Mehdi. He sat on the hard ground under the shade of a small lip of granite, catching his breath. This was no time to let doubt consume him. No, all he could do was wait, an ancient hunter for skittering prey, in silence.

★

With the call of the muezzin in the village, the morning's preparation for this mission concluded and they all went to their rooms to pray. No one expected Henry to do the same, but he did return to the attic space he'd taken. He'd made his bed, his military issue knapsack was firmly packed and ready to go by the ladder. He knelt on a patch of carpet and put his hands together and closed his eyes. The teenage Henry would have been horrified that this was what he was doing. But he was not going to take any chances with a higher power anymore; he no longer had the luxury of an agnostic's faint ache of despair.

He accepted, early on, that if he was going to be an artist, he would have to master solitude. It was the van Gogh deal. Nothing of any lasting power could be made from a sensibility shaped by a desire for approval. You had to pursue the vision relentlessly. It dictated your conception like you were sculpting the living image of your integrity, chiseling off all the received ideas until the inner form was revealed. It took all the faith he had to keep believing; he just never gave that faith a name and a god. Now it was probably too late, and his faith had taken him beyond any hope for grace. He had never felt so alone.

He pinched the tears out of his eyes as he heard the doors slam on the two vehicles outside. The voices of these strangers that never became anything more than his captors. They were bumbling, thuggish and vain but he forgave them now. All would be forgiven if they got through this, pulled off something like an act of justice, an act of war against the enemy that had always been inside him, the "infidel states" that made him a wealthy man of some fame and "market power." They were his true black sites.

Father, forgive me for what we are about to do. How fucked up was it to call for Nobodaddy in prayer? He'd gone through his own hours of therapy about his old man, the standard Oedipal jazz. He found peace, found even love in his heart, surprisingly enough. In his last puritan days of work in his studio, he'd wake before dawn, stare into the bathroom mirror, touch the grey hair at his temples, the new lines around his eyes and mouth and he sensed the old man ghosting in his bones. In Venice, on that morning they ran out to the Porta Magna together, he realized he had the same pigeon-toed shuffle, the same round shouldered, softball swing at the air. He gave himself the Raeburn name because he hoped for something mercurial and feminine to counter the force of this legacy within him, but nothing would, nothing could have, after all. Grandma Lizzie Raeburn died a suicide, checked herself out of Hotel Family History without really leaving a dent on the pillow. Father, we're always becoming, but it's just a return to the source.

"Mr. Raeburn, are you ready, sir?"

He turned to Gato at the ladder and gave him his best smile of contempt. "I am, sir. Let's get this done and get you your money."

★

After the longest three hours in memory, Gordon saw two vehicles approaching the back entrance of the facility. He pulled out his father's old field glasses and focused on the cube truck first. There was a logo in Arabic, the images of fruit and vegetables creating an oval lined in a laurel wreath. He shifted his view to the van and there was a figure of a plump baker pulling flat, golden brown disks from an oven with a long paddle. This could be a routine delivery; this could be the usual. The fence doors parted with that slow, calibrated speed of faceless automation. He felt calm about this because there was not one human he could see; this might all be carried out with machines talking to machines. No drama, he could slump back into the lull of this waiting.

But then, there was the pop-pop-pop of a semi-automatic round. Maybe he heard shouts—at least that's how he would remember it later. He tossed the field glasses in the open top of the knapsack, pinched the drawstring taut, slung it on his back and began to run down this hill towards the entrance. There was an explosion from somewhere under a guard tower. Flames and black smoke shot up and engulfed it in a black cloud. So this was happening, in all its strange, muted, sudden inevitability.

He reached into the side pocket of this knapsack and took out the pistol. He checked the safety and yes, it was ready—loaded chamber. It was all he could do to run with it in his hand. Old man turned toy soldier. He had no idea what he was going to do when he got to the entrance.

★

There were just twenty-six prisoners in this facility. It was staffed by over one hundred men—and yes, women—who have firearms and are considerably more practiced than, say, a visual artist who had only picked up an AK47 a few weeks ago. But there was much to be said about the effectiveness of ambush techniques. And plastic explosives. And quick, decisive action. In the dim, submarinish light of the corridors, with the piercing wails of the alarms and the yelling of the prisoners, Gato and Fayçal each abducted two sector wardens, placed the muzzles of their pistols behind their heads and marched these terrified men out to the cells to use their master keys in each slot of the doors like a cards slipped into ATMs. Maybe it was the acoustics, but it all sounded like a gymnasium in the hall, this operation transformed into a sport with a strange, darkly sexualized energy to it. Capture the flag.

Pop. Pop. Both wardens collapsed like rag dolls once the doors to the prisoners were opened and shrieking, terror stricken figures straight out of Goya's wartime sketches—wide eyed, ghostly pale—scurried out, ducking with their hands behind their heads as soon as they encountered their liberators. Shouts of praise to Allah. Gato pointed with his gun to a far exit where the truck and the van were parked, yelled for them to hurry in Arabic.

Henry found himself ten metres behind Fayçal and Karima as they rounded a corner, adrenalized and bellowing out warnings and demands for surrender to the guards. Karima sounded triumphant; as perhaps she should—she had a feline grace and precision to her movements with a gun and managed to take down two guards. But then she and Fayçal both halted in mid-bellow. Henry could not see what had stopped them in their tracks until he shuffled a few steps to slow down around a corner. It was then he heard the barking.

There were four German Shepherds moving surprisingly fast towards them, barely thirty metres away. They were all teeth and shiny dark eyes. The prey drive in them was a force propelling them forward with an intensity that would mean certain death for whoever was in their path. Henry could dimly make out two heavyset, bearded guards at the far end of the corridor. They each knelt on one knee as they were taking aim with their pistols.

Fayçal shot first and managed to wound one guard badly enough that he toppled to the floor. But he was too late taking aim for the dog who had leapt for his neck. Henry heard Fayçal's cry of agony as he took aim at the third dog that was just moments from lunging at him. In his periphery he glimpsed the quick, dance-like moves of Karima as she pivoted and fired, pivoted and fired.

And then Henry pulled the trigger. There was a thump in the dog's broad chest, a corona of blood that pulsed out with the faintest whimper from the animal. A female, he saw now. She dropped to the floor and one last spasm of life surged through her haunches, her one bright caramel coloured eye took in Henry, looming above her. Then that eye softly closed.

In this moment he could not imagine this dog ever wanting to do him harm. In this moment he was broken by his own power to kill. But this was what registered with the older self in him, not the adrenalized murdering self who was locked in this maze, running, firing, spraying bullets, wilded by his rage to stay alive.

"Loading docks! Now!"

He recognized this as Gato's voice, somewhere behind him. It halted Karima, this woman who saved his life, who had left no man or animal alive in the corridor directly ahead of him.

She turned and reversed her direction, roughly tugging at Henry's shoulder to do the same.

A door was half open at the end of the corridor, letting in sharp rays of sunlight and the sounds of rapid gunfire that portended a final battle to escape this place. Had this all just been six minutes? He felt like he'd been in this hell for hours.

Gato was in the driver's seat of the cube truck, waving them off. "I have them all in the back! You and Karima, you stay and wait for the others. Give them two minutes, you hear!"

"I thought we only had eight minutes!" Henry realized he was needlessly angry with Gato. What could he do? And from the sound of the gunfire just beyond the door, he doubted anyone from the group would survive and make it to them now.

"You abandon them, I kill you myself, Henry Raeburn." He waved his gun as he slammed the cube truck in drive and it lunged forward from the loading ramp.

Karima looked to Henry and she was clearly terrified. But then a thought transformed her. She raised her AK47 in the air with both hands and fired it at the ceiling, as if to scare Henry from her. "You try to drive away and I will kill you. Gato won't have to."

It was all he could do but just nod, pull his AK47 closer to his chest at the ready. He owed her his life, after all.

In a break in the gunfire, he heard footsteps, boots stomping on the tiles just beyond the doorway. It was Yasmin. She was screaming at the site of Gato driving the cube truck away. Henry ran to her, quickly grabbed her by her flailing arms. Her AK47 clattered to the ground as he guided her into the back of the van. He muttered words of reassurance that it would be all right now. How he wished he could have believed them.

He turned to Karima and it was something about her frightened look that made him realize what had really happened as Gato drove away. He had abandoned them. The timing was deliberately wrong; they were to be sacrificed. Within the depths of this prison was their only chance at saving their lives. He grabbed her roughly by the arm and they began to run, back in to a corridor lit only by the flickering lights on the blaring alarms.

★

Gordon was about fifty metres from the back entrance when he sensed a convoy of army trucks behind him. They were closing in, but he couldn't stop now. He was sizing up the fence, trying to figure out where he could try to scale it if he had to (the answer was nowhere, there was barbed wire) when the gates suddenly opened with a whirring sound. Speeding forward, like some crazed, gored beast, was the cube truck. It blared its horn for Gordon to get out of the way.

He veered to the right like he was tacking to the sidelines on a football field. No matter who was in this truck, it couldn't be Henry because he would have stopped. Of course he would have. As he heard the doors clang and begin to close again, he strained to pick up his pace. But he was breathless, cursing his old man's legs.

He was moments from the gate when he heard the sound of something launched with a sharp intake of air. He turned and took in the moment of contact: the cube truck went up with a boom and a fiery cloud, instantly incinerating everyone who was in it.

★

Please, please, please God, let me find Henry alive. He ran and made it into the compound before the gates closed. Whatever hell awaited on the other side of the fence, he could stop it happening if he could get to those who remained. Surrender had to be the only option.

He saw another van at a loading dock. As he approached, he could feel his heart pound, because he saw the dim outline of a figure crouched in the back. He turned the metal handle on the back door of the van, mumbling his son's name. But here was only Yasmin Raza. She was hyperventilating, rocking, hysterically weeping.

"My son, Henry, where is he?"

All she could do was motion to the open door of the loading area, shake her head through her tears. "He's… I'm so sorry…"

And then there was the metallic roar of the army trucks approaching—one, two, three—alongside them there must have been at least a hundred soldiers, firing into the air, shouting in Arabic. It was all Gordon could do to raise his hands in the air, bellowing out "Ne tire pas! Ne tire pas!"

The trucks screeched to a stop. More soldiers poured out of each vehicle. They ran past Gordon and Yasmin. A large, moustachioed man with epaulettes on his fatigues approached from the last vehicle, accompanied by three other soldiers. This group was walking slowly, casually, like weekend golfers approaching the green. One of the soldiers snarled loudly in Arabic, motioning to Yasmin and Gordon to drop to their knees as he poked the back of their thighs with his rifle.

"What did he say?"

"We're under arrest," Yasmin said.

As Gordon lay face down in the dirt, he felt the metal cuffs snap shut on his wrists.

The alarms stopped blaring. He could hear nothing but a few stray shouts of soldiers, somewhere in the corridors of the building behind him. It was over. And Henry was gone.

35.

The crew from the BBC did a good job of improvising a studio setting in the cramped Quonset hut that served as the administrative offices of the refugee camp. There was one video camera on a tripod, aimed over the shoulder of where Safae Hafidi, the correspondent for the region, was seated on a fold-out chair. A black cloth over the windows masked the blazing light of mid-afternoon. Henry could hear the faint, crackling sound of announcements made in English over loudspeakers. It was a flat, nasal, American-sounding voice. In here it was as quiet as an operating room as Henry took his seat opposite Hafidi, nodded his hello and allowed himself a smile. She smiled in return, but her gaze went back to the questions she'd prepared in a notebook that was perched on her thigh. A stocky, bearded old cameraman, introduced to Henry as simply Reg, attached a small microphone near the second pearl snap button from the collar of Henry's old western shirt, scrounged from a large blue bin near his tent.

"How's that, lad? Can you say testing?"

Henry did what he was asked. Lad, Reg called him. Now that he'd shaved off his beard and lost all this weight, he must look younger. This, despite feeling he'd aged a decade or more in the few months since he had first come to this part of the world.

"Are you ready, Mr. Raeburn?"

"Sure, I suppose."

Safae curtly waved to Reg, who barked that they were rolling.

"Henry Raeburn. What a journey this has been for you."

He paused, inhaled sharply. There were so many things to say about the last 72 hours, much of which he could not speak.

There will be nothing about the escape. He could not tell of how he had led Karima, from his memory of the blueprints the group had pored over, to the room next to the infirmary that had the concealed door to the infamous "catacombs." As his father advised, from a missive written by Ambassador Khadilkar, there would be no mention of all that he and Karima had seen down there, as they made their way through the 400 metres of tunnel: the large cage, hanging from heavy chains, the blood stained gurney in the white tiled room, the windowless cells that one would have to crawl into to languish for days, screaming through the darkness of confinement. The catacombs had been empty but you could smell death through the most powerful, scorching detergent, and you could feel how haunted the rooms were by all the souls that had perished from the horrors down there. These were the images seared in his mind now… images he'd wished he had had his camera for. They had only increased the panic he and Karima had felt, as they scurried along a corridor that narrowed, lit up like a subway track, until they could see a rusted steel door. Karima shot through the lock, he couldn't steady his hands at that point. There was every possibility that what would have been waiting for them on the other side of the door were soldiers with rifles pointed, ready to shoot first before they could scream their surrender.

"I feel very lucky to be alive."

"You were traveling either on foot or by boat for five days, I understand."

"'Bout that, yeah. We… my friend Karima and I… we made it to Tangier after the incident. We had a little help. Then the boat here… that was a little rough. But I think we knew once we got to Tangier we might be safe. Well… safer. "

"This marks the end of your imprisonment and your time as a hostage with this group that abducted you. The feeling of liberation must be profound. I wonder if you can talk about that."

Safae was speaking to him with a cautious, gentle tone. She leaned forward intently, but there was no gentleness as she looked him in the eye. He could tell she didn't quite trust him.

She sharply rapped the pen, tightly held in her small hand, just once, against the notepad in her lap.

"They rarely spoke to me in English, but from what I could gather, they hoped to topple the government, create another Arab spring. The money they had asked for…"

"Your ransom."

"My ransom, yes… it was my understanding this would fund their efforts."

"The woman found with you."

"Karima, yes."

"Karima Binebine. She was a part of this group, was she not?"

"Not by her own will, this is my understanding. But I can't really talk about her case. There is no extradition treaty here but I believe she hopes one day to return."

"I see." Safae took note of Henry's jiggling foot, his recrossed legs.

"What I can tell you is I had gone to Morocco for my photography first and foremost. I had never meant to involve myself in the politics of this region."

Henry looked up from Safae's gaze and there, just behind Reg and his camera, standing among Garry Fry and the two Irish aid workers who seemed to run this place, was Sylvain Marchessault, the new Canadian Head of the Political Section. So warm, bearish and helpful, this Mr. Marchessault, like an uncle from the Eastern townships. Yet he was also crystal clear about the lines Henry had to say to get through this interview. He slowly blinked as Henry spoke, allowed himself the smallest grin under his bushy beard.

"But your work itself is inherently political, is it not? I know you've done a series that focused on detention centres used by the west for those subjected to rendition."

"Black sites. Yes. I had trespassed in the area of one such centre that was alleged to be—"

"Alleged to be."

"It was the government's position, in the trial, that there had never been detainees who had been subject to rendition there."

"No political prisoners, arrested without trial?" There was a slight quaver in Safae's voice as she looked Henry in the eye. She'd stare him down on this.

He couldn't help but look up again at Marchessault. Yes, this was the deal. You wanted your father to get off with just a trespassing fine, you wanted your friend Karima to stand some chance of returning to her country without facing imprisonment herself? You don't deviate from the lines. And you sure as hell don't talk about what happened out there.

"There's never been any evidence of this, no."

"Yet you came to this region."

"I guess I was interested in this place from an aesthet... from an artistic perspective. I mean, I was interested in the whole country from this perspective. I just didn't really know. I was naïve. A tourist, really."

"Your involvement in this robbery, with this group. There was video footage."

"My understanding from the group who held me was that they were in a desperate position. They were losing hope that they would get my ransom money. But I want to be clear, there was no Stockholm Syndrome type thing going on."

"You did not at least understand what this group was hoping to achieve?"

"Of course I did. But the means by which they hoped to fund an opposition to their government... I mean you could never justify the crimes they had committed... the lives they had taken."

"So you were coerced..."

"They told me in no uncertain terms that I could either help them or I would be killed."

"I see."

"I was trying to survive."

"There is footage of you brandishing a weapon."

"In my head... I just reasoned that if I could get through all that was happening without hurting anyone, I could live a little longer."

"Self-preservation."

"Exactly, yes."

Safae leaned back in her chair, her gaze still locked on Henry, as if in close-up. She was going to play out the pause for as long as possible. Henry knew this was a tactic to extract more from his story. The guilty are compelled to fill the silence with words that only serve to cast further doubt. He looked over at Garry, who nodded in encouragement. You're doing fine, Henry. Just keep it together and get through this. It all gets easier after this first one.

"Henry Raeburn, you must be eager to get back home. I thank you for your time this afternoon."

"You're most welcome."

He heard the video camera click off, and then Reg approached him. Henry took the microphone off his collar. He couldn't get it off fast enough. It was his first step in getting out of this chair.

As Henry stood, Garry moved forward, with Sylvain close behind. Garry gently patted him on the shoulder. "Well done, mate."

"Mr. Raeburn, we have them here," Sylain said, quietly. "They are waiting in the kitchen area. I did not want them to be part of all this… with the camera…"

"Thank you, Sylvain. Thank you very much, that was thoughtful."

"Come, you can see them now."

Sylvain led Henry and Garry out of this room and down a dimly lit corridor. It smelled of fresh bread baking. There was something about the smell, the familiarity of it, that made Henry start to cry, even before Sylvain opened the door to the kitchen.

The face he saw first, when the door opened, was his mother Marithe's. She was already weeping as well. There, behind her, with his hand gently touching her shoulder, was his father. He was bearded, thinner, with a small abrasion on his cheek. First he tried to laugh, and then he too was in tears.

They wrapped their arms around each other and for this moment, like some enchanted spell, the years were scrubbed clean in the warmth of their embrace, the primal, ageless force of this love that overtook them. A family once again… if only in this moment.

36.

Gordon had to admit, despite his loathing of Ashwin, the ambassador turned out to be effective. He had managed to work behind the scenes and ensure that Gordon's trespassing fine would be negotiated with little fanfare. It was a straightforward transaction: if there was no public mention of what went on in the former black site—which was now officially closed, soon to be demolished—he would be released back to Canada. Whatever happened in the past within the walls of the site, whatever was discussed or redacted in the documents of the Canadian government, was now a matter of historical record. It was the culmination of Ashwin's skills of concealment.

Ashwin also deigned to give Gordon one of his last meetings at the embassy before departing himself—though he did not disclose when that was to be officially announced. Soul of discretion as always, it was the one quality that would surely serve him well in his next posting.

"I imagine you'll be looking forward to seeing Ottawa again, senator."

"Call me Gordon, Ashwin. I don't expect to be going back to work any time soon." He took in Ashwin's pensive look. So well done, this gentility, it was as if Ashwin had felt a twinge of remorse for all that occurred.

"I met with the Minister of Foreign Affairs here, just two days ago. He had a message for you. He said the Moroccan government had every intention to spare your son's life. They hoped to compel them to surrender. It is my understanding they will take this into account with the trial of this girl."

"Young woman."

"I'm sorry. Yes, this young woman Karima Binebine... if she ever returns." Ashwin twiddled his pen in the fingers of his right hand. He was already impatient, ready to usher Gordon out of his office. All the paintings were already off the walls, sent back to the art bank. It was just the messy human business that was an obstacle to a clean desk.

"And what about Yasmin?"

"Raza?"

"Who else?"

Ashwin wore a puzzled frown, play acting that it was a challenge for him to recall her particular case. "It is my understanding they have not decided on a trial date for her yet, given her statement to the police."

"But the bail conditions have allowed her to leave?"

"That, I'm not sure. I know they regard her as a special case and will likely try her accordingly. Of course, if she leaves, we don't have an extradition treaty, so…"

In the silence, Ashwin looked into Gordon's eyes, unwaveringly. Like a challenge. Gordon looked away first. He was too weary of this man's games to engage any further.

He thought of the last image of Yasmin that stayed with him: crouched down as if in prayer, holding her hands over her ears. She was silently crying, rocking back and forth. Gordon had called out to her as they took her away but she did not turn and look back.

"I had hoped to speak to her again. She won't return my calls or emails. I suppose it's all still too present. Too raw."

"As I'm sure it must be for you, Sen… Gordon. Once again, I'm deeply sorry."

Gordon didn't keep him. He shook Ashwin's hand, thanked him for all he had done for two fellow Canadians. And for a brief moment, before thoughts of Ottawa clouded back in, he had almost meant it.

★

Moments away from meeting Hannah and Hisham, in a hotel bar that overlooked the Vancouver harbour, Gordon parked his car, closed his eyes and took a deep breath. The only sound he heard was the whir of the power window closing. So much time, so much living behind him. It took close to forty years for Hannah to consent to—and okay, maybe embrace—the notion of his love, for Hisham to truly become his best friend. Yet something must have been imprinted from their beginnings, some quality of authenticity that could not be replicated with others over the years, through all the byways of careers, friendships, marriages, that brought them here to be with him.

He felt blessed. He had no self-consciousness at all about embracing them both in the bar.

Inevitably, just moments after their first drinks were served, Ashwin came up.

"His kind will always land on their feet. I wouldn't give him another thought, Gord." Hisham gave Hannah a conspiratorial look as he sipped from his glass of Sancerre. They had had dinner last night here in town, prior to Gordon arriving, and Ashwin was clearly a topic of conversation.

As was Henry, undoubtedly, but they were both too considerate, too cautious about the all Gordon had gone through to bring him up. For this he wanted to tell them both that he was grateful. For their very presence in his life. Yet it was more important to show them he was strong enough to discuss what must be taken on: his life after his brief political career, rebuilding a practice, some semblance of private life.

"I suppose you're not going to miss Ottawa now, yeah?" Hisham asked, with the start of a weary shake of his head.

"I am a little curious about how my exit will be perceived, sure. All those OLO flacks, they'll take their pals in the press gallery out for drinks and speak about me with the greatest sympathy as they portray me as just a crazy old guy. Always a bit unstable anyway... his kid and his fancy art career in Europe selling those photos that were actually an act of treason. No, there was definitely something off about father and son."

Hannah reached across the table and put her hand in his. With her fragile smile, as she looked into his eyes, she was all the future he cared about now. He could tell her he loved her but no, despite the last hippy years they remembered from their adolescence, they are not of a generation that said these things, especially with another man at the table.

"This is a bigger case than their parochial interests, Gord. There's a larger investigation that the government there is right to fear. At least from what you tell me."

"I swear to God, Hisham, I've thought about that whole operation from every angle, with all the knowledge I have." Hisham cocked his head, listening closely, but it was clear Gordon was really saying this for Hannah. It was as if he was finally debriefing her on all that had really happened. He looked at her directly as he gestured with his wine glass. "The armed forces could have gone in, backed up that security personnel. But no, they waited. They... along with our government... they sacrificed the key witnesses for any trial of what really went on in that black site, the key suspects if you tried the government for war crimes. And then, of course, they had known what vehicle had all those prisoners, and they ensured their testimonies would never be heard. So many birds, one stone."

Hisham let his gaze trail off out the window. The pleasure boats were moored along the boardwalk on this side of the harbour. Imagine the lives of those who were on board them. Monied enough to be oblivious to what went on just over that horizon, on other shores. Hisham looked to Hannah, encouraging her to speak.

But Gordon was not quite finished. "I mean, I just know they had to have some intel. Could have been that Gato himself who they turned. I've got so many questions for Yasmin. But once we got back to the city and she was freed on bail, it's like... poof... she disappeared."

"Gordon, you should know something... I mean I had to tell you this in person. A week ago, that guy from CSIS you were dealing with, Dennis Wilson... he came to my office. He said he knew I was trying to get in touch with Yasmin again, trying to connect with her parents. He told me to stop. He told me there was a reason I had never heard from her parents to begin with."

"She was working for them," Gordon said. He was looking out the window past her shoulder, trying to picture Yasmin as he knew her. He felt ashamed of his gullibility.

"Co-ordinated efforts, yes. She was with, as you called them, Christians in action. Probably while she was working for me, even. Wilson wouldn't say. But Gordon, this only broadens this case to a question of our own government's involvement."

"Of course it does," Hisham said. He patted Gordon's forearm.

"Hisham and I, we were discussing this last night," Hannah said. "This could take years in court. I mean there should be grounds for an inquiry, really."

"God… I don't know if I have it in me, Hannah. I mean I'm just tired… I've got to figure out how to earn a living again, how to patch everything together." He was focusing on a point beyond the harbour where the faint blur of a road snaked up a mountain.

"I know." And she reached for his hand again. "But it doesn't have to be just you handling all this," she said. "I just want you to know that."

★

Hisham retired early. They would have a full day of working through the briefs he'd prepared for Gordon, starting early in the morning. Over drinks he was probably relieved by what he saw happening between Gordon and Hannah. He had made his tactful exit as the sun was going down over the harbour, leaving them to walk to Gordon's home by themselves.

"The last time Henry and I were truly together, before all this happened, we were in Venice. He had a show there. People wanted to meet him, to hear his views on the world but all he really cared about was seeing his work on the wall, seeing people take it in, their moments of reflection, all to themselves. It seemed so right, so pure. It gives me some peace to know that he was at ease with himself then, and that he might be able to get back to all that now. That's all I want for him. When he was just a boy he was always happy, always at play. And then, in his teenage years, he became so serious. He took on the weight of the world. He was so angry."

"It was the same with my stepdaughter. For years we couldn't talk. It's still difficult, now that Isaac's passed away. Though we both try. I think now, with Yasmin, I wanted to complete something about that relationship. I wasn't even conscious of it." She shook her head as she gazed down at the planks along the boardwalk. "I'll always wonder if there were authentic moments of connection or if she was always just working for her masters. If she thought I was foolish… just naïve about the world."

"I'll take being naive over whatever sophistication might mean now. There's nothing that should make me hopeful. And yet…"

"And yet, yes." Hannah smiled, pulled her arm through his. "So what about you, Gordon? Were you happy there in Venice? I like how you described it. Were you falling in love with what your life was becoming?"

"Not quite then, no." He pulled her close as they reached the stone steps that would take them to the street where his home was. "But now, yes. Very much now. Despite the cost, it seems."

"Trust that love, Mr. Senator."

"I believe I will, Ms. Eisenberg."

ACKNOWLEDGMENTS

My thanks to Michael Redhill, Gregory Galligan, Marilyn Biderman and, as always, A.S..